ONE OF THE FAMILY

Widowed Mrs. Dawling was a charming but
limited creature with only one idea in her
pretty head: that her daughter Meryon
should marry money. Meryon's own ideas
were more romantic and it was a great shock
to her to find that the pair of them were re-
garded as unscrupulous gold-diggers by the
one man who really mattered to her. Somehow, it became very important to her that
Gregory should change his opinion.

Novels by Mary Burchell

WIFE TO CHRISTOPHER	WHEN LOVE'S BEGINNING
CALL AND I'LL COME	THE BROKEN WING
NOBODY ASKED ME	HOSPITAL CORRIDORS
WITH ALL MY WORLDLY GOODS	YOURS TO COMMAND
OTHER LIPS HAVE LOVED YOU	ON THE AIR
LITTLE SISTER	FOR EVER AND EVER
EXCEPT MY LOVE	LOVE IS MY REASON
BUT NOT FOR ME	LOYAL IN ALL
YET LOVE REMAINS	THE PRETTIEST GIRL
ONE OF THE FAMILY	TO JOURNEY TOGETHER
SUCH IS LOVE	LOVING IS GIVING
YOURS WITH LOVE	JOANNA AT THE GRANGE
I'LL GO WITH YOU	AND FALSELY PLEDGE MY LOVE
ALWAYS YOURS	THE GIRL IN THE BLUE DRESS
ACCOMPANIED BY HIS WIFE	DEAR TRUSTEE
WHERE SHALL I WANDER?	DEAR SIR
AFTER OFFICE HOURS	STAR QUALITY
PAY ME TOMORROW	CORNER HOUSE
STRANGERS MAY MARRY	PARIS AND MY LOVE
JUST A NICE GIRL	ACROSS THE COUNTER
THINE IS MY HEART	HONEY
DARE I BE HAPPY?	MY SISTER CELIA
TAKE ME WITH YOU	RELUCTANT RELATION
MEANT FOR EACH OTHER	THE WEDDING DRESS
FIRST LOVE, LAST LOVE	DESIGN FOR LOVING
WIFE BY ARRANGEMENT	HOUSE OF CONFLICT
NOT WITHOUT YOU	INHERIT MY HEART
UNDER JOINT MANAGEMENT	SWEET MEADOWS
CHOOSE WHICH YOU WILL	DANGEROUS LOVING
FIND OUT THE WAY	DO NOT GO, MY LOVE
IT'S RUMOURED IN THE VILLAGE	A SONG BEGINS
WARD OF LUCIFER	HER SISTER'S CHILDREN
THE BRAVE IN HEART	GIRL WITH A CHALLENGE
MY OLD LOVE CAME	THE STRANGE QUEST OF ANNE WESTON
THANKS TO ELIZABETH	THE MARSHALL FAMILY
CINDERELLA AFTER MIDNIGHT	THE OTHER LINDING GIRL
AWAY WENT LOVE	THOUGH WORLDS APART
IF THIS WERE ALL	WHEN LOVE IS BLIND
AT FIRST SIGHT	THEN COME KISS ME
A LETTER FOR DON	MISSING FROM HOME
HERE I BELONG	A HOME FOR JOY
TELL ME MY FORTUNE	THE CURTAIN RISES
I WILL LOVE YOU STILL	THE ROSEWOOD BOX
WISH ON THE MOON	CHILD OF MUSIC
LOVE HIM OR LEAVE HIM	SECOND MARRIAGE
MINE FOR A DAY	MUSIC OF THE HEART
SWEET ADVENTURE	UNBIDDEN MELODY
STOLEN HEART	SONG CYCLE
OVER THE BLUE MOUNTAINS	REMEMBERED SERENADE
THE HEART CANNOT FORGET	ELUSIVE HARMONY
THE HEART MUST CHOOSE	IF YOU STILL CARE
MEET ME AGAIN	ONE MAN'S HEART
UNDER THE STARS OF PARIS	LOVE MADE THE CHOICE
NO REAL RELATION	CHOOSE THE ONE YOU'LL MARRY
A RING ON HER FINGER	DEARLY BELOVED
	NIGHTINGALES
	MASQUERADE WITH MUSIC

ONE OF THE FAMILY

By

MARY BURCHELL

MILLS & BOON LIMITED
15–16 BROOK'S MEWS
LONDON W1A 1DR

*First published in Great Britain 1939
by Mills & Boon Limited*

*This edition published in 1985 by
Mills & Boon Limited, 15–16 Brook's Mews,
London W1A 1DR*

ISBN 0 263 75447 2

MADE AND PRINTED IN GREAT BRITAIN BY
COX & WYMAN LIMITED, READING

CHAPTER I

Mrs. Dawling thrust a shoe into one corner of the suit-case, and stood with the other dangling rather helplessly in her hand.

"It's so *odd*," she exclaimed plaintively as her daughter came into the room. "However well things fit in when one goes away, by the time one returns they all seem to have become different shapes and sizes. I *know* these shoes went into this case before, and look at them now! Not an inch anywhere."

"Let me see." Meryon crossed the room and took the shoe with a laugh. Packing never had been Mother's long suit, but that wasn't exactly her fault, poor darling. She was one of those people who ought always to be born into the world with a personal maid in attendance, and it was no good blaming her if, instead of adapting herself to circumstances, she spent her life expecting circumstances to adapt themselves miraculously to her.

"We-ell." Meryon surveyed the muddle doubtfully. "I think if—— Suppose you let me finish it, dear. Perhaps I could coax the things a bit better."

"I dare say that would be best," Mrs. Dawling agreed, immediately abandoning even the pretence of packing. Nor was she at all offended when Meryon's method of "finishing" consisted, perforce, in turning everything out and starting again. After all, Meryon *liked* doing these things. Much better, then, to let her do them, rather than wear oneself out for nothing.

With a little sigh of relief that her packing labours were over for this holiday anyway, Mrs. Dawling took a comfortable chair by the window and embarked on the much more interesting task of discussing the members of the house-party which was just breaking up.

"I can't get over the change in poor Muriel Varley," she remarked in a tone of enjoyable disgust. "No woman should let herself go like that. Should she?" as Meryon made no reply.

"Well, not every woman can keep her looks as well as you do, Mother," Meryon said indulgently, as she patiently disentangled belts and stockings from an odd ribbon or two.

"Perhaps not." Mrs. Dawling was pleased. "But there are limits."

"Not to Mrs. Varley," murmured Meryon.

"I know. That's just it! She *spreads* so. My dear, what does she look like in that check suit?"

Meryon didn't offer to say.

"Like a travelling rug. That's what she looks like," declared Mrs. Dawling. "Like a travelling rug all spread out and a felt hat put on top."

Meryon laughed, but a little deprecatingly.

"She's nice, though. I like her."

"Oh, she's *nice*," Mrs. Dawling admitted in a tone that would have deterred anybody from wanting to know her. "I'm very fond of Muriel. But she's so hearty, Meryon. So terribly hearty. And that girl of hers is going to be just the same."

"Jessie's a dear. Everybody likes her," protested Meryon quickly.

"Not everybody, darling." Her mother was firm. "That over-sporty kind of girl doesn't often attract men, you'll find."

"Well, I think she attracts Hugh Kinley all right."

Meryon smiled, and turned to go on with her packing. But a vexed exclamation from her mother stopped her.

"Hugh Kinley! What about him and Jessie? You can't mean—— Why, he's a baronet's son and they've *heaps* of money!"

"But Jessie's a dear girl and she's good family and——"

"But he's such a *catch*, dear," wailed Mrs. Dawling. "Why, he's *miles* too good for Jessie Varley."

"I think he's very lucky to get her," Meryon said just a trifle shortly, because Mother's conversation nowadays seemed to turn so very often on what Meryon grimly described to herself as "matches and catches."

"Oh, Meryon, you are *tiresome*. What makes you think—— I mean—— Well, is it serious?"

"I think so. I don't know why you shouldn't be pleased about it. I thought you liked Jessie. She's always sweet to you."

"I do like her. I like her very much indeed," protested Mrs. Dawling, in a tone from which affection was conspicuously absent. "Only, Hugh Kinley—oh, really, it's too bad! And she's six months younger than you, too."

"By which you mean—just what?" An involuntary smile lifted the corners of Meryon's mouth, although she was a little cross too. And then, without waiting for her mother to reply, "There!" She shut down the case. "Everything is in—*and* it shuts without your having to sit on the lid."

"Never mind the case." Mrs. Dawling looked almost childishly disconsolate. "And you know quite well what I mean. You're ten times as attractive as Jessie Varley, and Hugh Kinley isn't a fool. If you'd liked—— Really, Meryon, sometimes I think you don't *want* to get married."

Meryon came across and, leaning over the back of

her mother's chair, she put her arms round her with a consoling laugh.

"And sometimes I think you're nothing but a horrid little gold-digger," she said affectionately as she dropped a kiss on her mother's pretty copper-coloured hair. "You know perfectly well that Jessie and Hugh are ideally suited, and that Hugh and I just wouldn't have suited each other at all. So why try to engineer something quite unnatural?"

"You're just talking stupidly," Mrs. Dawling declared, that being her usual method of defence when her arguments were disposed of. "And, anyway, I wouldn't have minded if something had come of this friendship with Rex Treventon."

"Oh!" Meryon straightened up at once and looked rather intently out of the window.

"Meryon, I don't understand you. You're so *secretive*, dear, and it's not at all nice in a young girl." Mrs. Dawling looked so serious and accusing that Meryon laughed irresistibly at this most inaccurate description of herself.

"Oh, no—not secretive, surely," she protested mildly. "Or, if so, let me know which of my dark secrets is worrying you, and I'll tell you all about it."

"It's serious, Meryon."

"Very well—it's serious." Meryon composed her features and looked down at her mother with that air of affectionate indulgence that was her habitual attitude towards her. Indeed, anyone seeing them together just then would have found it hard to believe that they were really mother and daughter.

Barely seventeen years older than Meryon, Mrs. Dawling had an air of helpless fragility oddly out of character for the mother of a grown-up daughter, and they were much more often than not taken for sisters. They both had the same fine, creamy skin, the same slim, faultless figures, and the same striking copper-coloured hair.

But there the likeness ended. In place of the almost babyish blue eyes and pathetic ways of her mother, Meryon had inherited from her father remarkable greenish-hazel eyes, under strongly marked black eyebrows, a firm mouth that could be sweet when it smiled, but very determined when serious, and an air of calm self-reliance which lost nothing from the fact that she could look extremely gentle at times.

She was looking gentle now, because she knew that the only possible way to satisfy her mother was to let her explain herself at length, as though she were a child with a grievance.

"Meryon, don't you *like* Rex Treventon?" Mrs. Dawling began plaintively.

"Very much indeed." Meryon was completely in earnest. "He's the most interesting man I've met for a long time."

"Well, then!" Mrs. Dawling brightened. "And he likes you, child. I know he does. I couldn't be mistaken in the Signs." (Mother always gave "signs" a capital letter when they concerned matrimony.)

"Oh, yes." Meryon smiled slightly. "He likes me very much."

"I knew it!" Mrs. Dawling's spirits were rising at every sentence. "And he's such a charming man, darling. So finished, so travelled and sophisticated. And not very old really, you know."

"He's thirty-seven."

"Well, what's that? Nothing—absolutely nothing." Mrs. Dawling's tone seemed to reduce it almost to the period of baby-food. "Of course you can't expect that wonderful air of experience and sophistication in a very young man. Most of the attractive things about him are *because* he's—well, not so young and unformed.

And then the money, darling! Do you know, Agatha
Windridge told me that that uncle of his left him
three-quarters of a million pounds. *Three-quarters of a
million!* Apart from what he has already."

"Yes. I know he's very wealthy." Meryon felt that
the polite rejoinder fell terribly short of her mother's
ecstasies, but she couldn't help it.

"Did he say anything about it to you, then?"

"Well—a little."

"My dear, that's rather significant, you know." Mrs.
Dawling beamed. Then her face clouded again. "But
I can't think why he left so early this morning, without
any warning, before any of us were up, almost. It's so
odd, Meryon."

"Oh, no. That's a mystery I can explain," Meryon
said with a smile. "His sister was rushed to hospital last
night with appendicitis, and they wired for him. She's
married, but Rex is a great favourite of hers and she
wanted——"

"Darling, why didn't you *tell* me?" Mrs. Dawling was
smiling again like a delighted little girl. "I've been so
worried. I thought everything was over and——"

"Oh, but, Mother, please listen——"

"And now it's really going on as smoothly as ever.
Oh, my dear child, you don't know how delighted and
relieved I am. Such a charming man, too, and you
mustn't take any notice of what spiteful people say.
There are always a few tales about attractive men of
his age, especially when they've travelled so much.
And, anyway, one must be broad-minded these days
and——"

"Mother, really! You needn't make excuses for Rex
Treventon like that. You make him sound a sort of
reformed rake, whereas——"

"No, *no*, dear! I don't mean that at all."

"Well, anyway, we're quite good friends, but I

simply must insist that we're nothing else at all."
Meryon spoke very firmly at last, now that she had an
opportunity to stem the tide of her mother's eloquence.

"I know, darling. Not yet, but——"

"Not at all."

"Oh, Meryon dear, nonsense. You really must allow
your mother to know a few things without being told."
Mrs. Dawling laughed agreeably. "I haven't the slightest doubt myself that when you meet again in London
he will propose. In fact, I'm a little surprised he didn't
do it at the dance last night."

Meryon's expression showed for a moment how
greatly she disliked what she was going to have to say.
Then, with a sudden, defiant lift of her chin, she said
quite clearly:

"I'm awfully sorry to disappoint you, Mother, but
Rex *did* propose last night——"

"Meryon!"

"And I refused him."

"You re—— You said '*No!*' But you *couldn't* have.
You couldn't possibly have refused such a wonderful
match!"

Meryon gave a quick sigh and made a visible effort to
remain patient.

"Look here, darling. It's no good your getting upset
about it, because I'm quite determined. I like Rex as a
friend. I think he's charming and interesting. But I
don't love him in the least, and I am not going to bam-
boozle myself into thinking I do, just because he has
inherited three-quarters of a million pounds."

"But you'd *learn* to love him, child. You couldn't
help it. He's so charming and—well, anybody would."

Meryon didn't say anything. She wondered if Mother
knew just how horrid that sounded, when her whole air
made it obvious that she thought the greatest aid in
learning to love Rex Treventon would be his money.

But Mrs. Dawling's thoughts were running off on something else.

"Then this whole visit has been wasted! All the care and thought. All the new clothes. All my careful planning."

"Mother dear, you mustn't talk like that." Meryon was genuinely distressed. "You know it's been a perfectly lovely visit." For a moment her gaze strayed out of the window, across the still, dark beauty of the loch on which the Varleys' house stood.

There were some things about Glengalloch, she thought, that she at least would never forget. The pinky gold of the dawn stealing over the tops of the hills, while down in the valley everything was still dark and silent. Moonlight tracing a path of silver across the loch, so solid that one could almost have walked along it. Evening creeping down the glen, lengthening the shadows and softly blurring the outlines of the landscape, while the tinkle of distant sheep-bells and the twittering of sleepy birds seemed the only sound in the world.

It was a pity that Mother could take no pleasure in anything like that, thought Meryon with a sigh. It made her disappointment so bitter when her complicated yet artless little schemes went wrong. And at this moment, certainly, she was beyond taking pleasure in anything.

"Perfectly lovely visit!" she repeated indignantly. "It hasn't been anything of the sort. Who do you suppose really *wants* to come to Scotland on shooting parties? All this rushing north in droves just to shoot a lot of unoffending birds on the right date! It's nothing but an excuse for something much more interesting. And now look what's happened! Jessie Varley as good as engaged to a baronet's son, and you can't do anything but turn down one of the most eligible bachelors in England. Really, Meryon, I'm ashamed of you."

Meryon's soft mouth tightened suddenly in a way that reminded Mrs. Dawling uncomfortably of her dead husband in his most determined moods.

"Now look here, dear." Meryon sat down on the arm of her mother's chair. "I'm very sorry, but it looks to me as though nothing but very plain speaking will do. I know all this anxiety to get me a rich husband is simply because you have my own good at heart. But you've got to call this chase off. I'm not a husband-hunter by nature, and I'm not going to be made into one. It's no good your reckoning up incomes and checking up chances. You only embarrass me and make me very cross with you. The plain truth is that I shan't marry until I *want* to marry—and when I do, it'll be because I love someone, and not because he's got more money than he can count. See?" And she kissed her mother so affectionately that it ought to have softened the firmness of her words.

But, rather to Meryon's surprise, her mother refused to be mollified. Sitting up very straight, she turned to face her daughter, slightly pale and with her eyes dark and childishly obstinate.

"You're a very silly and wrong-headed girl, Meryon," she said sharply. "And you don't know what you're talking about. But one thing which you said *is* right, and that is that nothing but plain speaking will do. And I have some plain speaking for you. It's absolutely essential, my dear, that you marry soon, like a sensible girl, and marry well. The truth is that I broke into my last five hundred pounds in order to pay for this trip."

"You broke into your last—— Mother! what on earth are you saying? Are you mad?" Meryon had gone terribly pale.

Mrs. Dawling moved uncomfortably and looked very charmingly sulky.

"But—are you trying to tell me that you've been living on your capital?" Meryon strove to make that as calm as possible.

"It's not only *I*, my dear." Mrs Dawling bridled a little. "You have, too, you know."

Meryon winced.

"Yes, of course. I realise that. If you've really been selling capital, I—— But, Mother, why didn't you tell me? You never would say a word about your money affairs, except that Daddy left plenty, and——"

"So he did leave plenty—properly used," Mrs. Dawling explained quickly. "Of course the *interest* didn't amount to very much, but I worked out everything very carefully, and I made out that we could go on living just exactly as we always had, if we divided out the capital over the years until you were twenty-one. By then, I reckoned that you would be marrying well—I was *sure* of it, darling. You were so attractive, even as a little girl," she added irrelevantly.

"But, what a perfectly crazy——" Meryon stopped abruptly and bit her lip. It was hopeless, simply hopeless, trying to make Mother see. Besides, the grim, inescapable fact was that their money was gone. "I suppose it didn't strike you that I might *not* marry?" she said rather wearily.

"Certainly not, dear. Any really nice girl always gets married if she has the proper chances—and takes them. Look at me! I was married at sixteen and had you by the time I was seventeen."

Meryon said nothing to this. She had had this shining example of matrimonial success held up to her too often to find much enthusiasm.

"It was taking a frightful chance, Mother. Banking on my marrying before every penny was gone, I mean."

"Oh, no." Mrs. Dawling was almost cheerful again, now that her confession had been made. "You see, I faced the *really* important point from the very beginning."

"Did you? And what was that?" Meryon felt a sort of fascinated curiosity to hear what detail her mother considered important enough to warrant the spending of her whole capital.

"Well, you see, darling, I knew that if I reduced everything to such a standard that we lived on our poky little income, you'd never be fitted for a big position at all. Besides, you'd never meet anybody who was anybody. How *could* you marry well? No, I saw at once that the best thing was to live expensively, educate you expensively, dress you expensively and keep you from ever dropping out of an expensive world. Now here you are—admirably fitted to be a rich man's wife, admired and proposed to by men like Rex Treventon. It was really rather clever of me, darling, though I say it myself. And, really, the rest *is* up to you, and I know you won't let me down, now you understand."

Mrs. Dawling was so pleased with this exposition of the case that Meryon could only stare at her aghast. Then, because in her heart she was so frightened and stunned at the gulf which had opened, she said with almost brutal abruptness:

"I'm sorry, but I've told you already—I refused Rex Treventon."

"But you can get him back, dear. Any girl——"

"I don't want to 'get him back,' " Meryon retorted curtly. She had never spoken like that to her mother before. "I refused Rex because, although I like him, I don't love him. And I have no intention whatever of making an undignified and deceitful grab after him simply because I find we need his money badly."

"Meryon, it's simply *wicked*, the way you twist everything I say," wailed her mother. "I only meant——"

"Do you think we might leave the subject altogether

for the time," Meryon interrupted quietly, for she felt that she would literally scream if her mother went over all her absurd and illogical arguments once more.

"Well, if you like, my dear." Mrs. Dawling looked a little sulky again. "But it's all very important, you know," she added reproachfully.

"Yes," Meryon said, with a very cold feeling at her heart. "Yes, I do realise that. It's gruesomely important."

And then, to her unspeakable relief, the lunch-gong sounded, and she was saved any more of this futile discussion.

They went down together, crossing the big, square, polished hall, where sunlight poured in through an open door, and entering the panelled dining-room where windows all along one side looked over yet another view of the loch.

The party was much smaller now than it had been during the last week—some of the guests having departed the previous evening or early that morning. But even so, there was a pleasant air of informal gaiety which, until now, Meryon had thoroughly enjoyed.

To-day, however, it was terribly hard to sit there, laughing, talking, eating, chaffing, pretending to be very casual and not to have a care in the world, when all the while, at the back of her mind, anxiety was gnawing away like some indefatigable animal.

The things that Mother had said seemed fantastic now that she was surrounded by the friends and acquaintances of her familiar world. And yet that cold, horrid, inescapable phrase, "my last five hundred pounds," kept repeating itself in her head.

Five hundred pounds! A very great deal of money, no doubt, to some people, but Meryon had some idea of what it cost to live in the style her mother had always adopted. There was the rent of their charming little town flat, to begin with. The wages of Currie, their impeccable maid, and the cook. Clothes. Extravagant food bills——

At that point, Meryon thought her own excellent lunch would choke her, and only with an effort could she bring herself to notice Jessie's query.

"Are you staying with your mother at Oldkeep or going straight on to London, Meryon?"

"I'm going on to London. I'll just have time to see her settled with the Graydens, and then I take the train from Oldkeep Central just after midnight."

"My dear, how spartan of you. I do hate night journeys."

Meryon smiled.

"I don't mind if I have a sleeper," she said. And the most unwelcome thought came: "But I suppose having a sleeper is the sort of extravagance we simply can't afford now. How strange—and how perfectly terrible! I wish I'd known before and I wouldn't have booked it."

Good heavens! It had really come to that! She had to consider even the price of a sleeper in her attempt to stem the perfect tide of financial disaster which she could see sweeping towards them.

To Meryon, it was a genuine relief when the meal came to an end, and there was only time for a flurry of hasty "Good-byes" before she and her mother were in the car, driving to the station five miles away.

Once they and their luggage had been settled in a first-class compartment of the train, and the chauffeur from Glengalloch dismissed with Mrs. Dawling's usual lavish tip, it seemed to Meryon that the last links with the pleasant make-believe of false security were severed. They were rushing onward now through the afternoon sunlight towards stark and very unpleasant realities.

The very beat of the engine wheels seemed to chatter, "What's-to-be-done? What's-to-be-done? What's-to-be-done?"

But nothing supplied the answer.

It didn't even occur to her to discuss the subject again with her mother. Any solution, she knew, would have to be worked out and supplied by herself—a situation to which Meryon had become very used in the ten years since her father had died.

Even as a little girl, when the death of her father had been a scarcely understandable disaster, she had been aware in a vague, childish way that Mother was not someone to be relied upon, but rather a very distinct, though, of course, dear, responsibility. And the principle by which she had lived during the years since then might be summed up in the words, "I mustn't worry Mother about that."

Not that major problems had been at all inclined to arise—until now. Except for the death of her father, Meryon's childhood and girlhood had been remarkably free from shadow. She had been happy at school and happy at home. Friends and companions had always been there in plenty, and money had never been anything much but the everyday means by which the good things of life automatically made their appearance.

Now all that was to change. Unless she was prepared to accept her mother's complacent solution—and that she certainly was not—she was going to have to find some way of making money.

But how?

For one thing at least she was thankful, and that was that she was leaving her mother for a week or two with some very old friends of theirs. The Graydens were hospitable, well-to-do people who were genuinely fond of her mother, and Mrs. Dawling had been looking forward for some time to this visit.

Meanwhile, Meryon was to go on home to London, where various social engagements claimed her, and spend the week or two at their flat, in the care of the admirable Currie.

"That will give me time," reflected Meryon, with the feeling of panic lessening. "I'll have time to face up to things and see what is to be done, without having Mother making her fantastic matrimonial suggestions."

Even that small decision helped her to stave off the sense of disaster a little. And when Mrs. Dawling woke from a pleasant nap, it was to find a tranquil, even cheerful Meryon, who seemed in a much more sensible mood.

No more exclamations and uncomfortable questions about why one had done what one *had* done. (So silly, when, of course, anyone could see it had been the only thing to do!)

And, to Mrs. Dawling's relief, this satisfactory state of things lasted, not only through the rest of the journey, but during the hour or two Meryon was able to spend with the Graydens, and until she left them to take the night train to London.

For Meryon, the journey to London was completely uneventful, only remarkable for the fact that she slept exceedingly well, in spite of her worry. King's Cross looked cold and depressing in the early morning light, and as Meryon got out of the train she shivered slightly and wondered why she had insisted on taking the night train.

But, once she was in a taxi, driving homeward, the feeling of depression lifted. The flat would be ready to receive her—warm, welcoming, discreetly luxurious, and Currie would have a delicious breakfast prepared. There would be flowers everywhere, the gleam of silver and china, the subdued colourings of well-chosen furniture and hangings. Oh, it was good to be going home, when home was represented by comfort and—security.

The very smile with which Currie welcomed her seemed to repeat as much, and when, in answer to Meryon's "Everything all right, Currie?" she said, "Oh, yes, miss, of course," it seemed to Meryon that everything must indeed be all right. One felt that if anyone so well-trained as Currie said so, there was no possibility of doubt.

Over breakfast she opened the pile of letters which had arrived too late to be sent on to Scotland.

Invitations—invitations—invitations.

Odd how terribly filled one's time became the moment one was back in Town. "I suppose it just happens," thought Meryon with a sigh.

And then she paused. No, perhaps it didn't "just happen." Perhaps Mother, with her careful scheming had really worked for this too, as part of her extraordinarily complicated plan to make her daughter sought after by "everyone who mattered," whatever that vague term might mean.

"It's beyond me," murmured Meryon, pushing back her hair a little impatiently. "Anyway, I'm going to have a hot bath and then a walk in the Park. The rest of the dramatic future must simply wait until I've done that!"

But, actually, that was almost the only time she had to herself during the next week or ten days. Everybody seemed to know she was back in Town. Everybody seemed reproachful if she didn't drop in to see them. "Besides, you must be lonely without your mother," they all added.

"Lonely!" thought Meryon. "Sometimes I think the only way to be lonely in London would be to go and sit on top of the dome of St. Paul's. And *then* someone would probably organise parties of sightseers to come and look at one."

At any rate, she was ashamed to find that almost a fortnight had slipped away and still she had done nothing towards settling the problem so casually presented by her mother.

She supposed she had better start by a visit to their lawyer, and a request to know exactly how things stood. And then—that very morning—there arrived the astounding letter from her mother.

Even as Meryon slid her thumb under the envelope flap she had the peculiar feeling that the letter was important. And when she saw the length at which her mother had expressed herself, she was sure of it.

"*Meryon darling,*" wrote Mrs. Dawling with customary lack of restraint, "*You'll never guess what news I have for you, and, really, I'm afraid you will be shocked as well as pleased at first, because, of course, it must be very sudden to you. Not that I had any wish to be secretive.*"

Meryon glanced hastily down the page in an anxious endeavour to discover the real news in the forest of words. It was not easy, however. Then a name caught her eye. "Henry Monder." That seemed familiar. Wasn't he the man Mother had met and liked so much when she was at Cannes in the spring?

It seemed, on further investigation, that he was. Henry Monder had apparently turned up again as a friend of the Graydens: "*Such a delightful man, darling, and he is dying to meet you.*"

"Well, at any rate I'm not marrying *him*," murmured Meryon with grim humour. "He's over fifty, if I remember rightly."

But the next paragraph wiped both the idea and the amusement from her mind, for it seemed that something very, very far from a marriage for Meryon was in Mrs. Dawling's mind. Having gone round and round the point for two and a half pages, in the entirely mistaken idea that she had prepared Meryon, she suddenly dealt her bludgeon stroke!

"And I know, darling, I ought really to be saying that we think of getting married. But the fact is, Meryon, that we've done it. By special licence. Yesterday. So romantic, isn't it? Do please write (or even telephone) and tell me you are delighted. You'll love him, dear. You couldn't help it. He's quite the nicest man you can possibly imagine."

Meryon slowly laid down the letter and groped for a chair.

Married! Mother was not only "thinking of getting married"—she had "done it," to use her own expressive phrase.

Without warning, without so much as a hint! And Meryon had not even seen her new stepfather—could only recall the sketchiest description of him, supplied some months ago, when he was no more than one acquaintance among many.

For a moment she felt very much afraid, for the idea had come to her that perhaps Mother had rushed into some regrettable arrangement because she thought she had better recoup the family fortunes since Meryon would not.

But a further perusal of the letter reassured her. None of that spontaneous, artless outpouring could have come from anything but a very happy heart. And, with a relieved little laugh, Meryon suddenly realised that never once had her mother even mentioned Henry Monder's income.

"Then she must be fond of him," declared Meryon aloud, and there was no intentional cynicism in the remark. Crossing the room, she picked up the telephone receiver, and while she sat there, waiting for her connection, she tried once more to review the situation in its new light.

Of course, there was one thing. If Mother were really happily married, then more than half of the present problem had disappeared. If she could be quite sure there had been no ulterior motive, quite sure——

"You're through," the operator's voice informed her, and the next moment her mother's excited tones sounded in her ears.

"Hello, darling! What *did* you think? Aren't you surprised? And isn't it lovely?"

There was only one possible answer when Mother spoke like that.

"Of course it's lovely. And if you're as happy as you sound, then I think the idea is magnificent."

"Oh, Meryon, I *knew* you would!" The transparent relief in Mrs. Dawling's voice showed that she had not known anything of the kind, and that now she was delighted to find all her fears unfounded.

Meryon laughed.

"And when do I——"

"Oh, my dear, of course you must come up here at once. Oh, you *must*! Henry is longing to see you and so are Sally and John. . . . What, dear? . . . Why, they're Henry's children, of course? What? . . . Yes—my stepchildren. Isn't it extraordinary to think I'm a stepmother? . . . I didn't *tell* you about them? I must have, darling—surely. Anyway, they're sweet. . . . What? . . . Oh no, no, no—not *children*—at least not really. Sally's sixteen and John must be about fourteen, though, of course, poor boy, with his being ill so much—— Well, anyway, my dear, I'll tell you all about it when you come. Yes, yes, of course you must. To-morrow. I shall expect you. Yes—Henry says there's a splendid train that leaves King's Cross about ten—or, no, perhaps it's eleven, dear—I'm not sure. Anyway, you would be here just in time for tea. Good-bye, darling, good-bye! It will be so nice to see you."

Meryon replaced the receiver a little dazedly. It was rather as though an amiable hurricane had passed over her, and now she felt surprisingly flat and breathless.

So she had acquired not only a stepfather but a stepsister and a stepbrother too—all, or so it seemed, in the space of five minutes! Really, Mother's way of doing things was unexpected, to say the least. But she seemed happy—really happy—and that, after all, was the chief thing.

"I wonder if—and how—I am expected to fit into the new scheme," thought Meryon, amused and doubtful. And when the London train drew into Oldkeep Central the next afternoon, curiosity and a certain anxiety were still Meryon's uppermost feelings.

The slim, pretty figure of her mother detached itself from the waiting people the moment Meryon stepped from the train, and as she hugged her mother, Meryon was aware of a tall, pleasant, grey-haired man who stood watching the greeting with very much the same affectionate indulgence which she herself always showed towards her mother.

"And, darling, this is Henry." Taking Meryon by the hand, the new Mrs. Monder rather proudly presented her daughter to her husband. "Henry, what do you think of my grown-up daughter? Isn't she pretty?"

"Pretty enough to charm the most critical of stepfathers," Henry Monder said, and immediately took charge of the situation in a way which evidently delighted his wife. Almost before Meryon could reply to the greeting, she found herself being ushered out of the station to a big, dark blue Daimler, waiting impressively though discreetly by the kerb.

A chauffeur drove, and Henry Monder sat in front of Meryon and her mother, turned sideways so that he could talk to them. It did Meryon's heart good to see the way he looked at her mother, and his attitude towards herself was kind in the extreme.

Meryon was a quick judge of character, and after the first five minutes it was obvious to her that Henry Monder was one of those warm-hearted, expansive men who are invariably nice to everyone because they literally have no wish to be anything else.

"He's ideal for Mother!" thought Meryon with a certainty which astounded herself. "He'll never say a cross word to her, and it will be his real and constant pleasure to give her everything she wants."

Even from first appearance, she could not help guessing, too, that "everything Mother wanted" could include a good many material things without straining the resources of the generous Henry Monder.

The car, the chauffeur's uniform, the rug over her knees, the very way her new stepfather spoke, all told an unostentatious but unmistakable tale of wealth. And for that Meryon could only be thankful because, though Mother's true faults were not perhaps serious, extravagance was certainly one of them.

"You'll *love* the house, pet." Her mother interrupted her thoughts at that moment. "It has the most beautiful garden, and there is a tennis court and a sunk garden and lots of lovely things."

Meryon laughed at her mother's artless pleasure in her new acquisitions, and glanced a little diffidently at her stepfather. But she saw that there was no need for anxiety there. He was watching his new wife with open delight, only too pleased that she was pleased.

The car had left the business part of the town behind by now, and was making towards what Meryon knew to be the most charming of its several suburbs. Oldkeep itself, famous for its ruined castle and its many associations with the troubled history of the north, was not nowadays the most attractive of towns. Business houses, warehouses, offices and slums jostled each other along both sides of the river.

But, further out towards the open country, where the well-to-do men of its business world lived, Oldkeep could still show some very pleasant ways of living. And, as the car turned into a well-kept, semicircular drive, Meryon saw that Henry Monder's home was by no means the least luxurious of the houses which made up this district.

"Here we are, dear. Isn't it nice?" The new Mrs. Monder spoke as though she were personally responsible for the appearance of the house.

"Very nice," Meryon said with a smile, and then her stepfather took her hand.

"Welcome home, Meryon," he said, so kindly that the conventional phrase sounded almost original. "I hope you will always regard this *as* your home and spend as much of your time here as you like."

"Oh—thank you so very much. It's more than kind of you," Meryon said earnestly, for she felt genuinely moved by the warmth of the welcome. And then she followed her mother into the house.

Only a child showing off a doll's house, could have equalled Mrs. Monder's delight in displaying the beauties of her new home. She scarcely allowed Meryon to take off her things first.

"Never mind about your case, darling. Sanders will see to that. Oh, and put down your hat and coat here. I'll take you upstairs to your room afterwards—only you *must* come and see the south drawing-room first. It's the loveliest room you could imagine! I can't wait until you've seen it. Henry, do just go up and see if John feels like seeing a visitor, there's a dear. Sally isn't in yet, I know, so Meryon must wait to meet her. Come this way, darling."

Amused and, somehow, a little touched, Meryon

followed her mother across the wide hall into a very large and most beautifully proportioned room.

"There! Isn't that lovely?" Innocent pride of ownership was in every line of her mother, and Meryon had to smile.

"It's lovely," she agreed, taking a few steps forward into the room and looking round admiringly.

Along the whole of one end of the room ran windows which looked out over a sloping terrace to a charming formal garden, and then away to the open country beyond. The effect of distance was beautiful, and the room itself, with its admirable combination of the artistic old and the comfortable modern, was delightful.

It was a cool afternoon, and a cheerful wood fire rustled and crackled on the open hearth at the far side of the room. Drawn cosily round the fire were several big, high-backed chairs, into which one could sink with every sensation of luxurious comfort, and everywhere the warm, rich gleam of polished mahogany reflected back the soft glow of the firelight.

"It's so tasteful and yet so *rich*," Mrs. Monder said with a satisfied sigh. And at that Meryon really could not resist teasing her.

"Yes, the effect is certainly rich," she agreed, and then, putting her hands on her mother's shoulders, she added solemnly, "Mother, I congratulate you. You have certainly married money. Clever little person, aren't you?"

Her mother's expression of surprise and dismay was quite ludicrous, but Meryon remained perfectly serious.

"All these efforts to acquire a rich husband for me, and then what do I find?—That you've actually snapped up one of these matrimonial gilt-edged securities yourself!"

"Meryon! Really. I—— But, darling, you don't *mind*, do you? He's——"

"Mind that you've brought all this money into the family? You don't really expect a daughter of yours to mind that, do you?"

It was too bad, Meryon thought amusedly, because Mother always took these things so seriously. But, really, she deserved a little teasing. However, Mrs. Monder was full of explanations at once.

"You mustn't think for one moment that I forgot *your* interests too, Meryon. You really mustn't. And, my dear, it doesn't matter a bit about your not getting Rex Treventon." Meryon's eyebrows shot up, but her mother scarcely noticed. "There's more time now, of course, but, anyway—I was going to tell you—I've such a good idea, darling. I hope that *you* are going to like Henry's nephew more than a little. He's quite charming, just a nice age for you, and of course as rich as can be. It would be wonderful, wouldn't it? Of course, as I say, there's no *hurry*, but, anyway, you'll be meeting him this evening and—— Oh, my dear, there's Henry calling. Just a moment. I must go. But wait for me here. I won't be a minute or two, and I want to show you everything myself. Don't, *please*, go exploring until I come back." And with a little wave of her hand, Mrs. Monder hurried off, delighted, Meryon saw, to be doing her new husband's bidding.

Left alone, Meryon laughed softly. It was really very amusing to see her charming, absurd mother like this. And that, through it all, her match-making passion should have persisted! That was perhaps the funniest bit of all.

"No," thought Meryon. "No, the funniest bit is Mother's insistence on there being 'no hurry,' yet she has almost got me engaged and married before I have sat down in the house."

Still smiling, she strolled over to the fire and stood there holding out her hands to the blaze.

How pleasant a wood fire was! How pleasant this room was. She turned to look at it once more, and as she did so, she realised with a considerable start that a tall man, with rather ruffled fair hair and cynically amused grey eyes, was lounging in one of the big chairs, watching her.

For a moment she could only stare at him in astonishment, slowly taking in the fact that he must have been there all the time, hidden by the back of the chair— *hearing the whole of their ridiculous conversation!*

What on earth *had* they said? And what, in Heaven's name, must he think!

What he thought was pretty plain from the scornful little smile, and from the fact that only now did he get to his feet, although Meryon had been standing all the time. He didn't look the kind of man to be casual with his own womenfolk, but as he towered over Meryon now, she suddenly felt small and ridiculous and quite indescribably cheap.

Still he said nothing—only smiled that exceedingly disturbing smile. And so, after what seemed minutes, although it could have only been seconds, Meryon broke the silence, with what she immediately felt was an absurdly over-dignified:

"May I ask who you are?"

"You may." His voice was deep and pleasant and as amused as his smile. "I am the next victim proposed for the attention of this gold-digging syndicate." He bowed slightly. "Henry Monder's nephew, Gregory. Quite charming, just a nice age for you and, of course, as rich as can be."

Meryon gasped audibly. Then she drew herself up with a *hauteur* she was far from feeling.

"It isn't usually considered very gentlemanly to eavesdrop," she pointed out coldly.

"No?" he considered the point. "But then, is it

specially ladylike to prepare to lasso some poor fellow the moment you discover you like the look of his bank balance?"

"Oh!" Meryon went crimson and then very white. "Since you did overhear everything we said, I should scarcely have thought it was necessary to explain we were simply speaking in joke."

There was quite a long silence, while those contemptuous grey eyes travelled slowly over Meryon again, making her feel hot and cold by turns.

"Well, of course, it is possible that my sense of humour is stunted," he said at last, with a sort of polite insolence. "But it is only fair to warn you that, while my uncle seems to appreciate being the victim of a —joke, *I* most certainly should not."

"I think you're behaving abominably," Meryon said.

"And I don't know that I'm lost in admiration of your behaviour," he retorted carelessly. "But I think I hear my uncle and your mother coming. Shall we pretend to be conversing amiably?" And taking her coolly and resistlessly by the arm, he strolled over to the window with her.

"Will you *please*——"

"No, I will not. Now, all down that side of the garden my uncle decided he wanted to have—— Oh, hello, Uncle, I've just been showing Meryon how you altered the whole character of the garden last spring."

"Oh, yes, indeed." Mr. Monder was evidently an enthusiastic gardener and entered at once into the discussion. "It was just after I came home from Cannes— got one or two original notions from over there, you know."

"One or two very original notions," murmured Gregory thoughtfully, but only the angry Meryon heard, and she had to pretend not to have done so.

"Oh, so you and Gregory have introduced yourselves?" Meryon's mother smiled charmingly, quite unaware of any strain in the atmosphere.

"Yes," Gregory said, with a polite and thoughtful air. "Yes, I think Meryon and I might certainly be said to have introduced ourselves."

CHAPTER II

"Well, now!" Mr. Monder was as eager as his wife to make Meryon completely at home, and quite as unaware of any tension between her and his nephew. "Suppose you come upstairs to meet John."

"John is your son, isn't he?" Meryon tried to make that sound calmly interested, although she was still trembling angrily from what Gregory had said.

"Yes. Perhaps your mother told you——" Mr. Monder's pleasant face clouded. "He's something of an invalid, poor boy."

"I'm so very sorry," Meryon said, and she meant it. But as she turned to follow her stepfather, Gregory said regretfully:

"I'm afraid John is too young to interest you *very* much."

"Nonsense!" His uncle looked annoyed. "John is quite a young personality. And an intelligent boy of fourteen can be interesting in his way. I thought you always found him so."

"Oh, I do. But, of course, points of view differ, don't they?"

Henry Monder looked slightly puzzled and not very pleased. But Meryon, whose colour was becoming perilously high, exclaimed: "Well, let's go up and see John. I usually get on very well with schoolboys." And her stepfather was successfully side-tracked.

As they crossed the hall and went up the wide, shallow stairs, he said a little worriedly:

"John is not the—the average schoolboy, you know. He's been ill, on and off, ever since he was a baby, and that means no real school or proper sports or anything like that. He's a clever boy and all that but—well, anyway, you'll see for yourself."

For a moment Meryon wondered what she *would* see for herself, and then she realised that, of course, to the good-natured but unimaginative Henry Monder, it must be in the nature of a disaster to have a son who didn't run absolutely true to type. He would quite understand some hearty, football-playing boy who took things as they came, in the same way that he himself did. But anything at all out of the ordinary—particularly anything that could not run about and shout and make itself a healthy nuisance—puzzled and worried him.

"He's fond of the child, quite obviously," thought Meryon, "but I hope he doesn't wear that slightly apologetic air about him when the boy himself is there."

She had no time for further speculation, however, because at that moment Mr. Monder pushed open a door halfway along the upstairs passage, and ushered Meryon and her mother into a light, airy room that evidently did duty both for a bedroom and a boy's study.

So much Meryon took in in her first glance, and then her gaze came to rest on the occupant of the room. He was lying on a sofa in the big bay window, the strong light showing up the contrast between the pallor of his rather thin face and the startlingly dark eyes that looked back at Meryon with an amused interest quite beyond his years.

"Hello," he said, and held out his hand. "You're Meryon, aren't you? I know all about you. You're the most marvellous girl to be found between the Equator and the North Pole."

Meryon laughed as she took his hand.

"That's Mother, isn't it? You should never listen to the descriptions of parents. They're always much too partial."

"I don't know." His thin fingers held Meryon's rather tightly, and those uncompromising dark eyes examined her with embarrassing attention. "Anyway, she's quite right about one thing. You're awfully pretty. I'm glad. I like pretty people. Even when they're cats, they're restful to the eyes."

"Your new stepsister has a charming nature," Henry Monder said quite kindly, but with singular lack of humour.

"But I bet she's on her best behaviour now."

"Of course I am." Meryon smiled down at him. "When I really feel at home I throw terrible fits of temper, and even go into hysterics on very little provocation."

John grinned at her and said, "I guessed as much."

"Meryon dear, I never *heard* of anything so silly!" began her mother indignantly, but John went on almost immediately:

"Will you stay to tea with me? Just you, by yourself."

"Of course, if you——"

"Now, John, you mustn't be selfish." Henry Monder's patiently reasonable tone reduced John to the status of a dear but mentally defective child. "Meryon's mother hasn't seen her for some while and naturally wants to be with her. Perhaps another day."

John said nothing, but his eyes remained on Meryon as though he merely waited for her to finish her sentence.

"I don't think Mother will mind doing without me for a little while," Meryon said with a smile. "And if you'd like me to stay, John, I should like it, too."

"Perhaps we could all have tea up here," suggested Mrs. Monder brightly.

But John vetoed that with a polite formality that would not have disgraced a senior statesman.

"I'm sorry, but I'm afraid I should find that too tiring," he said gravely. And Meryon thought amusedly, 'Is he really only fourteen?'

"Well, if you're sure you would like that, Meryon?" That was her stepfather.

"Perfectly sure."

"All right, darling, of *course* I'll spare you." Mrs. Monder was pleased that the whole arrangement really turned on her own good nature. "Only don't go telling John any more silly stories about your having fits of temper and hysterics. There was never *anything* like that in our family. You know there wasn't."

And with this final admonition, she went out of the room with her husband.

When their footsteps had finally died away, Meryon and the boy on the sofa exchanged an extremely understanding and amused glance.

"Won't you sit down?" He leaned forward and rather feebly pulled up a chair for her. Then, as Meryon sat down: "I think your mother's an awful fool. I hope you don't mind."

"Not if you don't hurt her by letting her know you think so," Meryon said coolly.

"I say—that's awfully broad-minded of you."

"Why? Perhaps it just means that I don't attach much weight to your opinion." But Meryon smiled in a way that rather softened that, because she already liked this precocious, unusual boy with the too-bright eyes and thick, tumbled, dark hair.

He looked at her thoughtfully for a moment and then said:

"Is that a snub?"

"No." Meryon shook her head. "Just a friendly reminder that you're not the centre of the universe."

She received a half-startled glance of interest.

"You mean—invalids are apt to think they are?" he said quickly.

"Not if they are intelligent and try to keep their sense of proportion," Meryon told him.

"Oh!" Again that startled look. Then he drew slightly towards her, almost as though his liking for her found expression in literally wanting to be near her. "It's not easy, you know."

"What isn't?"

"Keeping your sense of proportion when everyone persists in regarding you as pitiable or—odd."

Meryon knew he was hoping she hadn't noticed the slight break in his voice, and she somehow suppressed the pity in her own.

"No, I'm sure it must be frightfully difficult. Particularly as most people are so silly where invalids are concerned. That's why I was glad to notice you are a realist," she added gravely. "It keeps you from sentimentalising the situation—or getting despondent about it."

"Oh, yes, of course." Then she saw him suddenly lift his chin determinedly. "Yes, certainly I'm a realist. That—that helps a lot."

"Of course. It would," Meryon agreed.

But while tea was being brought in, and she was pouring it out, she was really thinking:

"Poor child, if it's a comforting label, you hold on to it. For you're just a lovable, intelligent, unhappy boy, really."

John watched her in silence until she handed him his tea. Then he observed:

"You'll get on awfully well with my cousin, Gregory."

"Shall I?" Meryon managed not to make that too sharp.

"Yes. He's a wonderful chap. You'll meet him this evening. He's in and out here most days, you know."

"Is he?" Try as she would, she could not sound enthusiastically interested. "He—lives quite near you, then?"

"Oh, yes. He's Father's junior partner. Hasn't any family of his own, so he regards us more or less as belonging to him. He's what *you* would call—sensible about—sick people."

"You're very fond of him, aren't you?" Meryon said gently, and it struck her that perhaps she had judged Gregory Monder very hastily—as no doubt he had her.

"Very. So is Sally."

"Sally? Oh, of course. She's your sister, isn't she?" Here was a welcome chance of a diversion, Meryon thought. "And what is Sally like?"

"Killing," said Sally's brother succinctly.

"Do you mean she's amusing?"

"Well—much more so than she knows. She's very pretty, but an awful kid, of course," he added tolerantly. "She's in her last year or two at school, but I can't ever see that she's learnt anything. Even her spelling is frightful. She's dying to leave and have what she calls 'a good time.' I don't know what she means exactly, and I don't think she does either, but—anyway, here she is. That's her step."

Meryon looked up with interest as the door opened, and an extraordinarily pretty girl of about sixteen came into the room. She was as dark as her brother, but with enormous vitality and sparkle, and the yellow dress she was wearing set off her vivid colouring admirably.

"Hello."

"Hello."

"This is Meryon."

"I guessed as much. How d'you do?"

Pause. Then John said casually:

"It's all right. One can talk in front of her."

"Oh, good. You haven't got lots of stuffy ideas
then?" Sally looked at Meryon with engaging frankness

"I don't think so. I hope not." Meryon laughed.

"She hasn't," John explained. "Nor do you have to
tell her something is a joke before she'll laugh at it."

"Oh, you'll get on well with Gregory," Sally remarked
confidently. And Meryon was impelled to reflect on the
peculiarity of her having fallen foul, in a most unusual
degree, of the very person who was supposed to agree
best with her.

"Why are you so sure I shall like Gregory?" she asked
interestedly.

"Because we do," John said.

"Because nobody could help it," Sally said.

"Oh." Meryon laughed a little again at the logic, but
she couldn't help feeling flattered by the partiality of the
one reason and touched by the loyalty of the other.

"They are nice children," she thought with a warmth
of feeling that surprised her. "And interesting children
too. I'm glad they don't resent an elder stepsister
Perhaps I'll be able to do some things for them. Particu
larly as Mother said they've been without their own
mother most of their lives."

But at that moment, she thought, perhaps they
would rather be left alone, for it was evidently their
habit to exchange the day's news at some length and
with considerable candour.

As she rose to go, however, there was yet another
interruption, for the door opened once more, to admit
Gregory.

"Hello, Gregory!" John's face brightened indescrib
ably. "Did you get—— Oh, of course you did," as, with

smile, his cousin handed over a small, cloth-bound book. "I say, thanks most awfully. It was only published to-day, wasn't it?"

"Yes. But I've had it on order for the last fortnight."

"Even before I asked for it?"

"Well, I was pretty sure you'd want it." There was nothing at all indulgent about Gregory's tone. Nothing of his uncle's kindly but trying anxiety and fussiness. Just a sort of cool, affectionate good-temper which he might have shown towards any young cousin. Meryon saw at once how curiously it soothed and brightened the boy, and again she thought, "Perhaps I did misjudge Gregory."

"Oh—sorry." John looked up from the examination of his book and made a vague gesture indicative of introduction. "Of course, you two haven't met, have you? This is Gregory, Meryon. Our new stepsister, Gregory."

"But we have met," Gregory assured him agreeably. "We know quite a lot about each other already."

"Do you?" John looked surprised. "You didn't say so, Meryon, when I said you and Gregory would be sure to get on."

"Perhaps Meryon doubted your judgment on that point, but felt it is always better to say too little than too much," suggested Gregory. "But, anyway, I'm afraid I came to take her away. She is wanted downstairs now. Or rather, out in the garden. You're expected to make a tour of inspection before the daylight fades, I think," he explained to Meryon, quite as though he had no idea that the first half of his speech had made her very uncomfortable.

She said "Good night" to John and Sally, and came out of the room with Gregory. It was very tempting to say curtly that she would find her own way down to the garden, but he so obviously meant to escort her that it was difficult. Besides, perhaps this moment together might give her an opportunity to repair the early unfortunate breach.

The last thing she wanted was a permanent rift with one of her new relations. Indeed, she felt prepared to go to considerable lengths to put things right between them. Consequently, when they reached the drawing-room again, she put her hand impulsively on his arm before he could open the door into the garden.

"Mr. Monder—just a moment. There's something I want to say."

The grey eyes which were turned on her were cool and exceedingly amused.

"I believe the traditional reply is—'But this is so sudden,'" he said maliciously.

"Oh, please!" Meryon laughed annoyedly. "Haven't we developed that joke sufficiently? I just wanted to make you understand—to say that I know the conversation you overheard was silly and perhaps not in the best of taste, but there was not, of course, the slightest serious meaning in it. You really must accept my explanation. It's—it's so embarrassing and ridiculous for us both if you won't."

"I'm not in the least embarrassed," he assured her. "And as for explanations, let me assure you that considered in cold blood, your conversation needed no explanation whatever."

"But you *can't* mean that you're seriously making up your mind about two people on the unsupported evidence of some silly, frivolous conversation."

"Oh, not unsupported," protested Gregory gently. "Anything but unsupported."

"What do you *mean*?" Meryon stepped back from him and looked exceedingly dismayed.

He was not smiling or bantering now. He was looking exceedingly grim.

"My dear Miss Dawling, it is quite immaterial to me whether you did or did not intend me to replace the elusive—Rex Treventon, wasn't it? What does concern me is that my uncle—one of the nicest, and, incidentally, most stupid of men—took just ten days to be persuaded by your mother that he ought to marry again. You don't really suppose—and certainly I don't suppose—that she would have taken all that trouble about a poor man."

"But she's fond of him. She's most genuinely fond of him!" interrupted Meryon quickly. "You couldn't doubt——"

"Fondness usually takes longer than ten days to develop—unless there is financial assistance."

"But——"

"My uncle told me earnestly that 'the brave little woman was struggling along on her last few hundreds' —and a lot of other nonsense. Are you really asking me to believe that the brave little woman didn't take heart when she reckoned up my uncle's income? Come, Miss Dawling, you don't seem to credit me with much common gumption. If your mother is a gold-digger who has caught my uncle—well, that's his luck. If you are a gold-digger who accidentally warned me in advance— well, that's my luck. Only, please don't let's all pretend we're lost in affectionate respect for each other. Personally, I think you're a contemptible couple. And this afternoon's conversation did nothing to correct the impression."

For a moment Meryon could find no words to reply. Never before in her life had she felt so humiliated or so appalled. She had always been used to the unquestioning respect and liking of her friends and acquaintances. And now this man quite obviously—quite sincerely— thought her cheap and unscrupulous and contemptible.

"Shall we go out into the garden now?" He was holding the door open for her.

"No!" Meryon's words almost choked her, but she had to get them out. "No—I can't have you thinking such things of me—of us——"

"Aren't you putting an exaggerated value on my good opinion?" His glance flicked over her again.

"It isn't that. It's the justice of the thing!"

"Oh!" Gregory made an impatient little gesture. "Don't you think we might leave all these high-sounding words out of it. My views can't be of any importance to you now, and I assure you that your views are less than unimportant to me. Surely we may take *that* as the last word on the matter."

And they did.

There was nothing else to be said, Meryon thought. Nothing else at all. But never once, during the whole of that evening, did his stinging words leave her. And every time her mother reiterated her artless pleasure in some further attraction of her new home, Meryon found herself wondering uncomfortably if it sounded to Gregory like the exulting of a successful gold-digger.

Hateful word! Why had he used it?

And if only this hadn't followed so closely on her own uncomfortable impressions about Mother. Not that she was anything like—well, what Gregory Monder had said. But of course she *did* think money terribly important, she *was* happy to have married so well. That was what made it so dreadfully difficult to prove that the whole thing hadn't been a thoroughly discreditable business.

There *was* Gregory's side to it, too—little though she wanted to think so. The haste with which the whole thing had been arranged, Mother's transparent delight in everything, that ridiculous and unfortunate conversation—they must make a nasty sum-total. Particularly to someone who knew nothing about her mother and herself except what had happened in the last few weeks.

"Well, I can't do anything about it just now," Meryon told herself when, much later, she was alone at last in her large and beautiful bedroom. "He'll just have to see for himself, as time goes on, that we're not quite such a poisonous couple as he supposes."

But, during the next few weeks, Meryon began to find that the very generosity and kindness of her stepfather tended more and more to put her and her mother in the light of opportunists. He wanted to give them things. He insisted that Meryon must look on her mother's new home as her own. He pointed out (very truly) how exceedingly attached to her both the children were—particularly John. And when Meryon tried to get out of the position by pretending that she thought perhaps she preferred to live most of the time in London, he looked exceedingly disappointed and said:

"Well, of course, my dear, I quite understand your feeling, and I am arranging to keep on the London flat for you and your mother, in any case, because I'm sure he will want to have a place in Town. But I do hope you will spare us a good deal of your time."

"You're much too good to me," Meryon cried distressedly. "There isn't the least reason why you should take on the responsibility of me as well as Mother."

"But, my dear child!" Henry Monder was nearly as distressed in his turn. "I'm only too delighted to have you make your home with us. I don't expect you to put me in the place of your father, but I do hope you will regard me at least as an uncle who is very fond of you."

It was impossible to thrust back so much kindness and goodwill. Meryon could only accept as gracefully as possible, and decide very firmly to set about finding some opportunity of making a career for herself.

In the meantime, she had to put up with the scarcely
veiled contempt and dislike of Gregory Monder who
as John had said, was in and out of the house almost
every day.

About three weeks after Meryon had come to Old
keep, Henry Monder was persuaded to take a few days
holiday and accompany his wife to London.

"I know the old business is important, darling," she
said with, however, very scant respect for the old
business, "but you must have a holiday sometimes and
we didn't have a honeymoon, you know."

"I don't know that I can just now." Henry Monder
was doubtful. But his wife swept that aside.

"Oh, yes, you can. And a few theatres and dinners
and a day or two's gaiety is just exactly what you
want."

"Just exactly what *you* want, you mean," he
amended with a smile. But he gave in—as Meryon had
known he would.

"And it's perfectly all right, because we can leave
Meryon in charge, you see," Mrs. Monder added in a
satisfied tone.

So it was arranged that way, and not until they had
gone did Meryon realise what an unfortunate and
tactless decision that had been, because, as Sally told
her carelessly an evening or two later:

"Of course, Gregory always used to come and stay
when Daddy was away before. I hope he didn't feel—
well, sort of pushed out. Only, he hasn't called in
once, has he?"

"Good heavens!" Meryon looked dismayed. "I
hadn't realised that, Sally. Do you suppose he might
think that—that——"

"Well, of course, men are funny that way, you
know," explained Sally, who evidently thought that
she herself knew.

Meryon ignored this unhelpful generalisation.

"I do hope your father made it quite clear that the decision was his own."

"Well, of course." Sally stared rather. "Who else's would it be?" she asked, with a happy disregard of any cross-currents in the family circle.

Meryon didn't offer to say, but she decided on impulse that if only Gregory would call in, she would try yet again to come to a better understanding with him. She hated, more than she could say, to have to be at loggerheads with someone whom she felt instinctively she ought to like and respect.

However, the opportunity never offered itself, and the evening of her mother's return arrived without anything at all having been heard from Gregory.

Both John and Sally had gone to bed, for the travellers were not expected until fairly late, and Meryon sat up alone, reading, very much looking forward to the fact that her mother would be with her again in an hour or two.

It was nearly twelve o'clock by the time she laid down her book, and with something of a start she realised how late it was.

Funny—she was certain Mother had said they would be home just after eleven. But then, of course, Mother's information about trains was always doubtful, to say the least. And, anyway, they might easily have been delayed.

She went to the window and, pushing aside the curtain, peered out down the shadowy drive. She stood there for several minutes, until her eyes were quite used to the gloom. But although several cars flashed past in the road, none of them turned into the drive, and at last, with a slightly worried little frown, Meryon turned back into the room once more.

It was not really so very late, of course, and if she

had not been alone, she would hardly have noticed the
time. Only——

The sharp ring of the telephone bell interrupted her
thoughts, and eagerly she caught up the receiver.

"Hello! hello!" Meryon spoke more sharply than she
knew. "Who is that speaking?"

"It's Gregory."

"Oh!" She felt suddenly cool and steady, because his
voice was so matter-of-fact. "I'm afraid your uncle
isn't home yet."

"Isn't he? Do you know what train they were catching?"

"I don't. Mother said something about their being
home just after eleven——"

"You're sure she said that?"

"Yes. Why? Is there something——"

"Then it was the ten-fifty they were catching?"

"I don't know. Yes. I remember now. That sounds
familiar. Mr. Monder said that time. Because there's
nothing after that until the train that gets in something
after two. But I think they must have missed the ten-
fifty, so they won't——"

"I hope to God they have missed it." Gregory's voice
was not so matter-of-fact now, and she realised suddenly that it had sounded rather unnaturally deliberate
before.

"Gregory! What——"

"Listen, Meryon. Don't start panicking, and don't
let the kids know anything, but there's been an accident
to the ten-fifty. A bad accident, I'm afraid. And they
haven't been able to get much news through yet."

"What? What's that you say?" Meryon was clinging
to the telephone receiver as though she thought she
might wring some information out of it. "An accident?
Where? Oh, I must come down to the station!"

"No!" The ring of authority in his tone was

unmistakable, and Meryon was steadied again at once. "You're not to come near the place. Half Oldkeep is there already, and every second person's got hold of some sensational rumour. You couldn't do a bit of good and would get frightfully upset. I'll bring you news the moment I can."

"But where are *you*?"

"I'm speaking from a call-box outside the station, and there are fifty people waiting to come after me. I must go now. But I thought it best to call you in case someone else went scaring you. Try not to worry too much—and don't go frightening Sally and John."

"What sort of a fool does he think I am?" exclaimed Meryon furiously as the line went dead. "Of course I shan't wake them and tell them." And then she realised that her disproportionate anger over such a trifle only showed the degree of her anxiety and terror.

"I must keep absolutely calm and sensible," she told herself, speaking aloud in her agitation. "They're probably perfectly all right, both of them. Badly scared and shaken, of course, but perfectly all right. To-morrow we shall say, 'What an escape! To think that you're perfectly all right!' For, of course, they *must* be."

She got up and began to walk up and down the room, but quietly, so that the servant should not hear and wonder what she was doing. She didn't want to have to tell anyone yet.

How long would it take to get news through?

You'd think they could telephone. Yes, that's what the authorities ought to do—telephone through the news of the people who were safe, just as soon as they could check them off. A whole list of them.

But, of course, no one ever gave a list of the living. Only a list of——

Meryon sat down abruptly. It was silly to walk

about. It only made her tired, especially when her legs would tremble so.

It was awful, of course, waiting like this, but how wonderful the relief would be when they did come.

The sound of a car brought her to her feet once more. But it passed along the road and was gone again.

One o'clock! Nearly an hour since she had stopped reading. Perhaps if she tried to go on with her book it might be better.

She picked it up, turned the pages and tried to read, her ears strained for the sound of a car or the telephone. Slowly her eyes travelled down the page, but her mind took in nothing—not even the fact that she had really read this chapter before.

It was impossible! She threw the book down. They couldn't be long now—they *couldn't*. Oh, why didn't Gregory telephone again? He had no right to leave her in this anxiety. But then he probably knew no more than she did. Besides——

There was the sound of a car again! And this time, blessed relief! It was turning in at the gates.

In a second Meryon was out in the hall, wrenching open the front door, throwing a wide streak of light down the steps, as Gregory's car drew to a standstill.

He was slow getting out—maddeningly slow as he climbed the steps. And as he came into the hall at last, she saw to her stupefaction that he wore no coat, his dinner jacket was torn, and his left arm hung rather limply at his side.

"Gregory!" She could hardly get the words out. "What on earth—has happened? You're hurt."

"No. It's nothing. I've come straight from—there."

"*Where?* The accident? You didn't say it was near here."

"It was almost in the station."

"Oh, Heavens! And Mother? Is she—is she all right?"

"Yes." Gregory's nerve-strung weariness made him answer brutally. "Of course, she's all right. Her sort always are all right."

"How dare you!" Meryon could have struck him for that, for her nerves were jangling too, but something in his grey face stopped her.

"But then——" Her voice dropped to a frightened whisper. "Your uncle, Gregory? What about your uncle?"

"He's dead," Gregory said flatly. "He must have been killed instantly. I helped to get him out myself."

CHAPTER III

"He's—dead? But he can't be!" Meryon said stupidly.

"Of course he can. If you saw the wreck there is you'd wonder that anyone was alive."

"But——"

"For Heaven's sake!" Gregory spoke roughly again. "Do you mind getting me some brandy instead of standing there opening and shutting your mouth like a goldfish."

She went to get the brandy, ignoring the insult in the realisation that minor differences didn't matter for the moment. The overwhelming disaster of her step-father's death had wiped out everything else.

When she came back, Gregory was sitting in an armchair, trying rather clumsily to turn back his sleeve from his injured arm.

"Let me do that." She was beside him at once.

"You?" He didn't look grateful. "No. You'd probably cry or be sick. It's a nasty gash."

"Don't be ridiculous. Of course I shouldn't. Drink that brandy and I'll see after your arm."

He drank the brandy without another word, and lay back watching her, as she quickly and skilfully cut away his shirt sleeve. Then she fetched warm water and washed the big, ugly cut.

"I think you ought to have a stitch or two in that." It was the first word she had spoken. "It's really a case for a doctor."

"Every doctor in the place is busy with really serious

cases," he told her curtly. "Do the best you can with tight bandaging."

"All right. Am I hurting you?"

"A bit. It doesn't matter." But he had gone very white again.

"I won't be a minute. And then I'll get you some more brandy."

"There's no point in making me drunk," he said, and the faintest smile touched his lips. It was grim, but it gave her a grain of encouragement, and almost timidly she said:

"Gregory, you did say that Mother was *quite* all right, didn't you?"

"Oh, yes—I'm sorry. Of course you want to know. She's suffering badly from shock, but there's no real injury. It was best to let her stay in the hospital for the night, though. They'd given her something to make her sleep, and you needn't worry at all."

"Did she know about——"

"No."

There was a short silence until Meryon had finished the bandaging.

"There. I think that will be all right for the time. You mustn't use it at all or you'll start the bleeding again; but I think it won't trouble you if you're careful."

"Thanks. I'll manage to drive with one hand."

"You'll do nothing of the sort," Meryon said sharply. "You're not in a fit state to drive at all."

"But I can't walk home."

"Of course not. You're staying here for the night."

An indescribably obstinate look came over his pale face.

"I shall be perfectly all right, thank you. There isn't the slightest need to trespass on your hospitality."

"*My* hospitality!"

"Well, you're in charge here, aren't you?"

Something in the slightly truculent way he said that made him seem much more boyish and much less alarming than he had ever been before.

"Why, Gregory," she said, quite gently. "Don't be silly and make difficulties about *that*. You know the place is very much more yours than mine, and the really important thing is that you should get to bed."

She thought at first that he would refuse to be persuaded, but the weariness and shock were beginning to have their way.

"All right. I suppose you don't mind if I take my usual room," he said rather ungraciously.

"Not at all. Would you like to have my arm? I expect you feel a bit shaky."

"No, thanks."

She knew that was the sheerest obstinacy, but his acute unhappiness about his uncle and his over-whelming weariness had made him unreasonable.

"All right," she said, as though he were no older than John. "You get to bed, and I'll bring you something hot to pull you together."

"I don't want——" he began. But Meryon didn't wait to hear any more. She was not going to argue every point with a tired and overstrung Gregory. She went to the kitchen instead, where she began hastily to heat some strong soup.

It was not a task that took very much of her thoughts, and yet, even though her mind was free, it seemed impossible to make it grasp this tragic sequence of events. To-morrow she would understand better. To-morrow they would be more able to work out how they stood—how they were going to break it to Sally and John—whose responsibility it would be to complete the children's upbringing.

But to-night it seemed only important that she should heat the soup, take it to Gregory, and see that he was settled with some prospect of a good night's rest.

He was lying back in bed when she entered, in answer to his curt "Come in," and, as she looked at him, Meryon could not help thinking that he must have had a very harrowing and exhausting hour or two to make him look like that. But it was better not to let him speak about it just yet, and certainly best not to ask any questions. So she only said:

"You'd better drink this up while it's hot. It will help you to sleep."

"I don't want it," asserted Gregory without looking at it.

Meryon didn't say anything, but stood there smiling slightly, and he seemed slowly to become aware of the fact that he must have sounded young and undignified.

"Sorry." He sat up with difficulty. "Am I being a bit of a fool?"

"No," Meryon said. And then, suddenly realising that he could scarcely keep up, she sat down on the side of the bed and put a supporting arm round him.

She received a very dark look. But perhaps he considered he had piled up enough ungracious refusals for that evening, for he leant against her rather thankfully, after a moment, and drank the soup without a word.

"You're not hurt anywhere besides your arm, are you?" she said when he had finished.

"No. It's just that we had to work like blazes and some of the stuff was heavy. It was a bit unnerving, too."

"Yes, I understand. Now try to go to sleep."

He didn't reply, but lay down and tried, unsuccessfully, to hitch the bedclothes round him with his un-injured arm. Meryon calmly did it for him, aware that he watched her all the time.

"Good night."

"Good night, Meryon." And then, as she turned away: "Thanks for the maternal touch. It's quite dangerously soothing when one's all out. But do remember to-morrow that I'm a dozen years older than you, won't you? A little mothering goes a long way."

"I'll try to remember," Meryon said coolly, and, putting out the light, she went out of the room, closing the door behind her.

.   .   .   .   .

The next few days were something Meryon never forgot.

Not that Sally—and still less John—were anything but very brave about things. But to have them so quiet and stunned by the shock, instead of their usual high-spirited selves, distressed Meryon beyond measure. And she was moved almost to tears when John held her hand very tightly in his and said:

"You won't go away, Meryon, will you? You won't just pack up and go off with your mother again, now that Father's gone."

"I don't know, my dear." Meryon looked exceedingly troubled. "I don't think the decision will rest with me."

"You mean your mother will have something to say?"

"Well, naturally—and so will your cousin."

"Gregory!"

"Yes. Even if he hasn't been appointed your guardian —and I should imagine your father made some such provision—he is really the person most entitled to give a decision."

"But he'll be quite willing for you to stay. Why not?" John looked at her anxiously. And Sally, who had not taken part in the discussion until then, added eagerly:

"Yes. Why ever not?"

It was difficult to say, of course, and Meryon had to content herself with an unsatisfactory, "We'll see. There'll have to be some sort of discussion, of course, and I'll see what can be managed."

Of her mother, Meryon could make nothing. In the end, she stayed in the nursing home attached to the hospital until after the funeral. But even when she did come home, she scarcely seemed the same silly, obstinate but entirely lovable person Meryon had always known.

It was as though, in her bewilderment and resentment that Fate should have snatched away so much, she clung obstinately, and even greedily, to what was left.

"It's so unfair," she kept on saying to Meryon. "Such a little while with everything exactly as I could have wished it. And now it's all spoilt. Henry's gone, and there's no one to look after me, and I don't even know what is mine and what isn't."

"But I'll look after you, darling. I promise you shan't feel too much alone," Meryon assured her earnestly.

"It's not the same thing. It's not the same thing at all as being looked after by a man."

Meryon forebore to point out that it had answered very well for something like ten years, and her mother ran on almost at once:

"I shall stay on here, of course. Henry would have wanted me to stay on in the home I loved so much." She spoke as though she had known it since childhood. "I've told Gregory that, whatever happens, I intend to stay on here."

Meryon was galvanised into speech.

"Oh, Mother! You didn't say it just like that to Gregory, did you?"

"Certainly. Why shouldn't I? I'm poor Henry's widow. I have every right to stay on in his home. The lawyer said something ridiculous about Henry not having made a new will, and that everything was left to the children and Gregory in the last will. But it's absurd, of course. Gregory's scarcely even a relation— a nephew is nothing. And a widow must be provided for. The law insists on that nowadays."

"Oh, but are you sure?" Meryon found she was lamentably ignorant about the law of inheritance, and, in any case, the idea of her mother arguing things out with Gregory made her sick with apprehension.

"Of course I'm sure," Mrs. Monder said, almost querulously. "It's only common sense, anyway."

Meryon thought of telling her that the law and common sense were not always the same thing, but it didn't seem a very soothing reflection at the moment.

"I'll have to speak to Gregory myself," she thought. But never in her life had she felt such frightened distaste for any task.

However, it was Gregory himself who saved her the unpleasantness of introducing the subject. He rang her up a couple of mornings later with the request that, if she were free, she would call in at the office to see him.

"I want to talk business," he added in curt explanation, "and, if you'll excuse my saying so, I find it very difficult to talk business when your mother is around."

"I'll come," Meryon told him almost as curtly in reply, for, while she felt there was justification for Gregory's implication, it annoyed her extremely that criticism should come from him.

Actually, Meryon had never been before to the handsome suite of offices where "H. and G. Monder, Stockbrokers," had carried on their business. During her stepfather's lifetime there had been no occasion for her to go there, but she felt a certain uncontrollable interest now in seeing Gregory in the rôle of business man.

Her arrival in the outer office caused something of a flutter in the heart of the susceptible junior clerk, for the usual dealer in stocks and shares bore no resemblance to this slim, attractive creature whose copper-coloured hair and creamy skin were so admirably set off by the black suit and the silver fox she was wearing.

Meryon, however, was entirely unaware of any flutter —except her own slight nervous agitation—as she was shown into Gregory's office.

"Oh, good morning, Meryon." He got up at once and put a chair for her, but he didn't, she noticed, make any attempt to shake hands. But then he never did.

"How are you?" She was politely formal, too, for, except for the fact that his arm was in a sling, there was nothing whatever to remind her of the much more approachable Gregory of the night of the accident.

"I'm quite fit again, thanks. The arm's a bit stiff still, but nothing to bother about."

"I'm very glad."

She didn't know quite what else to say, and, if it had been left to her, there would have been an uncomfortable little silence at this point. Gregory, however, appeared to know exactly what he wanted to say, and had no hesitation in saying it. Sitting down opposite her on the other side of the heavy mahogany desk, he launched at once into the difficult subject.

"I suppose your mother has told you that we had a talk about—future financial arrangements."

"Yes. I'm afraid Mother confused the issue rather. You see——"

"On the contrary, she was admirably clear," Gregory assured her drily. "She is very anxious—I might say, determined—to stay on at the house, and, of course, I quite understand that." The tone became, if possible, even more dry. "On the other hand, it is the home of Sally and John also, and I feel that they, too, are entitled to stay on."

"But, of *course!*" Meryon was horrified at any other thought.

"Oh, good. I'm glad you agree. Because my instructions as executor of the earlier will, were that I should go on renting the house for the use of the children until they came of age. I was also made their guardian, with the implication that I should reside in the same house. But, quite apart from my uncle's second marriage having nullified the terms of the will, that arrangement is now impossible, of course."

"Why?" Meryon looked defiantly into those cool, hard grey eyes. But as she did so, Gregory's expression relaxed into one of mocking amusement.

"I couldn't dream of placing myself in such dangerous proximity to your charming self," he explained. "For I presume you also will feel unable to tear yourself away from the home which has come to mean so much to you. Though I'm afraid," he added reflectively, "that legally you come off rather badly in the division of the spoils. You're not actually *entitled*——"

Meryon sprang to her feet.

"If you only wanted to have me here in order to insult me, I can't see that there's any point in my staying. I thought——"

"Please sit down again, Meryon. It's always best to postpone the heroics until after the financial settlement, and I've got to explain this either to you or to your mother. Frankly, I'd rather make the explanations to you."

Trembling a little, Meryon sat down again, and Gregory went on in the grim and more businesslike tone of the first part of the interview.

"You probably know that my uncle made no will after his second marriage, but, both legally and morally, your mother is entitled to a certain part of his estate. The exact proportion—indeed, the exact total of the estate—has not yet been arrived at, but you can assure her that there will be plenty for her—or for both of you. You can fight that out between you," he added in a tone which almost drove Meryon from the office again. "Will you also assure her that she may consider that the house-she-loves-so-much is her place of residence until the whole question comes up again when Sally comes of age. That's all, I think."

"Very well. And now I should just like to say, in my turn, that I shall do everything I can to persuade my mother that it would be better to live elsewhere. She must, however, make the final decision for herself, but *I* shall most certainly find another home."

"Just as you like." Gregory reached absently for some document as though the interview were definitely at an end. And he rang the bell for the junior clerk to have the happiness of showing her out and wishing her "Good morning."

Out in the street once more, Meryon made no attempt to summon a taxi or board a bus. She felt that only by walking far and fast could she somehow get rid of this accumulation of anger and indignation.

How dared he speak to her the way he had? He had no right to cling to this ridiculous idea that they were a couple of spongers. *Other* men married a second time without their relations heaping every sort of insult on the second wife and her relatives. And even if the circumstances were most unfortunately suspicious——

Oh, why had things happened just as they had? And, above all, why did Mother heighten the unfortunate impression almost every time she opened her mouth? Meryon writhed to think of the things she had probably said to Gregory in the mistaken belief that she was being clear and businesslike.

It was true, of course, that Mother was entitled to some share in the estate. Even Gregory admitted that. But if only she hadn't embarked on this undignified wrangle over the house. Not, of course, that Gregory wrangled. He gave way with icy politeness and most unwelcome generosity. The very way he kept on repeating Mother's ridiculous phrase "the house she loved so much" made Meryon want to cry with vexation. It must seem to him only another attempt to grab more, under the cloak of inexcusable sentimentality.

"And the worst of it is that I don't expect anything will persuade her to move," thought Meryon unhappily. "But if that's so, I simply can't help it. I'll have to find something to do myself, and then perhaps she'll join me later. But the real point is that I *must find a job*, and get some sort of decent independence."

Which brought her, of course, to the very unpleasant reflection that her expensive education had probably not trained her to be anything more valuable than a social success.

Meryon was walking more slowly now. Her anger was evaporating, and a mood of grave consideration was taking its place.

"There must be lots of things that a moderately intelligent, moderately good-looking, perfectly healthy young woman can do," she told herself earnestly. The question was—did anyone want to pay for such things?

Oddly enough, considering her type of education, there was one thing at which she did excel in a modest way, and that was cookery and household management. She had enjoyed this at school and even—in spite of strong objections from Mother—gone on and taken an extension course at a domestic college, for her own enjoyment.

"That would probably make you into a fairly satisfactory cook-general, my dear," she told herself. "But you don't exactly look the part," she added with a rueful smile, as she caught the reflection of herself, in the Paris suit and silver fox, in a shop mirror as she passed.

What a pity that nothing she had ever done had been planned with the serious idea of being useful later!

"If I'd taken diplomas and things I could teach domestic subjects," thought Meryon with a sigh. "Now I'd have to start spending time and money on taking exams, when what I want is to *make* money and be independent of this whole wretched business."

It wasn't an encouraging prospect exactly. But *something* would have to be done, and, for a start, Meryon determined to go to London at the end of the week and make some definite enquiries. And, in between now and then, she would have to face the not very easy task of persuading her mother to something like her own point of view.

When she came to the task, however, it was rather like trying to bale out the sea with a penny dipper.

"But I don't see, darling," Mrs. Monder said—and that at least was very clear. "If we have money, why do you have this extraordinary idea of wanting to make more?"

"It isn't *my* money, you see," Meryon explained patiently.

"No, but it's mine, and you're welcome to your share of it," was the affectionate rejoinder. "Just as you were with your father's money, pet. He left it to me, but of *course*, I wanted to share it with you."

"That was different. He was my father. Mr. Monder was nothing to me—I hadn't the faintest claim on him, except what he insisted on in his generosity."

"Well, there you are! That was what he wanted, darling. I don't think you ought to go against the wishes of the dead." And Mrs. Monder began to cry.

It was impossible at that point to do anything at all but break off the argument and start comforting her mother.

"Well, never mind," thought Meryon. "It's no good trying to explain. I must just contrive to go to London on my own and make what enquiries I can." And since Mrs. Monder could always understand anyone wanting to go to London for a few days, that arrangement at least was quite easily made, and Meryon felt her mind rather more at rest.

After all, there was Effie Verne, she told herself, who ran that clever little dress-shop. She might have something useful to suggest. Did one have to have special training to become a mannequin, for instance? And what sort of life was it?

Then there was Helen Holmes, who was head of a big secretarial bureau. *She* was even more likely to be helpful, because she would have a much wider field of experience on which to draw.

Really, the situation was not too discouraging when you began to tackle it in a genuinely businesslike way. And Meryon's spirits began to rise insensibly.

On the evening before her departure, she and her mother were sitting reading in their favourite drawing-room, and Sally, as usual, was upstairs with John, when a maid came in to ask if Mrs. Monder were free to see Mr. Gregory Monder on business for a little while.

"Why, of course. Send him in. He knows he needn't ask permission first," cried Mrs. Monder. While Meryon thought that something out of the ordinary must surely have happened if he persuaded himself to come and talk business with her mother after all.

As Gregory came in, Mrs. Monder looked up with an

expression of pleased surprise. She was always completely unaware of his dislike of her—indeed, it would have been impossible for her to believe for one moment that anyone *did* seriously dislike her—and she genuinely welcomed a visitor in their quiet and rather sad household.

But nothing in Gregory's appearance suggested that he had come to brighten things. In fact, Meryon—much more observant than her mother—was exceedingly disquieted. He looked calm, it was true, but with a calmness that suggested unnatural restraint, and the odd little crinkles at the corners of his eyes suggested nervousness—a thing Meryon had never noticed in him before.

"Come and sit down, Gregory. This is nice!" Mrs. Monder smiled upon him with all the hospitable air of having been hostess in this house since long before he was born.

He sat down—rather heavily, Meryon thought—a little as though he were carrying a weighty burden. He didn't appear to pay much attention to the stream of affable remarks which Mrs. Monder immediately turned on him, and, finally, unable to bear a growing and inexplicable dread, Meryon said:

"Gregory, is anything the matter?"

He raised his eyes then and looked across at her, and she was shocked to see a suspicion of dark circles round them.

"Yes." He spoke slowly and in rather a low voice, but his words were perfectly clear. "I'm afraid something is the matter. Something very serious indeed——"

"Not *more* bad news," wailed Mrs. Monder, as though Gregory were personally responsible.

"Hush, Mother." Meryon saw that Gregory was under a great strain, and she guessed that the interruption was hardly helpful. "Please go on, Gregory."

"It's to do with my uncle's financial position. I'd been hoping for the last few days that things were not so bad as the first signs suggested. But almost immediately after that conversation I had with you, Meryon, information began to trickle in that he was very heavily committed in certain quarters quite unknown to me."

"You mean he had been speculating?"

"Well—yes. In a sense, he had been speculating. It was the sort of risk one does take sometimes, and had he lived, I don't doubt he would have come out of it all right. As it is, the whole structure collapsed, and as I had no knowledge of this special transaction, of course, I had no possible chance of covering the risks as they came."

"But he ought to have *told* you," Mrs. Monder exclaimed.

"Yes." Gregory's mouth tightened with the effort of hiding his dislike of her. "He most certainly ought to have told me. But I don't know that blaming a dead man is going to help us much now."

"Is it—very bad, Gregory?" That was Meryon.

"It's ruin," he said quietly, and she saw with a pity quite distinct from her fears, that he had gone terribly pale.

"Ruin! It isn't possible," Mrs. Monder insisted almost angrily. "It isn't possible. Henry was a very rich man."

"Rich men fail in business sometimes, Mrs. Monder," Gregory told her curtly.

"But what do you mean? How much is there left?"

"Nothing."

"*Nothing*? But the house? That must be worth a lot."

"We rent it. We don't own it. The contents belong to the children—and partly, I suppose, to you."

"Gregory"—Meryon was struggling to cope with

each successive wave of disaster—"what about you? *Your* interests were all in the business, too, weren't they?"

"Yes," he said almost conversationally. "Yes, I've lost everything, too."

"It's like the Flood," cried poor Mrs. Monder, not very accurately, but at least it showed the measure of the disaster.

"You really mean that there literally won't be a penny left from the business, Gregory?" Meryon spoke again, perfectly calmly, just as Gregory had, but she was wide-eyed now and almost as pale as he.

"I'm afraid not. We can wash that straight out. I think I can get a smallish job with a firm I know in London, and, of course, I'll take Sally and John with me. I don't know how they're going to adapt themselves, poor kids, but we'll have to see what can be done. When the place is sold up and the various adjustments made, there may be about five hundred for them. I can't imagine there'll be much else. It's not as if—— Just a moment! There's Sally calling me. They must have heard the car. I'll go up, or else she will be coming down." Gregory went to the door, then he turned, his hand on the handle. "There's no need to tell the children yet. They'll know soon enough. I'll be back in ten minutes, in case there's anything else you want to know." And he went out of the room.

"What are we to *do*, Meryon?"

But, for once, Meryon paid no attention to her mother's appeals.

"Five hundred pounds," she repeated thoughtfully. "That's what he said." Then suddenly she laughed unsteadily. "The last five hundred pounds! Why, that's much the same as with us. If we put it together that makes a thousand. We must try very hard not to touch that, because the children——"

"Are you crazy, Meryon?" her mother said sharply. "You've heard Gregory say—Sally and John are his responsibility. And, of course, it's true. How lucky he has a job and can support them. I wish we could say as much. But, of course, we must manage for ourselves now, difficult though it will be. Some of the proceeds of the sale will be mine, and then——"

"*Mother!*" The word was only a whisper, but it was somehow more penetrating than a shout. "Are you suggesting we should desert the children and Gregory now?"

"My dear child, what ridiculous words you use. It's not a question of desertion. They have their own lives to live. We have ours."

"And how do you suppose Gregory is going to manage with Sally not yet out of school and John needing attention. He says he hopes to get a 'smallish job.' He *hopes* to get it. He hasn't got it. And then, if he does— are you suggesting he should pay nearly everything he has to someone who'll make nothing but a substitute of a home for the three of them? That's what he'd have to do, you know. He couldn't manage without—not with John an invalid and Sally not old enough to keep house."

"But"—Mrs. Monder faced her daughter in utter bewilderment—"it's nothing to do with us. What do you suggest *we* can do?"

"Do? We're going to stand by them, of course. We were staying with them in prosperity. We'll have the honesty to do the same thing now. I'll keep house and look after John, and do it with half the expense a paid housekeeper would entail. That at least I can do. I'll not have it said of me—or of you either—that we deserted people we once made use of, not if I have to go out by the day charring to help to keep them."

"Meryon!" It was the only word Mrs. Monder could find, and it had no effect at all.

"You can make what decision you like yourself," Meryon said passionately, "but I'm staying with them until Gregory himself tells me to go—and perhaps even after that, if I think it best," she added grimly.

CHAPTER IV

FOR SEVERAL SECONDS Meryon's mother gazed at her in helpless bewilderment. Then at last, as though grasping something intelligible in the tangle of her daughter's preposterous views, she said:

"Well, of course, there is one thing. We should at least have a home if we did what you suggest." And on this unlucky remark Gregory came back into the room.

Mrs. Monder turned to him at once.

"Gregory, Meryon thinks it would be best if we all stayed together even now. After all, we should at least have *each other* then, shouldn't we?"

"That's a very moving thought," Gregory agreed coldly, while the contemptuous look he gave Meryon made her wince angrily. "But I'm afraid that, as things are, I could not take on the added responsibility of providing a home for two more people."

"Only we've got to have a home *somewhere*, haven't we?" Mrs. Monder pointed out. But Meryon broke in, in great distress:

"That's not the point at all, Mother." She turned to Gregory, pale and very much in earnest, hating the embarrassment it caused her to have to face the coldly speculative look in his eyes. "You see, Gregory, it's going to be terribly difficult for you, trying to keep a home going for Sally and John—particularly with money so short. I thought I might do that, and then——"

"You mean that seems the simplest way of getting a home for nothing?"

His tone was so casual that it was a second before the full meaning of his words sank in. And, even then, it was Mrs. Monder who spoke first.

"Gregory! How *could* you think such a thing of Meryon—much less say it!" Her astonishment that anyone should think anything but well of her daughter and herself was almost laughable.

"'Just a moment.' Meryon held up her hand and stopped Gregory's reply with a little air of dignity that was oddly touching. "I don't blame you for putting a bad construction on that, because I know you must be beside yourself with anxiety. But I *didn't* mean what you suggest at all, and this time I insist that you understand the truth."

"*This* time?" murmured Mrs. Monder interrogatively, but no one took any notice of her.

"Well?" Gregory stood in front of Meryon, his hands thrust into his pockets, his mouth faintly sulky, but his eyes so genuinely unhappy that she spoke much more gently than she had intended.

"Why, you see, Gregory, it's only common sense. If you get this post you speak of, that will ease things considerably, but the other half of the problem will be running a home for the children and yourself. A paid housekeeper would cost much more than you could afford, and it wouldn't be a very happy arrangement for John. I could look after him much better and—and we're fond of each other, and I could run the home. I really can do that well."

"You can?" He had been staring at the ground with unnecessary attention, but now he glanced up in unflattering surprise.

"Of *course*." That was Mrs. Monder. "Why, she was always head of her class for cookery at school."

"Really." Gregory seemed unimpressed by this corroborative evidence.

Meryon smiled faintly.

"Well, that's only part of it, of course. But I really have some talent for that sort of thing. It's one of the few things I can do really well."

"You're too modest," murmured Gregory ironically, but she saw he was slightly impressed.

"Anyway, the housekeeping wouldn't cost you anything except room in the house for Mother and me. And we would, of course, contribute something towards the household expenses."

"From what, my dear?" Mrs. Monder spoke quickly, and pushed out her under-lip with a childishly obstinate air that was not without its attraction.

"Well, Mother, we shall have to sell up everything in the flat now, you know." It was strange how clearly things seemed to fall into place. "And I expect we could live on the proceeds for quite a long time, especially if we have no rent to pay."

"Live on capital, darling!" cried Mrs. Monder in a scandalised tone. "I never heard of such a thing." And indeed, at that moment, she really thought she hadn't.

"I couldn't allow you to do that," Gregory said coldly. "If you are playing the part of unpaid housekeeper, Meryon, the least I can do is to see that you and your mother have no living expenses."

"Don't be silly." Meryon spoke with such cool positiveness that, she saw, it was almost a shock to him. "We can none of us afford to make expensive gestures just now. We must be severely practical and show a little common sense. Mother and I have roughly five hundred pounds left in capital. You think the children will have something the same. Very well, we must do our best to leave that untouched in each case. It will provide something of a bulwark against emergencies. Then, if you will give Mother and me—well, house-room, I'll run the home for you and save you the expense of a housekeeper. That balances things up. But we must make some small contribution towards general expenses, and we *can* do that out of the proceeds of the things at our flat."

"And what about the time when that may be all gone?" Mrs. Monder's voice became almost tearful in its plaintiveness.

"Oh, lots of things will have happened before then," Meryon assured her cheerfully. "Sally will be earning, and Gregory will have worked up a wonderful salary again. Then he'll be able to pay a housekeeper and I shall be free to take a job myself and keep you in luxury for the rest of your life." She hugged her mother affectionately and smiled at her rather pleadingly, in an attempt to make her take a happier view of things.

"Suppose Gregory *doesn't* make money again?"

"But he will—of course he will," declared Meryon stoutly. "You'll see."

"Do you really believe that?" The interruption came so very quietly from Gregory that Meryon swung round in astonishment. For a moment she could make nothing of that sombre, almost melancholy expression of his. And then suddenly she realised with an acute flash of understanding that, worse than any present disaster, was the overwhelming shock Gregory had received to his confidence and his belief in himself.

She went over to him and took his hand in hers.

"Why, Gregory," she said gently, "I haven't the slightest doubt of it."

"You mean one has to believe in fairy stories at a moment like this," he retorted a little cynically, but his hand closed tightly on hers.

"No. I don't mean anything of the sort. I mean that we've got to build our hopes on the few things we're certain of now. And thank Heaven, one of them is your strength and reliability."

He didn't say anything, but she saw the slow colour come back into his face. Then, still without a word, he bent his head and impulsively kissed the hand he was holding.

Meryon was so much moved that she could say nothing for a moment. It was Mrs. Monder who broke the short silence, and she, too, had found something to make things look a little less black.

"Of course, Meryon dear—I'd forgotten—there *is* always Rex Treventon, isn't there?" she said brightly.

"We'll leave Rex out of this, I think," Meryon said shortly. But she thought angrily, "There are times when I could slap Mother—and slap her *hard*." And she felt instinctively that something else besides her voice had suddenly gone cold.

"Well—about telling the children——" That was Gregory, very brusque and very much himself again. "If you agree, I think we'll wait until we have things more cut and dried before we talk things over with them. Anything indefinite is always terrifying at their age."

"Yes, I agree with you," Meryon said, while Mrs. Monder added as her helpful contribution:

"It does seem such a pity that we have to tell them at all."

Gregory glanced at her drily.

"I'm afraid that, as we shall have to move from Old-keep to London, live in a small house instead of a large one, and alter our whole style of living, it will be necessary to give them some sort of explanation," he said curtly.

"Well, yes—I suppose you're right," conceded Mrs. Monder reluctantly. "But it does seem a pity."

No one was able to deny the truth of that, so she was allowed the final conclusion. And, after a word or two more, Gregory left them, promising to return the next morning to discuss the whole future on a practical basis.

Meryon had very much feared that Gregory's departure would be the signal for an outburst from her mother. But either Mrs. Monder had no more reproaches or suggestions to make, or else she recognised that little could be said now to move her daughter from the decision she had taken.

In any case, even to Mrs. Monder, it was possibly something of a relief that, in the midst of all this uncertainty and anxiety, some definite course had been decided upon.

Fortunately this fairly manageable state of mind lasted during the exceedingly difficult weeks which followed. From time to time she had odd and always unpractical suggestions to make, but Meryon—practised in the art of side-tracking her mother—was usually able to dispose of them without causing any ill-feeling.

Telling Sally and John was the most unpleasant task of all, and Gregory and Meryon undertook it jointly, with Mrs. Monder insisting on supplying a running commentary on her own, rather original lines. This irritated Gregory profoundly, but Meryon thought it caused some secret amusement to John at least, which helped to soften the force of the shock.

"But do you mean"—Sally's dark eyes were very large and horrified—"do you mean we're *poor*?"

"I'm afraid so, Sally—at least in comparison with what we have been."

"Almost destitute, in fact," added Mrs. Monder, with picturesque exaggeration. "Though, of course, we didn't want you children to know."

Gregory made a movement of impatience, but John said gravely:

"Well, I shall be a great asset to you, sitting at the

side of the pavement in a bath-chair, selling matches."

"John dear!" Mrs. Monder was horrified. "That won't be at *all* necessary!"

"No, but it might be interesting, and very good for my soul," John told her.

"Nonsense——" began Mrs. Monder, but Gregory interrupted.

"We're getting rather far from the point. The fact is that we shall have to leave the house—in fact, leave Oldkeep altogether, because I have been offered a post in London, and we have no choice but to go there."

"I don't want to go to London," Sally announced rather stormily.

"My dear child, of *course* you do," Mrs. Monder assured her. "You'll love it. It's so much more lively. Theatres and restaurants and——"

"You're giving Sally a rather inaccurate idea of the London she will know," Gregory said drily. " I'm sorry, Sally, my dear, but I'm afraid you've got to take your share in helping us out of this bad corner. And, believe me, I do realise that perhaps it is harder for you than any of us. You were just arriving at the age when you might reasonably expect to have a good time, and instead we'll have to ask you to share responsibilities I would willingly have spared you."

Sally's pretty, flushed face softened immeasurably at this appeal, and Meryon saw that she was exceedingly gratified at being treated as a responsible grown-up.

"Well—what do you suggest I should do?" she asked more quietly.

Gregory's troubled grey eyes rested on her very kindly, but his mouth was quite firm.

"I think the best thing is to put you into a business college as soon as we get to London, and train you for office life."

Sally looked dismayed, and Meryon said hastily:

"I have a friend who runs a big secretarial bureau— you know, Mother, Helen Holmes. I expect she could help in getting you an interesting post, Sally."

"It doesn't sound exactly interesting to me," Sally said rather gloomily.

"Nonsense, my dear. Why some of Helen Holmes's girls end by working for *Cabinet Ministers*," declared Mrs. Monder, dangling this tempting bait before the unimpressed Sally.

"Well, if any Cabinet Minister trusts to Sally's spelling the country will be plunged into a major European crisis," remarked John thoughtfully.

"That isn't at all kind, John," Mrs. Monder said reprovingly, perhaps because she had a fellow-feeling with Sally on the subject of spelling. "The fact that you can't do anything yourself towards helping does *not* entitle you to criticise your sister."

"He wasn't criticising. He was only ragging," retorted Sally indignantly, while John drew down his brows in a most unusual scowl and said nothing at all.

"There's no need to start apportioning the amount of sacrifice and help yet," Meryon said quietly. "The fact is that we've all got to do the utmost we can to adapt ourselves to a new life and make a success of it. It isn't going to be specially nice for any of us, but if we support each other and don't start quarrelling it will have plenty of compensations, I don't doubt."

"An admirable point of view," commented Gregory a little sarcastically.

"And, anyway, it won't last for always," Meryon declared, her colour rising slightly at his remark. "I'm *sure* we'll come out of it well in the end."

"Your faith in the future is very touching," Gregory told her, still a little sarcastically, but this time his expression was softer.

"It isn't only faith in the future. It's faith in *us*," Meryon said earnestly.

"In a minute, Meryon dear, you'll have us singing 'Rule, Britannia,' " remarked John teasingly. At which they all laughed and felt rather better.

The family conference had taken place in John's room, and when at last the others were going, he called Meryon back for a word with her alone.

"What is it, John?" She stood there looking down at him, suddenly aware that the laughter on which the conversation had ended was all gone now, and in its place was a troubled restlessness.

He shot a look at her out of those almost resentful dark eyes.

"I suppose *I'm* the real problem?" he said shortly.

"No, my dear. No more than each of us is part of the problem," Meryon told him quite coolly.

"Oh, yes—I know." He turned away with an unhappy impatience that worried her. "You and Gregory and Sally will all be awfully sweet about it, and pretend it doesn't matter in the least having a perfectly useless and helpless person to look after, when every penny counts. But I know—I'm not such a fool. If I were not here the problem would be twice as easy to solve."

"On the contrary," Meryon said slowly. "It was only your presence which solved most of the problem for me."

"What do you mean?" John twisted round again to gaze at her with nervous eagerness.

Meryon sat down by his sofa and clasped her hands rather tightly together.

"I think I'll tell you something that the others know nothing about, John. You see, Gregory didn't really want me to come and share your home at all. He'd much rather that Mother and I went off on our own."

"Would he?" John looked astonished. "Why?"

"Because he doesn't like me, I suppose."

"But he must. Why doesn't he like you?"

"Well—he thinks he has his own good reasons, and—and, in the ordinary way, he would have decided against my coming with you."

"Did you want to come, Meryon?"

"Yes," Meryon said. "I wanted to come very much."

"To look after me?"

"And Sally." Then, with an odd little smile, she added: "And Gregory."

John gave her a quick glance, but, with admirable tact, refrained from saying anything else. After a moment Meryon went on:

"I couldn't *insist* on looking after Gregory and Sally, because I suppose, in a way, they could look after themselves. But fortunately you were there, and even Gregory couldn't deny that it would be a happier arrangement for you if I kept house than if a paid housekeeper did. In fact, John"—the smile deepened—"I owe you a considerable debt of thanks."

John laughed slightly.

"You have a very nice way of turning things round," he told her, but she saw that his face had grown much brighter.

"Well, my dear, it's the truth. Only, of course, you mustn't say anything about what I've told you."

"Of course not." Then, as she got up to go: "You don't return Gregory's dislike, do you, Meryon?" he said gravely.

There was a short pause before Meryon raised her eyes and met his glance squarely.

"No," she said quite coolly. "No, I don't return Gregory's dislike at all. In fact, I'm really quite attached to him in a—sisterly way."

"I see," John said, and didn't try to detain her any longer.

After that, the arrangements for the great change-over went forward without delay. Of necessity, the brunt of it all fell on Meryon, and from morning until night there seemed an endless stream of matters to be settled. The selling-up of the present home, the renting of a new one, the transfer of whatever furniture was necessary to the smaller house, arrangements for the journey, decisions on what could be taken and what, very definitely, could not.

But here at least was something to take hold of, something which made her feel that she was justifying her existence in the family at last, and she welcomed it.

A medium-sized and very unpretentious house in one of the inner suburbs was rented, in spite of Mrs. Monder's protest that it was "quite the wrong quarter, darling. No one would *dream* of living there."

Meryon pointed out patiently that several thousands of people had already not only dreamed of living there, but had actually set up house there.

"Oh, but, my dear—I don't want to be snobbish— only what sort of people *are* they?"

"The same sort that we are, probably," Meryon told her grimly. "Hard-working middle-class, who are trying to make both ends meet. And I only hope we do it as successfully as they do."

"Meryon," Mrs. Monder's voice quivered, "you're quite changed these days! I hope our misfortunes aren't going to make you *bitter*, darling. Your dear father always used to say that there was nothing quite so distressing as an embittered woman. That was one reason why he was always so fond of me—that I never *was* bitter, I mean."

Meryon knew that quotations from her dear father always meant that her mother was feeling miserable and uncertain of things, so she very easily forgave the rather startling reference to embittered women, and, kissing Mrs. Monder affectionately, she said:

"That's all right, Mother dear. I promise not to grow embittered, and you just go on being sweet. Only, you know, we've got to look facts in the face occasionally." She ignored her mother's movement of protest at this unusual and unwelcome thought. "And the truth is that we couldn't possibly afford to live in a fashionable district now. We have the choice of going very much further out to perhaps a rather nicer house, or taking the kind of place we have chosen which means we're more conveniently situated for Town."

"I don't see that being nearer Town is going to help us much," Mrs. Monder argued disconsolately. "If one hasn't money to spend, what's the use of going to Town?"

"Gregory will have to go every day, and so will Sally," Meryon pointed out. "I can't have them wearying themselves with a long double journey every day. Besides, that means two season tickets to consider, and we must keep those as low as possible."

"Season tickets!" murmured poor Mrs. Monder. And then, as the full implication sank in: "Oh dear, of course, there'll be no car now, will there?"

"No," Meryon said. "I'm afraid there won't be any car, dear. We couldn't possibly manage that, you know."

"Not even a small, second-hand one?" Mrs. Monder was making a considerable effort to readjust her ideas.

Meryon shook her head.

"I'm afraid not. The running of it would be too expensive, at any rate at present, when *really* every penny counts."

There was a slight pause, then Mrs. Monder made a last, rather artless effort.

"I don't know that that isn't rather *false* economy, dear," she said earnestly. "Taxi fares can run away with a great deal of money, you know."

"I dare say. But buses, trains and trams are all remarkably cheap," Meryon reminded her inexorably.

"I suppose you're right," her mother agreed with a sigh, but her final capitulation was not marked by the brightness of outlook for which Meryon's dear father had so justly admired her.

The house which they had chosen was really a great deal pleasanter than Mrs. Monder's objections would have led one to believe. A little old-fashioned and ugly from the outside, it had, nevertheless, the advantage of fairly large and lofty rooms, considerable window space, and a general air of brightness not always to be found in that type of house. There was, in addition, a quite exceptionally large and pleasant garden, and the house itself was situated near one of the big commons of South London.

It fell rather far short, perhaps, of the house agent's description of it, but might, at a pinch, still be covered by the term "desirable residence."

"Of course, it's simply *dreadful* as it is," Mrs. Monder informed the astonished house agent. "But redecorated from top to bottom it would at least be *habitable*."

"Pardon *me*, madam, it's a very fine property," began the house agent indignantly—and launched into a catalogue of its advantages.

With excellent, though unconscious, generalship, however, Mrs. Monder immediately countered with a remarkably comprehensive list of its defects, interspersed with such unanswerable appeals as: "And, of course, no one with a grain of *taste* could tolerate that, could they?"

"Come away, and let's look at the garden," whispered Meryon to Gregory. "Mother will have everything but a marble bath by the time she's through with that poor man. She is ten times better at this than you or I."

Laughing a little, Gregory came with her, and together they strolled down the garden path to inspect the untidy but effective border of early spring flowers.

"It isn't too bad, is it?" Gregory looked round with a lightening of that grave air that was nearly always with him nowadays.

"No. I think we might make something very nice of it," Meryon declared. "Do you know anything about gardening?"

"Not in the least. Do you?"

"No," Meryon said, and they both laughed.

"I suppose we can find out enough to keep the place decent," he added after a moment.

"Or even enough to get a good deal of pleasure out of it," she suggested.

"You are optimistic about everything, Meryon."

"Stupidly so, you mean?"

"No. Blessedly so," he told her coolly. And then, before she could answer, he turned away to walk back to the house, remarking, "Perhaps it's a shame to let your mother tackle the agent on her own."

"Don't you believe it," Meryon said with a smile. "He is the one who will probably retire to a bewildered counting of his losses at the end."

And, sure enough, when they joined the other two, it was to hear the house agent agreeing with something like fervour, that a really satisfied tenant was the first essential in the eyes of an intelligent landlord, and he would "see what he could do about it."

It always seemed to Meryon afterwards that he must have tested the landlord's intelligence rather severely, because she could not imagine that all in-coming tenants had so much done for them. Even Gregory said to Mrs. Monder:

"Really, I congratulate you. I can't imagine how you did it."

But, though pleased, Mrs. Monder was faintly puzzled.

"I'm so glad you think I helped," she said. "But, of course, *no* one could have been expected to live in the place as it was, and, as I explained to the agent, cheap decorations are always poor economy. It's just common sense, isn't it?"

"We must hope he is still seeing it in that light now," Gregory agreed gravely. And the matter was left there.

It was not until everything was settled and the furniture installed that Meryon had Sally and John brought to the house. She felt very keenly that to children who had never known anything but the best and easiest of everything, the discomfort and upset of a move, in addition to all the other changes, would be an unnecessarily severe trial.

"And they really are only children—even Sally," thought Meryon with a smile as she watched their genuine pleasure and enthusiasm over even small novelties in their new surroundings.

"Do you mind having your room on the ground floor, John?" she wanted to know.

"Not in the least. And it makes things a bit better for you, not having to run up and down stairs, doesn't it?"

Meryon was touched that he should have seen the significance of that at once, and, squeezing his hand rather tightly, she said:

"Thanks, dear. I see you're going to look after my interests very well while the others are away."

He looked pleased and gratified, although it was only a small point, and Meryon thought: "I must remember in future—most of our happiness or unhappiness is going to be made up of small points."

Gregory had already started work in his new office,

and, if he found a very distasteful change in having to obey orders rather than give them, not a word of complaint was heard at home about it. He looked a good deal more fagged and white than Meryon liked to see, and she was afraid that he was over-working seriously. But she knew that even sympathy from her would probably be resented, and, with something of an effort, she refrained from making any comment.

As soon as they had settled down in the house, Sally was introduced to her new rôle—that of student in a business-training college—both Meryon and Gregory judging it best that she should not have too much time for reflection between leaving her school in the North and embarking on more specialised training.

Rather unexpectedly, Sally seemed to enjoy the change. She liked the practical, common-sense atmosphere, the suggestion that grown-up independence was only just round the corner, and, above all, she enjoyed the sensation of being definitely useful in the new scheme of things.

"I don't think Sally can be at all *sensitive*," Mrs. Monder told Meryon, with some air of criticism. "Really, I hardly think she minds this disaster at all."

As Mrs. Monder was the only one who firmly continued to describe their changed circumstances as "this disaster," Meryon found some difficulty in answering her patiently.

"Sally is doing her best to adapt herself," Meryon said a little sharply. "And it does her great credit that she is succeeding so well."

"Yes, I know, dear. But she almost *likes* it."

"And don't you think it's just as well that she should?"

"No, I don't," declared Mrs. Monder energetically. "Oh, Meryon, this is just what I was afraid of years ago, when I refused to alter *our* standard of living. One gets *used* to being what one never expected to have to be," she explained plaintively and not very lucidly.

"Well, never mind, if it makes one feel a little happier," Meryon said soothingly.

"But it does matter. Suppose Rex Treventon were to come in now, for instance. What would he see? Not the elegant, charming, leisurely girl he's always known. But someone in an overall. Yes, I know it's a very pretty overall, but that makes no difference. Someone whose chief concern is to get a meal ready in time to suit a lot of people coming in from other sordid jobs."

"Mother, dear, not *sordid*!" protested Meryon with a laugh. "Just humdrum, but decent. And, in any case," she added flippantly, "if it's any comfort to you, I don't imagine Rex would love me any the less for seeing me in an overall."

There was a pause, and then Mrs. Monder remarked in a rather thoughtful voice:

"Perhaps you're right."

"I'm sure I am," Meryon said consolingly, too busy with her dinner preparations to notice her mother's change of tone.

Indeed, the casual remarks passed entirely from her mind for the moment, and it was not until the following Saturday that something happened to remind her forcibly of them.

It was just about tea-time. Meryon was setting the table and Sally was spasmodically helping her, when John, who was lying on his sofa by the window, exclaimed suddenly:

"I say, there's a very exciting looking car just drawing up outside. And I should say it's the local millionaire who's getting out."

"Let me see." Sally came to the window. "Goodness, what a beauty! Cream and plum-coloured Packard.

And he's coming in here," she added a little ambiguously.

"Cream and plum-coloured Packard?" There was an odd note in Meryon's voice as she too glanced out of the window. "Why—that's Rex Treventon's car! How on earth did he know where we were?"

No one offered to answer this question, and Meryon turned quickly to her mother. Mrs. Monder at that moment was extremely reminiscent of a kitten with drops of stolen cream on its whiskers.

"Yes," she said defiantly, in answer to Meryon's look. "Yes, I did let him know we had moved, *and* I told him you'd be very pleased to see him. You needn't look so severe, Meryon. It wasn't a crime. And, anyway, you'd better go and answer the door to him, my dear."

CHAPTER V

For a moment Meryon stood quite still in the middle of the room, divided between surprise, chagrin, and a certain amount of genuine pleasure. Then John said gravely:

"Well, if we still have a Packard-owner on our visiting list, don't let's keep him on the doorstep." And Meryon went to open the door.

Rex Treventon, of all her friends, was perhaps the one who most completely epitomised everything she had now left behind, and in the first second that she faced him across the narrow hall of their new home, Meryon felt that she gazed at him from another world. The next moment his charmingly infectious and self-possessed smile had bridged the gap, and Meryon found that her hands were in his, and he was greeting her with the same air of unstudied admiration and cordiality as he would have used at a cocktail party in Mayfair or in the ballroom of a West End hotel.

"Meryon, my dear! I can't tell you how delighted I was when your mother's letter came."

"And I am so glad to see you, Rex—so very glad."

It was true, she realised. His affectionate admiration warmed her to the very core of her being, and everything about him was a reminder of the pleasant, easy, worthwhile things, so ruthlessly banished now from the stern struggle that life had become. It was like coming unexpectedly into hot sunshine after weeks of cold and rain.

"You'll stay to tea, of course?"

"If I may."

"Please. I'm just getting it now."

She hung up his heavy motoring coat, and, as she did so, was slightly ashamed to find she was thinking, "I suppose the price of this would pay our rent for six months."

In the old days, the idea of even a passing thought on the value of one's friends' belongings would have been incredible. Now——

"I must stop that," Meryon told herself quickly. "It's what Mother calls being sordid. But, all the same, it *would* pay the rent," the practical side of her added.

As they came into the fuller light of the dining-room, and her mother fluttered forward to meet him, Meryon found herself thinking:

"How extraordinarily good-looking Rex is. And how easy and charming and *approving*." Perhaps that was the nicest part of all. Approval had been singularly lacking from her life in the last few months, and it was lovely to have someone implying by every word and look that you gave pleasure by simply being there.

She never had the impression that she gave Gregory pleasure by simply being there. And then that reminded her.

"Why, how late Gregory is!" she exclaimed, breaking across her mother's little Niagara of greetings.

"Well, darling"—Mrs. Monder was not very pleased at this stemming of the flow—"I expect he is busy. We won't wait for him, anyway, as we have a visitor."

"He said he would be working this afternoon, Meryon," John reminded her, and Mrs. Monder murmured at once:

"So wrapped up in his work, you know." She always preferred to regard work as something in which one engaged from choice or eccentricity. Never, never from stern necessity.

Meryon went out into the kitchen to make tea, and left her mother to complete the introductions. Almost immediately Sally followed her—theoretically to help, but actually to sit on the corner of the kitchen table and say with great candour:

"Meryon, what a frightfully handsome man! Is he an old flame?"

"We are very good friends."

"I should think so. He's what I call really exciting. So very much The Other Man."

"What other man?" Meryon asked obtusely.

"Well—you know—there's always Another Man in really romantic films and books. Frightfully man-of-the-worldish, and usually much more interesting than the hero, anyway. Experienced and charming, with a bit of a past. Meryon, has he got a past?"

"He never told me so."

"No, of *course* not! Though I dare say if he were to ask you to marry him he'd tell you everything beforehand and ask your forgiveness."

"I can't imagine it. And, anyway, wouldn't it be a bit late?" Meryon asked practically.

"Oh, no, Meryon! It would be only *right*, if he wanted to turn over a new leaf and reform for your sake."

"It all sounds very embarrassing," Meryon said, as she poured the water into the teapot.

"I don't believe you have a scrap of romance in you!" Sally exclaimed.

"Never mind, dear. I'm sure you have enough for us both," Meryon told her with a smile. And, laughing crossly, Sally snatched up the tea-tray with more enthusiasm than judgment, and marched off into the dining-room, followed more slowly by Meryon.

When they came in an animated conversation was in

progress, and Meryon was touched to notice that, however much her mother might try to monopolise Rex, he had quite obviously insisted on including John in the circle.

"That's just like Rex," she thought. "The children are sure to adore him." And then she reflected that Sally's romantic description of him was really somewhere near the truth.

At thirty-seven, Rex Treventon had acquired all the poise and charm that much travel and varied experience can give. But in doing so he had never lost that essential touch of interest in other people which establishes contact at once with any age and any class.

Sally was right in one other particular, too. He was quite unusually good-looking—with the sort of good looks from which age takes nothing. Tall and rather heavily built, he had thick, dark hair with more than a touch of grey in it, dark eyes which sparkled with a faintly cynical kindliness, and an attractive, slightly full-lipped mouth in which natural self-indulgence warred with deliberate self-restraint.

Not that Sally recognised those signs, however. She only knew that he was "frightfully good-looking," and that Meryon must be very cold-hearted if she was not thrilled by his obvious partiality.

Meryon was not entirely unmoved, of course, and each time she met his smiling eyes across the table she warmed afresh to the realisation that life was not, after all, entirely made up of getting meals, seeing that Sally and Gregory left in good time in the morning, running an old-fashioned house, and generally trying to make both ends meet on a terrifyingly small income.

"Fancy, darling, Rex has been in Egypt and the Near (or is it Far?) East nearly all the winter," Mrs. Monder said. "No wonder we didn't see much of him."

"I remember you were going." Meryon coloured very

slightly, because she had been almost sure, at the time, that his departure was not unconnected with her own refusal to marry him.

"It was not until I came back a few weeks ago," Rex explained, "and tried to get into touch with you, that I found so much had happened and that no one seemed to know your new address."

"We didn't want just *anyone* to know, of course," Mrs. Monder said, speaking with dignified melancholy, as though they had been suppressing a family scandal. "Only our real *friends*."

"The implication is very flattering." Rex gave her his most charming smile.

"Well, of course, Rex, I have always felt that you and Meryon——"

"Here's Gregory!" exclaimed Meryon, and the relief in her tone might have sprung from a variety of causes. For a moment Rex's observant eyes narrowed very slightly in a speculative glance. Then Gregory came into the room, and the last of the introductions were made.

If Gregory remembered Rex's name with any curiosity, he showed none, and certainly he was not wasting any overwhelming cordiality on their visitor. Meryon hoped uneasily that his curtness was obviously due to overwork and weariness, but she wished he would take just a little more trouble to meet Rex's easy charm with something similar.

"I'm sorry I'm late, Meryon. No, don't bother about fresh tea—this will do."

"It won't take a moment," Meryon said, and went out of the room.

When she came back, her mother and Rex and the children were talking in complete friendliness, but Gregory, leaning back in his chair, seemed to be making very little attempt to join in the conversation.

"Did you have a heavy afternoon?" she asked as she handed him his tea.

"Yes." Gregory gave just the bare monosyllable— nothing else.

"Really! On Saturday afternoon, too," exclaimed Mrs. Monder. "You shouldn't, Gregory dear. It's too much of a good thing." She spoke as though Gregory's curious self-indulgence must definitely be checked.

He didn't even answer, only glanced at her with a weary dislike which he made no attempt to conceal. It was pardonable, perhaps, in a tired and harassed man, but it was in very unfortunate contrast to Rex's pleasant, indulgent air, and Mrs. Monder bridled slightly.

"I daresay Mr. Monder had very little choice," Rex said easily. "A rush of work isn't something you can argue with, you know."

"Quite." Gregory's tone was entirely unfriendly.

"Yes, but, after all, a half-day *is* a half-day," protested Mrs. Monder. "I mean—there's an Act of Parliament about it or something, isn't there?"

"It was not an occasion for invoking Acts of Parliament," Gregory told her drily.

"No, I suppose not." Mrs. Monder looked doubtful. Then, turning to Rex, she added in a hushed but perfectly audible tone: "So many changes for *all* of us, you know. Imagine! head of your own business one week and then—well, almost office boy, one might say, the next."

"He's *not* an office boy," cried Sally, greatly incensed by this affront to her cousin's dignity. He's got quite an important position."

"Hush, Sally. It's merely an irresistible figure of speech." Gregory spoke quite coolly, but his colour had risen.

"The City's champion stamp-licker, aren't you?"

John grinned, but without a shadow of malice, and the faintest smile passed over his cousin's grim face.

"No, no, my dear, of course I didn't mean *that*," Mrs. Monder hastened to explain. "It's stocks and shares and things like that. Very clever, really, except that I just don't *believe* in them, after what happened to poor Henry."

There was a moment's silence, while everyone tried to decide whether Mrs. Monder had ceased to believe in the existence of stocks and shares, or whether this was simply her way of expressing her disapproval of stockbroking. In any case, she herself rushed on in a moment:

"Of course, one knows there was no *disgrace* about it, only with everything gone, and Meryon doing a servant's work (though I will say she does it better than many who are paid for it), and poor Sally slaving at a business school—well, one does feel so *chastened*."

"But why?" Rex's lightest touch of sympathy was entirely inoffensive. "I should think one would get a considerable kick out of having squared up to things so well. Isn't that so, Miss Sally?" He turned suddenly to Sally, who beamed at once and said:

"It's not too frightful, you know. I really like the business college. And it's nice to feel I'm helping."

"Oh, of course, the children are *wonderful*," Mrs. Monder agreed. "So cheerful and loyal. But then" —once more she dropped her voice dramatically but ineffectually—"they hardly understand, of course. And, anyway, they adore poor Gregory."

Poor Gregory's eyebrows shot up at this unfortunate sequence of remarks.

"Do you *have* to make me sound something between a swindler and a half-wit?" he enquired with a kind of casual rudeness that made everyone gasp.

"Really," thought Meryon, "I know Mother is trying, but Gregory is impossible!"

And then she realised from the slight rattle of the cup in his saucer, that Gregory's hand was shaking a little, and immediately a great wave of angry pity swamped every other emotion.

"Mother means that we—that Sally and John—feel an affectionate loyalty to you as—as the head of the family, and that makes it so much easier," she broke in eagerly. She had no time to put it less clumsily, and she was not at all sure that she improved matters. At any rate, Gregory pushed back his chair without a word, and getting up, strolled over to the window and stood looking out—possibly in contemplation of their visitor's magnificent car.

Again it was Rex who made an effort to patch the ragged surface of the conversation.

"I've been wondering whether I can persuade you to forsake your family for once, Meryon, and come out with me this evening. Would they spare you?"

"Oh, I don't think——" began Meryon. But both her mother and—rather surprisingly—Gregory spoke with one voice.

"Of course you must go."

Meryon still hesitated.

"It will do you good, my dear. You haven't had any pleasure for ages," Mrs. Monder urged, while Gregory merely added, a little ungraciously:

"Why on earth shouldn't you?"

"There are several things I ought——"

"Nonsense." Gregory didn't allow her to get any further. "Your mother has just observed that you do the work of a servant." He smiled, but not very kindly. "You had surely better claim the privilege, then, of your evening out."

There was a moment's uncomfortable silence, and then:

"Do come, Meryon," Rex said, and for a chilly

second his eyes rested on Gregory with no more liking than Gregory's glance had expressed for him.

"Very well." Meryon spoke nervously, and a little breathlessly, for she had an idea that some awkward currents were running just below the surface of their conversation, and it disturbed her very much to realise that Rex and Gregory very definitely did not like each other.

"I'll clear up everything and housekeep for the evening," volunteered Sally, and she seemed to consider herself amply repaid by the smile of approval which this drew from their visitor.

"All right. I won't be long getting ready," Meryon promised, and made her escape upstairs to her room, hoping most profoundly that during her absence everyone would manage to keep off any more thorny subjects.

If only Mother hadn't made those unfortunate remarks! If only Gregory hadn't resented them so fiercely! Surely—surely there had been no need though for him to say such sharp and bitter things. Rex, now, would have passed things off with a touch of banter or an amusing comment.

But then, of course, Rex was in a very different position. Firmly entrenched behind unvarying security —wealthy, popular, leisurely—*he* could afford to laugh at stupid, two-edged remarks that might mean nothing at all or might mean galling criticism.

But Gregory, still sore and shaken from his sudden collapse into undeserved failure—harassed, anxious, struggling under a crushing load of responsibility—no wonder he was super-sensitive and winced angrily at any hint of pity or patronage or blame.

He *had* been rude to Mother, of course, and it *was* silly of him to take up her absurd remarks like that— but, oh, he had flushed and paled with such angry

nervousness, thought Meryon with sudden pain, and
his hand had actually been trembling. Her heart ached
over him as though he were a naughty but very dear
child, and she longed absurdly to protect him—she
scarcely knew from what.

But her business just now, of course, was to go out
and enjoy herself with Rex, while her family (she was
glad he had called them that!) made shift for themselves without her.

She opened the door of her bedroom cupboard—and
immediately it came over her with overwhelming force
that indeed she was stepping back into a different
life for one evening. For, of course, she must wear
the green two-piece with the great silver-fox cuffs.
It was the obvious—the only—choice for an informal
evening's pleasure with Rex. It would not be the
slightest bit over-done or out-of-place now. And yet
when she had kept that over from her one-time ward-
robe, and hung it in the narrow cupboard of her unpretentious bedroom, she had thought, "How silly,
really, for, of course, I shall never wear it. I should
just look hopelessly overdressed for anything we're
likely to do now."

But for an informal evening's pleasure—so long as it
was with Rex—the outfit was perfect.

As she dressed, she began to feel little stirrings of
excitement. It was impossible not to, for she was to
play at being rich again for one evening, and the
thought was very sweet.

Oh, the days when one used to pay forty, fifty, sixty
pounds for a dress or coat, and then go out and enjoy
oneself so carelessly! Those *were* good times—there
was no denying it. It wasn't that those things were
necessary. It wasn't even that one couldn't be quite,
quite happy without them. Only there was something
so incredibly carefree and gay and heart-warming in

escaping for a few hours now from care and responsibility.

For the whole of one evening she was to be beautifully dressed, expensively entertained, affectionately and admiringly looked after. And it was Rex—dear, charming Rex—to whom she owed this pleasure. It was such a happy thought that he had come into her life again. There wasn't any *harm* in slipping away and pretending for once that everything was just as it used to be. And yet she had the oddest little feeling of guilt as she looked at herself in the glass.

Who was this expensive, copper-haired girl in the wonderful green outfit? Meryon Dawling, who had thrown in her lot with a set of impecunious half-relations? She didn't look like that. Much more she was the popular friend of Rex Treventon, turning her back on everything serious and responsible, and going out to have an incredible amount of money spent on her entertainment.

Rather soberly Meryon went downstairs.

Nobody commented on her appearance, but everyone noticed it, she knew.

Nothing but admiration showed in Rex's dark eyes. Mother's expression of gratification would have been funny if it hadn't been somehow a little touching. While the quick way Sally sucked in her breath delightedly showed *her* appreciation. John gave Meryon the slightest nod which meant, "You look a peach! Be sure you enjoy yourself." Only Gregory's expression she could not fathom.

Disapproval—approval—indifference? It was hard to say which, and yet she knew, as she turned to go with Rex, that it was Gregory's expression which she would most willingly have read.

"Enjoy yourself, darling," her mother said. "I'm sure Rex will give you a lovely time."

"That's a promise." Rex smiled at her with apparently lazy pleasure, but she knew that deceptively casual expression hid an eager, even passionate, interest.

"I suppose you won't be very late?" Gregory's enquiry sounded strangely curt and ungracious, almost as though he didn't think she ought to go, although he himself had urged her. It struck a very unwelcome note in the otherwise friendly atmosphere, and Meryon said, with almost guilty haste:

"No, no. Of course I shan't be very late."

"That depends entirely on what we decide to do with our evening," Rex said smoothly, and as he ushered her out into the hall, he unmistakably passed his arm lightly round her for a moment.

She knew quite well that Rex was thinking very hard things of Gregory—and she could hardly wonder. He said nothing, however, as he handed her into the car, tucked a rug round her with solicitous care, and then got into the driving seat himself.

With a luxurious purr, the great Packard slid away from Beechcroft Crescent, that row of "desirable residences," and the young housekeeper of Number Twenty-Two was heading for an evening of extravagant pleasure.

For a minute or two there was silence. Then Rex spoke, a little drily:

"Does your family rough diamond make you all clock in and out, or does he keep a time-book for you?"

"Who? Gregory?" She was startled and a little dismayed. "Oh, Rex, you mustn't pay any attention to the way he spoke just now. He's tired, you know—and worried and overworked."

"And aren't you sometimes tired and worried and overworked?"

"Oh!" She frowned. "That's different."

"Why is it different, my dear?"

"Because——" Meryon hesitated. "Well, I suppose, because the final responsibility doesn't rest with me. He knows we have to look to him really for everything that keeps us going. There must be something rather frightening about that, don't you think?"

"No," Rex said deliberately. "I think there's something darned lucky about being allowed to work really hard for you. And if that ungrateful hound can do nothing but snarl at you, I don't think he deserves his luck."

She saw then, of course, why Rex could never have liked Gregory much, in any circumstances, but she wished most earnestly that he could do him just a little more justice.

It was a hard situation—hard on Rex too, come to that, because he wanted nothing more than to look after her and give her the best of everything. And because she could not love him, she had had to refuse him, and another man—who cared less than nothing about her—lived in the same house with her, worked for her in a sense, however reluctantly, and shared some part of his life with her.

No wonder Rex was a little bitter.

Diffidently she put her hand on his arm, and immediately he turned his head to give her that quick smile of his.

"Rex, I'm frightfully sorry it works out like this, but —try not to think too hardly of Gregory. He's really behaved wonderfully over this difficult business, and if his nerves and temper do get a bit frayed at times, it isn't to be wondered at."

"My dear, you're charming, making excuses for the brute," Rex told her lightly. "And I'm genuinely sorry that he came a financial cropper. It must be very—hard." His good-tempered tone was exactly that of the perfectly successful man towards someone who had failed—however undeservedly. Then his expression became sterner. "But I must confess that a certain inclination to kick him does come over me when I see him taking out his bad temper on you—standing there telling you to be home early, and, I suppose, waiting on the doorstep with a watch in his hand when you do return."

"Rex! You're absurd. He didn't *mean* what he said. It was just—oh well, he had to say something—and he was a little bit cross and nervous and——"

"Why nervous?"

She hesitated. It was impossible to explain, without giving Gregory away further, and she said hastily instead:

"Anyway, it's ridiculous to suggest he would—would wait up for me or question what time I came in."

"He doesn't consider himself sufficiently the head of the family for that?"

"Of *course* not."

"You're sure?"

"Quite sure."

"Good. Then we can dismiss the uncongenial subject of friend Gregory from our talk and enjoy our evening in peace."

She didn't want to leave things quite like that, really, but there was simply nothing more that she could say. Rex had an entirely wrong impression of Gregory, of course—well, an impression of one side only, that was to say. But argument was obviously serving no useful purpose—and, in any case, she really had not come out with him for the purpose of arguing about Gregory. And reluctantly she allowed him to drop from their conversation.

She thought, as they drove through the darkening streets towards the West End, that perhaps she should suggest to Rex that they went nowhere fashionable or well-known to-night. For she had no wish to meet any of her one-time acquaintances just now—there had been enough explanation and readjustment for one night.

But she need not have troubled. Rex seemed to know by instinct just where she would like to go, and the little place he chose—in that indefinable area between Soho and Mayfair where anything may or may not be fashionable—was quiet and exclusive and intimate.

The food was perfect, the service unobtrusive but faultless, and the wine-cellar obviously stocked by a man of imagination. And as Meryon sat opposite Rex, savouring each delicious course as it was set before her, she thought:

"Heavens, isn't it lovely to eat food you haven't cooked yourself!"

She almost said so to Rex, but caught back the words just in time. After all, he had probably heard and seen enough for one evening of a life where trifles were apt to assume very large and disagreeable proportions.

It was easy after that to give herself up to the sheer enjoyment of the evening.

From the restaurant they went to a brilliant and witty revue which had made quite a stir in the theatrical world a couple of weeks before.

"You haven't seen it yet, I hope?" Rex said, and as Meryon assured him that she had not, she thought:

"It's no good, of course. He can't really understand our position. Seen this show indeed! Why, where does he suppose I should find even the price of a pit seat nowadays?"

But it was lovely to sit in the stalls once more, and pretend there was no greater concern in the world than the risk that someone might take you to a theatre show you had already seen.

She really meant to go home immediately they came out of the theatre, but Rex scouted the notion.

"Why, Meryon dear, of course not! You're having supper with me first—if only to give our excellent Gregory some reason for frowning at the clock."

"Rex—*please* don't say these things. I assure you Gregory won't have given my return another thought." She hoped that was strictly true, and gave it extra emphasis in case it was not.

"No?" Rex smiled at her. "Then you certainly must stay out later—in order to prove his innocent and un-suspicious mind."

She laughed vexedly, but she stayed, of course, and they went somewhere very gay and charming which had sprung up in London night-life since Meryon had dropped out of things. And they talked so long and were so happy recalling past days that it was very much nearer two o'clock than one before they turned the Packard southwards again and drove in the direction of home and responsibility.

As they turned at last into Beechcroft Crescent, Rex gave vent to a chuckle of unmistakable amusement.

"What——" began Meryon, and then she stopped, in real exasperation and annoyance.

The powerful headlamps of the car sprayed their light down the centre of the road, and a street lamp here and there shed an isolated patch of yellow. But over and above these there was one light—and one light only— and unmistakably it shone from the dining-room of Number Twenty-Two.

Meryon felt furious in that moment—not only that Gregory should do anything so ridiculous as sit up for her, but that he should actually prove Rex right in his teasing assertion! She never for one minute supposed that anyone else was concerned, for she knew it could not be one of the children, and nothing would persuade her mother to stay up until this hour.

It was as though Gregory imagined he had authority

over her, or distrusted her, or something equally absurd. And just then Rex observed amusedly:

"I think perhaps I am the element he distrusts. Moneyed scoundrel decoys virtuous, hard-working girl into haunts of vice."

"Rex, don't be so absurd!" Meryon laughed angrily. "He—he's probably just been sitting up reading and forgotten the time." But she didn't think that really. She knew they all studied every penny of the electric-light bill much too closely for that.

However, Rex appeared to accept that explanation, even if the whole situation amused him unduly.

"Would you like me to come in and tackle him?" he asked lazily.

But her hurried "No, no, of course not. There's no question of 'tackling' anyone," stopped his teasing.

He got out of the car and stood there on the pavement holding her hand in his.

"It's been a wonderful evening, my dear. I hope it's only one of many, now that I've found you again."

"Oh, thank you, Rex." She was touched and pleased out of all proportion, she felt, but the fact that someone was actually having the effrontery to wait in the background to scold her, made Rex's tenderness all the more acceptable. Not that she intended to have nonsense like this from Gregory, of course. He would have to understand clearly, once and for all, that her time and her concerns were her own.

But as she said "Good night" to Rex, and mounted the old-fashioned steps to the door of Twenty-Two, she wished and wished that her gay and happy evening need not end in hard words.

She opened the door rather quietly with her key, half expecting to find a grim Gregory standing in the hall. But there was no one there, and with a final wave to

Rex as he got into the car, she softly closed the door behind her.

Well—she supposed he was sitting there in the dining-room now, with that preposterous air of disapproval which he presumed to use towards her. She realised then how she had allowed his attitude to affect her, because she found that her heart was thumping quite loudly. And, suddenly determining that this absurd business must end, she went over and, impatiently opening the door, marched straight into the room.

Then she stopped.

The light was full on and Gregory was sitting there— but not at all as she had expected. He was at the table, surrounded by a mass of papers, but entirely oblivious of them all. His head had fallen forward and his cheek was pillowed on his arms. And as she tiptoed forward to look at his sleeping face, every scrap of anger left her, and a very great tenderness took its place. For the exhausted expression on Gregory's face was that of an overworked schoolboy who had fallen asleep surrounded by his homework.

CHAPTER VI

"WHY, GREGORY," she said softly, and instinctively she put her arm round him. He sighed deeply, but didn't wake up, even when she raised him gently and drew his head against her. "Gregory, dear, you must go to bed."

"I'm so terribly tired," he said in a whisper, but quite uncomplainingly, and then he opened his eyes. His heavy lids drooped with weariness still, and he looked up at her in some bewilderment. "What on earth——" he muttered.

"You must have fallen asleep over your work," she explained. "I found you when I came in."

"Oh!" He stared uncomprehendingly at the papers on the table, and then he seemed to recollect himself. Sitting up, he put her from him, gently but very definitely. "Oh, yes, I——" He frowned. "I brought one or two things home from the office—urgent things— better to clear them up before starting another week."

She saw that in his over-strung state he expected her to make the sort of idiotic remark that Mother did.

"Yes, of course. It's best sometimes," she agreed soothingly. "But you'll go to bed now, won't you? It's very late."

He glanced at the clock.

"Lord! Is that the time?"

"I'm afraid so." This was the moment when he ought to make some sharp comment on her late return, of course, and so apprehensive had her conversation with

Rex made her that she held her breath and waited for what was to come.

But nothing came. Gregory simply pushed back his chair and got up.

"Yes, of course, I'll go now."

"I'm going to make myself a hot drink first," she exclaimed on sudden impulse. "You go along up and I'll bring you one in bed."

"No, no," he said automatically. "I don't want anything."

But she felt as she had on the night of the accident —that she knew best what he wanted and she didn't intend to have arguments.

She went up to her room first, and changed her beautiful coat and dress for her dressing-gown. Because, of course, one didn't go wandering about the kitchen at night wearing the only decent outfit one possessed—at least, not if one hadn't the faintest idea where the next one was coming from.

It didn't take long to prepare the drink, but when she came into his room he was already in bed, sitting up rather straight, but with his hair a good bit tumbled. Again she thought he looked like a tired schoolboy, and she experienced an absurd but intense desire to hug him comfortingly.

He accepted the drink with a faint smile, and began to sip it gratefully.

"He *did* want it," thought Meryon. "Of course—I knew he did."

Then he looked up and said, "Did you enjoy yourself?"

"Very much indeed, thank you. We had dinner at a very nice place in Soho and went to the show at the Corinthian. Then we had supper afterwards at some gay place whose name I've forgotten. It was new since my time."

He smiled again slightly, perhaps at the expression which seemed to relegate her to the position of a back number.

"And after all that," he said reflectively, "you felt the need of a hot drink?"

"Oh!" She coloured deeply and laughed a little uncomfortably. "Well, you wouldn't have let me make it if it had been only for you."

"No?" He looked thoughtfully into the cup and didn't elaborate on that theme, and after a moment she said, "Good night," and turned away.

"Meryon!" He caught at her dressing-gown with his disengaged hand and detained her.

"Yes?" She turned back in surprise.

"I just—wanted to say"—he fingered the fold of stuff in a faintly nervous way—"you didn't think that I didn't *want* you to go out and enjoy yourself, did you?"

"Why, Gregory!" She was exceedingly touched by the amount of effort which she guessed must have gone into this. "What makes you say that, I wonder?" She sat down on the side of the bed and looked at him.

"Well——" He didn't seem to be finding this an easy conversation. "Your mother said I must have—spoilt half your pleasure, and even John thought it sounded as though I—grudged you your evening's enjoyment. I didn't, you know." He raised those troubled grey eyes and looked at her very earnestly. "I didn't like that self-satisfied lounge lizard, but I was quite glad for you to have a good time with him if that was what you wanted."

Meryon swallowed this insult to Rex because she saw Gregory was under the impression that he was making amends, and it made him feel better.

"I know you didn't grudge me a good time," she

said gently, taking the cup from him and putting it on the side table. "I never thought you did." This was not entirely true, of course, but very nearly so, and his slight sigh of relief made her glad she had said it anyway. "It was just that you were tired and worried, wasn't it? And you didn't take to Rex much, did you?"

"No. He's not my sort at all; and we should never be likely to fall on each other's necks in friendship. Still, according to your mother he is perfection in mankind." He grinned suddenly. "And she thinks I could hardly do better than stumble inadequately in his footsteps."

Meryon laughed, but just a little vexedly. She wished Mother hadn't pushed Rex's good points down Gregory's reluctant throat, and she wished the two men hadn't decided to dislike each other so heartily.

"He's really a very good sort, you know," she explained, a little put out to find how much of her evening seemed to have been given up to making Rex appreciate Gregory, and Gregory appreciate Rex—particularly as the results had been so poor.

"I'm sure he's a combination of all the virtues," Gregory agreed as he slid down under the bedclothes. "But it's much too late—or, rather, too early—to sing hymns of praise just now."

"Yes, of course." She leant over absently and tucked in the bedclothes, very much as she might have with John. Then she found his amused eyes on her and coloured slightly, remembering once more, very forcibly, the night of the accident, when he had told her that "a little of the maternal touch went a long way."

"Good night," she said rather hastily.

"Good night," he replied very gravely. "And,

Meryon—I'm genuinely glad you enjoyed yourself. You know that, don't you?"

"I know." She smiled at him. And then, as three o'clock struck from the clock downstairs, she went at last to her own room.

.   .   .   .

"Well!" Sally stirred her coffee and gazed at Meryon across the breakfast table the next morning. "Did you have a perfectly marvellous time?"

Sunday morning's breakfast was apt to be a rather late affair, because being world's workers for six days of the week made them appreciate the week-end relaxation, in a way that had never applied in the days when Meryon and her mother at least could indulge themselves any day.

"Um-hm! Lovely, thanks," Meryon said, smiling at even the memory of the pleasant evening she had had.

"I'm so glad, darling." Mrs. Monder beamed with self-congratulatory pleasure. "It was *such* a happy idea of mine to think of looking Rex up again. After all, it's absurd of us really to feel any shame about the change in our circumstances. We must realise that *misfortune* does not imply *blame*."

With the sole exception of Mrs. Monder, no one had ever supposed such a thing, of course, but Meryon and Gregory maintained an heroic silence.

"Three cheers for the sackcloth and ashes," murmured John, selecting a piece of toast, while Sally looked very much surprised and said:

"Who was blaming us, anyway?"

"No one, dear. It was just a very natural feeling," Mrs. Monder explained patiently.

"Was it? Well, I didn't feel it," Sally said cheerfully.

"No, Sally. But then you're very *young* and not very sensitive," Mrs. Monder said forgivingly, whereat Sally wriggled a little uncomfortably and looked faintly bored. She never could quite understand why youth should be a minor crime and sensitiveness a major virtue, but it didn't matter, anyway.

"Were you very late home, dear? I don't think I heard you," Mrs. Monder said, turning to Meryon.

"Very late," Meryon said, and for a moment her eyes sought Gregory's. To her surprise, there was a shadow of a smile in his, and it warmed her very deliciously. Funny that she had thought the lateness of her return would be a bone of contention. It was almost like a bond of amused friendliness instead.

"I suppose he took you to all sorts of exciting places?" That was Sally, determined to extract all the thrills she could at second hand.

"Well, we had dinner and went to the new revue at the Corinthian, and then we had supper afterwards."

"That's what I call doing things properly," declared Sally.

"Well, of course, Rex is a *very* wealthy man," Mrs. Monder explained gently, a little as though the credit were partly hers.

"Nearly a millionaire?" Sally wanted to know.

"Very nearly, I should say," Mrs. Monder agreed with a touch of childlike complacency.

"In fact"—Gregory stirred his coffee with thoughtful deliberation—"in fact, a gilt-edged security."

Meryon started quite violently at the familiar ring of that phrase, and immediately there rose before her that wretched scene with Mother in the drawing-room at Oldkeep, when Gregory had overheard their unfortunate remarks about rich husbands.

Then he hadn't forgotten! She had thought, perhaps, lately that he had, but the memory evidently was still at the back of his mind—and not very far back either.

"I should call that a rather *vulgar* expression, Gregory," Mrs. Monder said at that moment. She tended more and more to treat him as though he were her own son, and therefore to be praised or reproved in much the same way she adopted to Meryon.

"Would you?" Gregory smiled at her in a much more friendly manner this morning. "Well, it's your own daughter's expression."

"Meryon's! I'm sure it isn't," Mrs. Monder retorted, going rather pink.

"Oh, yes, Mother. I did use it once in fun," Meryon said hastily, and Gregory added gravely:

"Oh, purely in fun, of course."

"Anyway, it's quite an attractive expression," John pointed out. "Think how delighted we should be if anyone could apply it to us at the moment."

"I—should—say!" declared Sally with emphasis, but quite happily. "It's funny how you don't think about money when you have it, and then when you haven't you do."

"Involved, but correct," agreed her brother. "I'm all for Meryon marrying the tame millionaire myself, and letting us sponge on her."

"*John!*" cried Mrs. Monder, genuinely horrified to have her own ideas presented in a different form.

"He's only joking," Sally explained patiently.

"Well, it's not a joking matter at all," Mrs. Monder said, a trifle ambiguously. "Rex Treventon is a very old friend of ours, and—well, anyway, he is a *very* old friend of ours," she finished lamely.

"Bit of a rip, isn't he?" Gregory said, so gravely that, if she hadn't known it was so out of character, Meryon would have suspected him of teasing Mrs. Monder in his turn.

"There! *I* said he had a past too!" exclaimed Sally, while Mrs, Monder said indignantly:

"I hope you're not going to say that *that* vulgar expression is Meryon's too, and, anyway, I very much resent it. Rex is a man of charm and experience, and I was very sorry to see, Gregory, that you evidently didn't appreciate him in the least."

"He's not my type," Gregory agreed, pleasantly but firmly. And Meryon thought:

"Really, these two are tiresome! Rex's superior dislike of Gregory is just about matched by Gregory's superior dislike of Rex."

Her mother, however, was not following that line of thought. She said, with unnecessary dignity:

"Then I'm afraid, my dear Gregory, that if Rex is 'not your type,' the loss is yours. And, anyway, I suppose there is a little bit of jealousy about it, too."

"Eh?" Gregory sat up then with a particularly penetrating and annoyed look. "Why on earth should I be jealous of the fellow?"

"Well—it's .only—that is, I suppose——" Mrs Monder floundered badly when faced by the enquiry direct, and her eyes rather innocently shifted to Meryon. Poor, partial Mrs. Monder couldn't really suppose that anyone could be in her daughter's company so long and remain quite impervious to her charms.

Gregory's eyes followed hers, with an expression which he deliberately allowed to become bewildered.

Meryon wished frantically that the ground would open and swallow her up. Then Gregory gave a cool, astonished laugh and made the one remark! "Good Heavens!" And Meryon was conscious of nothing but a cold, sick weight of depression.

She got up quickly and began to clear away the breakfast things. Last night's pleasure seemed halved

—oh, more than halved—for, of course, the nicest part of it all had been that it had ended with her on such happy terms with Gregory. Now that was all altered. He was scornful and unfriendly and remote once more—and really it was Mother's fault, however little she had meant to cause trouble.

Indeed, the innocence of her intentions was plain on her face now, and, after a puzzled moment or two, she said, with obvious truth:

"Really, Gregory, I don't think I understand you."

"No? Well, perhaps it's just as well," Gregory told her with a slightly contrite smile. "I had so far departed from the Rex model as to be almost rude. You must forgive me."

Mrs. Monder was so pleased at being in a position to forgive Gregory—even if she were very doubtful of what—that she smiled charmingly at once and said:

"Well, dear, never mind. I dare say you have a great deal to make you cross sometimes."

But Meryon thought she noticed during the next few days that, though he might be on good terms with her mother once more, for herself he seemed to maintain the most complete indifference.

They had been in the house nearly three months by now, and the first warmth of early summer was beginning to make itself felt. To most of them it came as a pleasure, but, after a while, Meryon noticed that John seemed to be flagging in some indefinable way. To all enquiries, he answered that he was perfectly all right, thank you—a bit fed up with the heat, but that was all. And at first Meryon tried to silence her vague fears with this.

A dozen times she was tempted to speak to Gregory about it, but she knew that he had his own anxieties at the office, without her adding any worries which perhaps were groundless, anyway. Mother, of course, was very little good in a case like this—which left only Sally.

"Well, why not speak to Sally about it?" Meryon thought suddenly. In spite of her wide streak of romanticism, she was a sensible and level-headed child, and, in addition, she probably knew John better than anyone, and could hazard a real opinion about his present state of health.

A little to Meryon's disquiet, Sally showed no surprise at the subject being introduced. She said at once:

"I know. He's not a bit well. I notice it more each day. He was always like this in the hot weather, you know—only, of course, before, he was able to have treatment."

"What sort of treatment, Sally? Why didn't you say something before? And why didn't Gregory mention it?"

"Well, you see"—Sally looked faintly uncomfortable—"I know it used to be frightfully expensive. Even Daddy said so once, and he very seldom counted any cost. I don't expect Gregory even knew about it."

"But, my dear, he must! He was like one of your own family. Your father would be bound to have spoken of it."

"No." Sally pressed her lips rather tightly together. "Daddy was a bit—stupid about John, you know. I don't mean that he wasn't frightfully fond of him and all that, and, of course, he would have done anything for him. But he always acted as though John's illness were almost something to be a bit ashamed of. At any rate, something to talk about as little as possible. I know it sounds idiotic, but he was like that, really, and I don't expect he talked of this special treatment to Gregory."

"I see. I remember now that I had the same impression." Meryon looked thoughtful. "You say it's really very expensive?" (Oh, why did money have to play this sickeningly important rôle in everything, now that one had so little of it?)

"I'm afraid so."

"But very necessary?"

Sally nodded regretfully. "That's why John didn't want me to mention it."

"Well, I'm very glad you did. Of course in a case like this, one—one finds the money somehow." (There was their reserve fund, after all—terrifyingly smaller than they had expected at first—but still *something*.) "I suppose the truth is that he *must* have this treatment if—if he's not to get worse. Is that it, Sally?"

For a moment Sally's lower lip actually quivered, and then she nodded.

"It means a good deal of pain for him, and—much less chance of his getting better later, I think," she explained slowly.

"I see." Meryon set her mouth with absolute determination. "Then I'll have Dr. Trellor to-morrow and hear exactly what is necessary."

"Are you going to say anything to Gregory?"

"No," Meryon said after a minute's hesitation. "No, I shan't tell him until it's absolutely necessary. I think his work makes enough demands on him already. We needn't add extra anxieties until we have to."

"He's quite right, Meryon. You *are* a brick," Sally said with sudden fervour.

"Who's quite right?" Meryon's very beautiful eyes opened to their fullest extent.

"Gregory. He said—well, I don't know that he meant me to repeat it."

"Why? Did he tell you not to?"

"Oh, *no*. Only—well, it was when we were going up to Town one morning, and he was giving me a pat on the back for not grousing too much about the business college. And I said I really liked it—I do, you know—and that I was afraid he couldn't say the same of his office. Then he said, 'Well, it's been killing work getting something-or-other into running order' (I didn't understand that bit) 'but three months more should see me out of the wood, so there's nothing to grumble about.' And then it was he added, 'Thank God, Meryon's such a brick! She shoulders far more than her share at home, and that gives me just the relief that makes things possible. I hate that she should have to do it, but I'll make it up to her later.' And I think he will, Meryon—he was terribly in earnest."

"He said—that?" Meryon had an absurd desire to weep.

"Yes." Sally was rather awed to see the degree to which Meryon was moved. "But you *knew* we all thought the world of you, didn't you?"

"I—I didn't know Gregory did," murmured Meryon. "Anyway, of course, he doesn't."

Sally looked at her rather curiously.

"I shouldn't be so sure," was all she said.

And then Meryon laughed a little shakily, and actually blinked a couple of tears from her lashes. Sally didn't know the real facts, of course—but that scarcely seemed to matter. He had said—that. He did appreciate the fact that she was trying to help in every way. And it was doubly sweet because it was so unexpected.

"He *shall* be kept free from anxiety at home!" Meryon told herself almost passionately. "He has all that he can manage, making money to keep us. The home is my concern, and it's nothing more than my duty to see that he's not worried about it. They're my family too—I've *made* them mine. And I'll look after them properly, even if it kills me!"

But she didn't make any heroic speeches of this sort to Sally, of course. She just said:

"Well, Sally dear, it's very nice to know you all feel confidence in me, and I'll find a solution somehow to this problem about John."

"That's good!" Sally gave an immense sigh of relief. "I can't imagine how we got along without you, Meryon, even in our prosperous days. You seem to make a sort of centre of things," she added vaguely.

Meryon patted her shoulder affectionately, but said no more. And the next day, when Gregory and Sally had both gone to Town, she spoke to John quite casually.

"I've been hearing that once or twice before, when you were run down you had some marvellous special treatment, John. I'm going to have Dr. Trellor in to-day, and we'll discuss whether it's necessary again."

"Oh, but"—John looked startled—"we couldn't afford it. It's frightfully expensive, Meryon. And, anyway, I'm all right," he added hastily.

Meryon bit her lip to see how determined he was about that, even though his pallor and listlessness told a very different tale.

"Well, Dr. Trellor won't recommend anything that isn't necessary," she pointed out soothingly. "And as for the expense, there are always arrangements for people of limited means to have medical treatment free or, at any rate, for very little money."

"Even anything as unusual as this?" John's expression was doubtful, but with an underlying eagerness that made Meryon's throat contract.

"Oh, yes. I'm sure of it," she declared cheerfully.

"Anyway, was it so very unusual? Tell me about it."

John hesitated a moment, as though, even then, he thought it wiser to keep silent. Then at last he said:

"Well, I think there are only about two places in England where it's done. Have you ever heard of the Kurt Brahlen Clinic?"

Meryon shook her head.

"No, I don't expect you would, unless you'd had some special reason to," John said. "Kurt Brahlen is a German Swiss, I think. Anyway, he's done marvellous research work in connection with spinal trouble, and he has one clinic in London, I know, and a smaller one was opened in Oldkeep about a couple of years ago. There may be one in Edinburgh, too—I'm not sure— but, anyway, of course it was very lucky for me that he started one in Oldkeep."

"And you're sure there is one in London?" After all, that was the important thing now.

"Yes. Somewhere in North London. But"—he broke off suddenly—"it really isn't possible, Meryon. It means three or four visits a week at least, and we couldn't manage that on travelling grounds alone."

"We'll see. We'll see. No doubt we could arrange something," Meryon said cheerfully. But she was really thinking with unhappy impatience: "Oh, why ever didn't we settle in *North* London?"

John fixed his large, dark eyes on her—much too large and much too dark they looked at that moment.

"I wish I hadn't told you anything about it," he said with that attractive air of responsibility that was so much older than his age. "Now you'll worry yourself sick about it."

"No, I shan't." Meryon smiled determinedly. "I shall merely arrange that you have this treatment."

"I can't imagine that it won't be terribly expensive —quite beyond anything we could afford. You see, the actual equipment of the place—electrical appliances and all that sort of thing—must have cost a mint of money to begin with, and probably takes a fortune to keep up. I could see that, even at the smaller place in Oldkeep. And then each patient has to have individual and expert attention of the very first order. You can't get that sort of thing cheaply, Meryon dear."

"I'm practically sure one can," Meryon said, with something like desperation just below the surface of her obstinate optimism. "Anyway, I'm determined you shall have the treatment if it's going to make all this difference, so it's no good arguing."

"Dear Meryon!" John smiled at her with a shadow of his old roguishness. "What an attractive mule you can be."

But she knew, without being told, that he was painfully anxious to find her optimism well-founded.

Dr. Trellor had remarkably little to say while he was actually examining John that afternoon, but later he came into the sitting-room with Meryon, his expression very much graver than she liked to see. It was true that, on the two or three occasions they had had to call him in before, he had seemed to her a serious-minded person, but she thought it was no fancy of hers that now he looked significantly solemn.

"Well?" she said more sharply than she had meant to. "Is he very seriously ill?"

The doctor hesitated a moment before replying.

"He is never in a good state of health. That's rather too much to expect."

"Yes, yes, I know. But he's not so well as when you saw him in April, is he?"

Again that slight pause, not so much as though the doctor was unsure of his replies as that he wished he could frame them differently.

"He is not so well," he admitted. And then, as though deciding that frankness was best, "There is a definite deterioration in the general level of health."

Meryon locked her fingers together nervously until the knuckles cracked.

"What can we do?" she asked abruptly.

"Very little, I'm afraid. You are doing everything possible at the moment. Plenty of rest, no excitement, good food——"

"Oh, that's just playing with the problem!" Meryon exclaimed despairingly. "It's what one might do for a bilious attack or a cold."

The doctor was silent.

"What about special treatment? I thought there was so much that could be done nowadays."

"So there is, my dear Miss Dawling—but only for certain complaints."

"Well, there must be *something*! What about the work at the Kurt Brahlen Clinic?"

Dr. Trellor looked up quickly.

"Well, of course, if I suggested sending him there it would be the counsel of perfection, but unfortunately——"

"Yes?"

"It would cost you a very great deal of money."

"How much?" Meryon said, so crudely that she was faintly shocked herself.

He was much too polite to say, "Very much more than you could afford," but his deprecating little shrug said it for him.

"Can't you give me any idea?"

"Well, to begin with, you would have to move him within easy reach of the Clinic. It's the other side of London. And you would have——" The doctor broke off, and then added thoughtfully: "Probably the only practical plan would be to send him to the

Kurt Brahlen Home in Buckinghamshire for, say, six or eight weeks. They have resident patients there. The other idea of having him in a boarding-house near the Clinic would never work. Taking him backwards and forwards, and having him among strangers who didn't understand the case would undo all the good that was done, I'm afraid."

"And how much would the home cost?" Meryon wondered if there had ever been a time when money was not the most important thing in the world.

"Twelve or fifteen guineas a week, without any question. It doesn't come under the National Health Service, I'm afraid."

Meryon caught her breath and whitened slightly as she did a terrifying little sum in her head.

"You said six or eight weeks?"

The doctor nodded.

"Anything between a hundred and a hundred and fifty pounds before you had covered all the extras and incidental expenses."

One hundred and fifty pounds! She would have spent that sum on a Continental holiday in the old days. Now it seemed almost the price of John's life.

"It would make all the difference to him, wouldn't it? Having this treatment, I mean."

"Yes. I feel reluctant to say how much difference since"—he paused and gave Meryon a sympathetic glance—"I'm afraid it is a practical impossibility?" he finished, half questioningly.

"But, surely, Dr. Trellor, there are cases where allowance is made. I mean, the—the charges are reduced or—or even waived altogether. Aren't there great surgeons who do operations for—well, almost for nothing and that sort of thing?" She flushed deeply. It all sounded horribly like begging somehow. But, anyway, it was for John, so she didn't care.

Dr. Trellor didn't seem to think it was like begging, however. He took up the subject kindly, though regretfully.

"It is true, of course, that people of limited means can have the very best attention for little or nothing. But in this particular case there is no doubt whatever that there is a big waiting list for the three or four free places the Home can support. It may even be that there is difficulty in entering as a paying patient. You see, the treatment is highly specialised and, in any case, a comparatively new discovery. The demand for it is bound to exceed the supply, so to speak."

"And those who can pay come first," Meryon said a little bitterly.

"It is a practical necessity, you know." The doctor smiled, but not unsympathetically.

"It seems hard that what is perhaps life or death can be measured in money."

"It *is* hard," the doctor agreed gravely. "But you must not forget that, in the case of a nursing home of this type, only the existence of the paying patients can make it possible to carry out essential research."

"Yes, of course, you're right. I shouldn't have spoken like that." Meryon pushed back the loose wave of hair over her forehead and smiled bravely at the doctor. "So the problem is simply to find a hundred and fifty pounds. I'll see what I can do, Doctor."

He laughed slightly, and looked at her with something like puzzled admiration. She sounded so very much as though she meant what she said. And yet —he glanced involuntarily round the simply furnished room, and again round the bare hall as he took his leave. There didn't seem to be many signs of unexpected wealth there.

It must just have been a manner of speaking. She was a good, brave girl, obviously. Only, even good, brave girls had to recognise the inevitable sometimes.

But perhaps Dr. Trellor would have changed his mind if he could have seen Meryon's expression as she stood the other side of the closed front door, sunk in thought. She didn't look at all as though she had recognised the inevitable. She looked much more like throwing down a challenge to Fate.

CHAPTER VII

As THE SOUND of the doctor's car died away down the road, Meryon turned and went slowly back into John's room.

It was very quiet there, and she saw immediately that he was asleep. Not a very good sleep—just the exhausted slumber of someone who had little strength.

Crossing the room, Meryon stood looking down at him—at the thin, rather delicately moulded face, the slightly untidy dark hair, and the childishly long lashes.

It was extraordinary how dear both the children had become to her, and John, with the extra appeal of his unspoken need, perhaps had the closer hold on her heart. She couldn't imagine what she would do if anything—well, if anything serious happened to him. He was such a lovable and important factor in their lives—amusing, endearing, philosophical, a personality in spite of his physical inactivity.

"I couldn't possibly have anything happen to him," Meryon whispered. "I *couldn't*."

One hundred and fifty pounds.

There was a sort of grim rhythm about the phrase, as though it took pleasure in mocking her, and for a moment she thought:

"I know why some people commit crimes for money."

However, it had not come to a question of crime yet, and presently, stealing quietly out of the room, she went upstairs to see if her mother had woken up from

the little afternoon nap in which she regularly indulged
but as regularly denied.

Mrs. Monder was sitting on the side of her bed when
Meryon entered in answer to her sleepy "Come in."

"Do you know, dear, I believe I actually dropped
off to sleep for a minute or two," she said with a
disarmingly surprised little laugh. "It must be this
warm weather. So fatiguing, isn't it?"

"Yes. I'm afraid it is." Meryon seized the opening
immediately. "As a matter of fact, I'm very worried
about the effect on John. I can't help wondering if
we're doing all that can be done for him."

"What else could we do?" Mrs. Monder was agreeable,
but unhelpful.

Meryon took the plunge.

"I'm afraid anything that could be done would cost
money."

"*Everything* costs money," her mother observed
plaintively. "And the funny thing is that the less one
has, the more it seems to cost," she added, not very
clearly.

"Yes, but you and I *have* got a little in hand,"
Meryon ventured to point out.

"Not much when you consider that we're living on
it, and not on interest," her mother countered quickly,
for she was not without her gleams of shrewdness,
particularly, it must be confessed, where her own
interests were concerned.

"I know. But I thought that if perhaps something
could be done for John and it—it wouldn't cost *too*
much, we might put up the money." It was a terribly
feeble way of inserting the thin end of the hundred-and-
fifty-pound wedge, but she could think of nothing
better at present.

Out came Mrs. Monder's underlip in that characteristic pout of protest.

"Isn't that more Gregory's business, dear? He has some capital—or, at least, it's for the children, isn't it? which means he can spend it on them, surely. After all, several hundred pounds will go a long way."

"Oh, Mother dear, don't be silly! It isn't several hundred pounds, you know. We hoped it might be nearly five hundred, but it wasn't more than two hundred in the end."

"Two hundred pounds is a lot of money," Mrs. Monder stated, with that good-tempered obstinacy that was so pretty if it didn't concern one personally, so infuriating if it did.

"But it's absolutely the only thing that stands between the children and disaster if—well, if Gregory should be ill or lose his job or anything like that." Meryon couldn't add that, in any case, she wanted to keep Gregory out of this at all costs.

Mrs. Monder considered the position with an air of intelligent concentration that was entirely deceptive.

"How much money have we got, dear?" she produced finally. "I mean, one draws some of it out and doesn't put it back, of course, and then there ought to be some money from the furniture, only there were expenses too. Anyway, it's very difficult to understand."

"I think," Meryon said very patiently, "that it would be quite a good idea if I went up to see Mr. Framden myself." Until now, her mother had had the monopoly of visits to their lawyer, partly because she had an odd childish jealousy of letting Meryon handle her money affairs. "And it might help if you let me have your pass-book," Meryon added.

"There's nothing in it, dear. At least, I mean nothing on the important side."

"I see." Meryon suppressed a slight smile. "Well, I think I'll go and see Mr. Framden this afternoon."

"But is there any need for hurry?" Mrs. Monder looked surprised.

Meryon thought of John's pale, sleeping face, and knew, with a chill of dread, that there *was* need for hurry. But she said quite coolly:

"It's a fine afternoon and I might just as well go now. Besides, it's nice to know exactly where one stands, isn't it?"

"Not always," Mrs. Monder said with engaging frankness. "Sometimes it's much nicer to go on pretending."

"You hopeless little ostrich!" Meryon exclaimed with a laugh and kissed her. Occasionally the sheer absurdity of Mother's outlook was almost cheering.

"Not that I've been entirely unlike an ostrich myself," reflected Meryon, as she sat looking out of the bus window on her way to Town. "I ought to have got this completely straight before. Only, of course, there's been so much else to do, and Mother always handled or mishandled the money for so many years that it seems almost an intrusion now to be interfering."

However, interfere she must, particularly as Mother had artlessly intimated that her bank balance was exhausted. That meant that Meryon must inspect the main balance of their tiny capital before Mother started taking dangerous and illogical nibbles at it.

Meryon was not entirely unknown to Mr. Framden, although their few previous meetings had been confined to such things as congratulatory phrases and the presentation of a cheque on her eighteenth birthday, according to the terms of her father's will. (Why had she spent that cheque so carelessly and happily?)

Now, however, he had no cheque to give her, and few congratulatory phrases.

"Well, Miss Dawling," he said regretfully, when she had put the all-important question about their financial situation, "you are, of course, aware that there have been large and regular sales of capital for many years? That was your mother's definite policy, though I may say that I did everything in my power to dissuade her."

"Yes, of course. I understand that. I'm afraid I didn't know anything about it myself until—well, until it was too late."

"Quite, quite." The lawyer took off his rimless spectacles and balanced them thoughtfully in his hand, as though that helped to make his ideas flow more freely. "Unfortunately—if you will pardon my saying so—your father left everything to your mother unreservedly, until you were twenty-one. The residue was then to be divided between you."

Meryon privately thought that "unfortunately" scarcely covered the case, especially when one reflected on the amount of the residue, but she merely inclined her head.

"Consequently, of course, that meant that there were no means, other than those of argument, by which your mother might be persuaded to leave even the smallest part untouched. And—again if you will pardon my saying so—your mother is singularly unresponsive to argument."

"I know." Meryon had a fleeting memory of certain scenes in which she had tried to persuade Mother to something against her will. "Then the plain fact is that we have—— Well, how much *is* there left, Mr. Framden? I think, quite frankly, that Mother is afraid to find out for herself, but she seems willing that I should do so. I know that there was something like five hundred pounds left a week or two before her marriage."

"Ah, yes, but"—Mr. Framden checked any undue optimism by an emphatic wave of his spectacles—"I am afraid Mrs. Dawling—or, rather, Mrs. Monder—considered her second marriage an occasion for a certain amount of—I might say, lavish expenditure."

"Oh, dear," Meryon said hopelessly. She knew what lavish expenditure could mean where her mother was concerned, and it was possible, of course, that Mr. Monder had not paid for all the beautiful clothes in which his new wife had blossomed forth in their earlier, carefree days.

"There was, of course, the money from the sale of the furniture at the flat."

"Oh, yes?" Meryon brightened a little, but Mr. Framden immediately curbed that with another ominous wave of the spectacles.

"But there was a quarter's rent due, and another had to be paid in lieu of notice, I'm afraid."

Meryon didn't even say "Oh, dear," this time. She saw that they were much more likely to reach the ultimate goal of their conversation if she let Mr. Framden work things out in his own way, free of interruption.

And, sure enough, after a minute or two, he pressed a bell and bade an obsequious junior clerk bring him "the papers in Dawling, B. J."

The papers were brought, and, putting on his spectacles once more, Mr. Framden turned some of the pages, clearing his throat the while, and finally announced:

"Yes, here are the full details for the current financial year, and, of course, those of previous years are open to your inspection at any time, now you are of age. When all out-goings have been paid (I see there is a note of them here) and interest to date added, the full sum available amounts to three hundred and ten pounds, nine shillings and elevenpence. Say three hundred and ten pounds ten," he added generously.

"I see." Meryon twisted her gloves rather nervously round her hand, but before she could add anything, Mr. Framden spoke again:

"And I do *beg* of you, Miss Dawling, that you will use all the influence you have with Mrs. Monder to see that she makes as few inroads as possible on this sum. Your mother is a very charming woman, but entirely devoid—if I may say so—of any sense of the value of money."

"Yes, I know."

Meryon was silent again, thinking of that one hundred and fifty pounds. It was hopeless, of course. Half their capital. It would be criminal, even if Mother could be persuaded—which she certainly could not.

"Anyway, I couldn't do it," Meryon thought. "It would be terribly wrong—just a case of sacrificing Mother to John. But, oh! what can I *do*?"

She said "Good-bye," with slightly forced composure, to Mr. Framden, having promised to do her utmost to keep a brake on Mother's expenditure.

When she came out of the office into the sunshine of Kingsway, it was still only ten minutes past four, although it seemed to her that it had taken hours to extract this miserable bit of information from the lawyer.

She paused for a moment on the edge of the pavement. There was nothing to do, of course, except go home. And yet to do so seemed like an acceptance of defeat, almost a betrayal of John.

Perhaps, after all, she ought to tell Gregory and see what he thought. He might say at once that they would spend the money out of the tiny bit left for the children. And yet—to leave scarcely anything in the event of

Gregory's losing his job or falling ill! That seemed suicidal too. And perhaps John was not so very ill— not dangerously ill. Only——

"Hello, Meryon!" A familiar cream and plum-coloured car slid to a standstill almost beside her, and, sitting at the steering wheel, smiling in a carefree way that defied all anxieties, was Rex.

"Oh, Rex, I *am* glad to see you!"

The exclamation came from Meryon's very heart, because somehow the very sight of anything so secure and easy-going as Rex made one feel that disaster and poverty and anxiety were unreal things that stood a long way off.

Leaning forward, he opened the door.

"Jump in, and we'll go and have tea somewhere. No, no!" as she began to speak. "I know all about the claims of the precious family, and I promise to get you home in time to present an evening meal to Sally and the ungrateful Gregory. But at the moment you're coming to have tea with me. You look a little fagged and as though you need a quiet half-hour. Come along."

Meryon went. And it was typical of Rex that he said nothing at all to her for a while—just let her sit back and relax, while the powerful car nosed its way through the traffic, guided by Rex's unerring hands.

Only when they were seated in the secluded corner of a quiet Bond Street tea-room did he say anything of importance, and then it was so much to the point that even that in itself was a relief.

"What is the matter, Meryon? I know you wouldn't have been looking so serious and worried for nothing, and I think I must be allowed a friend's privilege of helping if possible."

"Oh, Rex dear!" She laughed a trifle unsteadily.

"How nice and straightforward you make everything sound."

For a moment a strange light flickered in his dark eyes, but it was gone almost immediately.

"You know that I would ask nothing better than to make everything in the world straightforward for you," he said almost curtly.

"Yes. I—I know. You're much too good to me," Meryon told him hastily.

"No, not too good," he corrected, and then, as a very dry little smile touched the corners of his slightly cynical mouth. "Well, what is the matter with Gregory now?"

"Gregory! It's not Gregory," Meryon replied almost indignantly. "It's John."

"Oh, it's John, is it, who is making you look so worried? And what is the matter with John?"

"He's ill." Meryon spoke in a low voice. "He's never well, you know. It's some spinal trouble—the kind of thing that doctors find very difficult to treat. One doesn't even hope for a complete recovery, short of a miracle, but the trouble can be kept stationary most of the time."

"Yes?" Rex prompted her gently as she seemed inclined to hesitate.

"Well, he's been worse lately." Meryon's words came quickly and a little breathlessly. "I can't help seeing it for myself, even without the doctor's word for it. I had him to see John this afternoon. He *says* he is worse and that he ought to have treatment—terribly expensive treatment. And it's true, I'm sure. He used to have it in the old days, but now——" she broke off. Then she added flatly and more despairingly than she knew, "It would cost a hundred and fifty pounds. I've just been to see our lawyer. I was coming away when I met you. It just can't be done, that's all."

There was a second's silence as her voice trailed away. Then Rex said:

"But you can have the money, Meryon. You can have it now. At least"—he took out his note-case—"you can have a hundred now and the rest to-morrow. Of course you can. Surely you knew you had only to ask me?"

"A hundred now," repeated Meryon stupidly, staring at the notes in his hands. Then she laughed hysterically. "Oh, Rex, you're like the Count of Monte Cristo, who carried a million francs in his note-case just to produce them at the most dramatic moments."

Rex looked slightly taken aback.

"I'm not in the least like the Count of Monte Cristo," he said with a laugh. "He was an unconscionable snob, if I remember rightly. But do take the money, Meryon dear. You're doubly, trebly welcome. I'd rather pay a thousand than see you look so troubled."

"But I couldn't. One simply doesn't." Meryon murmured the words automatically, though she felt a little like someone refusing to be rescued from some perilous place on a cliff.

It was perfectly true, of course. One *didn't* accept large presents of money from one's men friends. One didn't allow a sheaf of ten-pound notes to pass over a tea-table like that.

But, oh the simplicity of it if one could! And the special circumstances might justify it. Oh, surely, surely they might justify it! Rex had so much money —though that, of course, was not the point. If he had seen John as a poor boy in a hospital and made this offer, everyone would have said, "How generous! How fortunate!" and it would have been all right.

Then why not now?

She knew perfectly well why not, of course. She didn't dare to raise her eyes and look at him, because she knew the expression in his would give her the reason why she should refuse this money. Perhaps in some cases one could take money from one's friends—even men friends. But one did not take money from a man who was in love with one—particularly if one could not love him in return.

"Don't be silly, Meryon." He was speaking quite gently. "Think again. I've got far more of this rotten money than I know what to do with. Why should John go on being ill for the sake of some conventional quibble? And why should you go on killing yourself with worry about it?"

If only he hadn't added that last bit! If only it could be an issue between him and John! But she knew that he was giving *her* the money because *she* must not be allowed to look anxious and worried.

"Or am I just being a squeamish little idiot? Just sacrificing John to my false sense of pride?" she thought unhappily, aware that she was keeping Rex waiting an absurd length of time for an answer.

She raised her eyes slightly, though her head remained bent. The notes were lying carelessly on the table now, just within her range of vision.

How absurd she was! Why, only a few hours ago she had told herself she understood why people committed crimes for money, and here she was now, having heroics over what Rex rightly described as a conventional quibble.

Taking a sudden resolution, she raised her head and looked straight at him.

"It's only fair to say that I have no idea when I could pay it back," she said breathlessly.

"I never lend money to my friends, my dear. This

is a gift," Rex told her coolly. "That is clearly understood."

"Rex, I don't know how to thank you."

She did know of one way, of course, but neither of them mentioned that. He only said:

"You agree, then?"

She nodded.

"Good. I'm more glad than I can say." He pushed the notes towards her across the table. "And now suppose we have our tea."

Meryon folded the notes slowly and put them in her handbag.

"Thank you," she said, baldly and inadequately. And then, with a hand that trembled slightly, she began to pour out the tea.

Most men would have found it impossible to create a cool and normal atmosphere after such an incident, Meryon supposed, but Rex achieved it with apparently no effort. A few minutes after she had accepted the gift of a hundred pounds from him, he had contrived that they should be discussing general topics in a completely normal manner.

And he was quite as good as his word about getting her home in good time. It was he who said finally:

"Much though I should like to keep you, isn't it time that we were going?"

Meryon glanced at her watch.

"Oh, yes, it is." A little reluctantly her mind came back to the necessity of having dinner ready when Gregory and Sally came in. But, actually, she had herself so well-disciplined by now that only the faintest regret lingered as she left the pleasant, luxurious place with Rex.

As they reached the door, it swung open to admit a slim, wonderfully dressed woman. Even in a second's encounter, Meryon took in that she was extremely beautiful, in that slightly outrageous manner that either attracts or repels according to one's disposition.

The next moment, to Meryon's surprise, the woman was greeting Rex with a "Hello, darling," that somehow sounded just a little less casual than the tone was went to imply.

Meryon walked on out of earshot, but she knew instinctively that this was someone to whom Rex would not introduce her. There was nothing *wrong* with the woman, she told herself. She was beautiful, she was tastefully dressed, and in spite of the "darling" she might be only an acquaintance, in any case.

But, even so, Meryon found herself thinking: "I suppose there are some sides of Rex that I know nothing about." And, for some reason, she remembered the hundred pounds in her bag with more acute discomfort than ever.

He rejoined her a moment or two later, and she was not at all surprised to find that, not only was there no question of an introduction—he made no reference to the woman either. He handed Meryon into the car with all his usual care and kindliness, and a moment later they were driving down Bond Street towards Piccadilly, with a careless remark from Rex on the difficulty of regulating the traffic in such a narrow street.

Oh, well, of course, it was no business of hers, really. *Rex* was no business of hers. She had made that decision for herself. But the incident was the kind that stayed in the back of one's mind.

Not until they were almost home did he mention the question of the rest of the money.

"Would you rather have the extra fifty in notes, Meryon, or as a cheque?" he asked coolly, adding almost immediately: "Notes, I expect?"

That was true, of course. A cheque with Rex's name

on it might be a little embarrassing to deal with, and
she said quickly:

"It would be more convenient in notes, if you don't
mind."

"Not at all. I'll call in at the bank to-morrow morning and register the money to you at once. You'll get
it by the evening post."

Meryon was silent for a moment. It was difficult to
explain that in the close ring that their family had
now become, a registered letter could hardly come without comment. Still more difficult was it to explain
that she didn't want anyone in the family to know
about this.

However, it had to be done, and, gripping her hands
rather tightly together, she said:

"Rex, there—there isn't any hurry about the rest of
the money. You needn't send it."

"I might just as well. I'd like you to have it at once,"
he explained with characteristic careless generosity.

"Thank you. It's sweet of you, but—you see—I'm
not telling them at home—at any rate, not just yet.
It might——"

"My dear, I understand. This is entirely between you
and me." The quiet satisfaction in his tone was unmistakable. "I see, of course, that to have it arrive in
a registered envelope would hardly be tactful. We must
arrange to meet somewhere, Meryon, and I'll have it
for you then."

It was wonderfully kind of him, of course, to understand so completely, but Meryon began to wish passionately that the whole thing could be much less
personal. Already the arrangement was rapidly taking
on the character of an intimate secret, shared by them
alone. And that was the last way she wanted Rex to
regard it!

However, things were rather out of her hands by now

and, still unable to steer the course of the conversation differently, she found herself promising to meet him two or three evenings later and, if possible, to have dinner with him.

As she said "Good-bye" and let herself into Number Twenty-Two, Meryon wondered a little grimly if she had less—or more—reason to be worried than when she had left the house a few hours ago.

The moment she came into the hall she noticed that Gregory's hat was hanging there. It was early for him to be home, and she was immediately and rather absurdly aware that she would much rather not have had him see her drive up in Rex's car.

The next moment, she told herself she was ridiculous. It was a perfectly natural and understandable thing for her to have tea with Rex. Why on earth should there be any comment?

Pulling herself together, she went into the dining-room. Gregory was sitting there alone, reading the paper, but he got up as she came in, and crumpled the paper slightly in his hand, with an expression that oddly suggested nervousness to her.

"Hello, Gregory. You're home early."

"Yes. Things were slack for once, and as I've had a good many late evenings in the last weeks, there was a chance of getting off early and I took it."

"I'm so glad. You can do with it. I—I've just been up in Town myself and I ran into Rex Treventon. We had tea together."

"Did you? I suppose that was his car I heard just now?"

"Yes."

"He wouldn't come in?"

"No, he——"

"Thought he might not be welcome," suggested Gregory, and his grim little smile suggested that in thinking that Rex would have been perfectly correct.

"Nothing of the sort," Meryon said a trifle sharply. She turned away, and as she did so her eye fell on a vase of tall crimson roses, an unheard-of luxury in their household nowadays.

"Why, what wonderful roses!" she exclaimed. "Who-ever brought them."

Gregory cleared his throat.

"I did," he said almost defensively.

She knew she ought to say something, however mild, about unnecessary luxuries, but she couldn't. Not with Gregory standing by, looking like that. Besides, they were so beautiful and gave her such spontaneous pleasure that perhaps one might even excuse the extravagance.

Meryon put down her gloves and bag, and touched the roses with almost loving fingers.

"They're lovely, Gregory. They make the room look quite different."

"They weren't meant for the room," Gregory said in that abrupt way of his. "They were meant for you."

"For *me*? You bought them specially for me?" She could hardly believe her ears. "Oh, Gregory, how nice of you! But why? It's not my birthday or a celebration or anything."

"No, I know." He frowned and examined the pattern of the carpet with unnecessary attention. "I just thought I'd like to get them. It's pay-day, anyway. And"—he hesitated—"Oh well, I do notice how much you do in this place, you know."

She crossed the room and took his hand.

"Thank you, Gregory. You can't imagine how much pleasure you've given me."

"That's all right." He slightly patted the fingers that were curled round his. "It's nothing, but I'm very glad if you're pleased."

"I *am* pleased." She let go his hand and began to arrange the flowers, more to hide how much she was moved than anything else.

He watched her for a minute in silence. Then he spoke—almost diffidently for him—but this time it had nothing to do with the roses.

"Meryon, are you and Treventon really great friends?"

"Well"—she was slightly nonplussed—"we've known each other quite a long while. Why?"

"Because"—again he hesitated—"well, if you were my sister, I should tell you I damn well didn't like you running around with a fellow of that type."

"What a good thing I'm not your sister, then," Meryon told him sweetly. And then, as he seemed disinclined to regard that as an answer: "But why would you want to play the heavy Victorian brother in this particular case?"

Gregory frowned.

"I'm sorry if I seem pompous, but—Treventon hasn't an impeccable reputation, you know."

Meryon gave an angry little laugh.

"Who has?" she said with most uncharacteristic flippancy, but annoyance and a certain faint alarm made her speak so.

"That isn't worthy of you, Meryon," Gregory said coolly, and this time his tone was very much that of an elder brother.

"No, I know. It was stupid to speak like that. Only, please, Gregory, don't go trying to dig up things against Rex simply because you don't like him personally."

"I'm not 'digging things up,' and it isn't because I don't like him—though, incidentally, I don't," Gregory added in parenthesis. "And I know his being a friend of your mother and all that sort of thing makes it sound good. But just remember there have been a few stories about him in the past and——"

"There are always stories about anyone so wealthy and attractive," Meryon countered quickly, aware that that sounded singularly like Mother.

"Yes, I know. But—— Oh, well, hang it, Meryon! Unless you're perfectly serious with him, don't forget to let him know which side of the fence he's sitting. Personally, of course, I think the fellow's a bounder, but——"

"I'm perfectly aware of your opinion of Rex," Meryon said very coldly, "and it happens to be a ridiculously prejudiced and inaccurate one. In any case, I hope I can be trusted to behave with a certain amount of decency and discretion where *any* of my men friends are concerned. It seems rather absurd that I can't have tea with Rex without provoking this sort of nonsense."

"Well, I'm sorry, Meryon," began Gregory impulsively. "I'll grovel if you like, only——"

But Meryon had turned away and was going towards the door.

Gregory gave an exasperated little laugh and shrugged.

"Oh, very well." And then: "Your gloves and bag, Meryon. You've forgotten them." He picked them up and Meryon turned back quickly.

He held out the bag, and in her annoyance she almost snatched at it. Without the slightest warning, the clasp came undone, and, as the bag tipped in her hand, the whole contents deposited itself on the floor.

"Oh, I am sorry! Was that my fault?" Gregory went down on hands and knees to collect rolling coins, a compact, lip-stick, a pencil and one or two papers and envelopes.

"It doesn't matter. Let me do it." Meryon spoke

with frantic anxiety. But she saw she was already too late.

Gregory was kneeling there, looking up at her with an expression of angry incredulity, and in his hand was a roll of ten-pound notes.

CHAPTER VIII

FOR A MOMENT Meryon panicked badly. Then she made
an effort at recovery.

"There's no need to start making melodramatic
guesses. And for heaven's sake don't indulge in
weighty demands to know how I came by it, because
I——"

"All the same"—Gregory got slowly to his feet—
"I should like to know how you did come by it."

His voice was perfectly quiet, but the line of his jaw
was grim.

"Gregory, don't be so ridiculous! One would think
you imagined I'd stolen it!" She was so scared that her
voice ran up unexpectedly, and instinctively she put her
hand against her throat.

"How did you come by this money?"

Gregory repeated the question, still in that quiet
voice.

"I'm not going to tell you. It's absurd! Can't I have
any private concerns? Surely my money affairs are my
own."

He didn't answer that. He simply said:

"Did Treventon give it to you?"

"I tell you I won't be catechised· like this! If I
choose——"

"Did Treventon give it to you?" Gregory caught her
wrist suddenly and jerked her to his side.

"Gregory! Are you crazy? It's no business of yours—

I'm no business of yours. How dare you take it on yourself to dictate to me?" Meryon was trembling all over, but she stuck to her guns.

"I'm not dictating to you. I'm asking you a question," he said. "And you shall answer me if I have to wring your neck."

"Gregory!"

"Did Treventon have the damned impudence to give you money?"

"It was *not* impudence."

"Then he gave it to you?"

"Yes, he did, if you must know," Meryon exclaimed desperately. "Now will you let me go?"

He dropped her wrist and took a step backwards, but he still held the precious notes.

"You took money from a man like Treventon! Did you ask for it?"

"Gregory, you don't understand. There are times when one *can* accept money from a friend."

"There is no time when a girl accepts money from some man who is infatuated with her—unless she's going to give something very definite in return. Is that the arrangement?"

"How dare you say such a thing?" Meryon was white, and her eyes looked almost black as the pupils distended with anger. "You haven't the least right to make such an insinuation against me. No—nor against Rex either."

"Rex!" Gregory's tone expressed measureless contempt. "You don't suppose you're the first woman to whom he's given money, do you?" But he seemed to realise that in his anger he had gone much too far, for he added more quietly: "I'm sorry. I shouldn't have said that about you, of course. But I don't think you realise the position you're putting yourself in."

"I understand very much better than you do the

exact situation." Meryon felt that the cold dignity of her tone was a hollow thing, but it was her only refuge. "And now will you please hand over *my* money and finish this ridiculous scene."

"No, I won't," Gregory retorted flatly. "You're going to send this money back to Treventon or I'll cram it down his throat myself."

"Gregory!" Meryon was beside herself with indignation and fear. "Are you quite mad? Is this the twentieth century or are we in some Victorian melodrama? I never heard——"

"Now, look here, Meryon." Gregory's interruption was quite quiet, but lost none of its point for that. "It isn't any good your ridiculing my attitude. That's the second time you've accused me of being Victorian— whatever that may be—but that doesn't hurt me. The Victorians had their points, come to that, and certainly their womenfolk would have been ashamed to run around picking ten-pound notes off any moneyed bounder who liked to leer their way."

"Please——"

"No. I haven't finished." He came over and took her hand. His voice was much quieter now, and she saw most of his anger was gone. "I know there are lots of things about this rotten, lean way of living that must make you nearly frantic, but one doesn't sacrifice one's self-respect over it, Meryon. In the ordinary way, you'd see that yourself. You've let things get you down. Do just send this money back and forget the whole thing."

She wanted then, most passionately, to explain why she had accepted the money—why it was impossible that she should give it back. But now it was much too late, even more impossible than in the beginning. The whole incident had been presented to Gregory in its very worst light. Nothing on earth would convince him that the end justified the means. Even John's need would weigh little against his conviction that Rex was anything but disinterested. That meant that either he would insist on using their desperately tiny capital after all, or else that John must go without the means to health—and perhaps even life.

At this point Meryon's resolution hardened implacably. Neither Gregory nor anyone else should turn her from her purpose, whatever she had to say or do.

"I'm sorry, Gregory"—her voice was quite steady—"but I shall *not* send back that money. There are special circumstances which, I think, justify my taking it."

"Special circumstances?" He seized on that. "What special circumstances?"

And she couldn't say, of course. It was like some silly play, she thought bitterly. She had made this rather dramatic assertion and could only back it up by a feeble refusal to say more.

At her silence, the shadow on Gregory's face deepened. But it was not a shadow of anger now. There was an anxiety and genuine distress there that made her heart ache.

"Gregory," she said almost pleadingly, "can't you believe that there *might* be circumstances that would justify it?"

"No, I can't. Even if you were engaged to the fellow——"

"Well—suppose I were?" Meryon scarcely knew that she snatched at this passing straw, but Gregory's expression changed almost violently.

"If you were engaged——" He stopped, swallowed slightly, and then went on: "I shouldn't like the idea of the money even then, but, of course, it—well, it would be entirely a matter for yourselves," he finished jerkily.

"Thank you, Gregory. I'm glad you see that."
Meryon had the sensation of treading a tight-rope
at this moment.

"Then you are engaged?"

She thought she saw a desperate, though very
narrow, way out.

"Well—it's an absolute secret. We're not saying a
word to anyone at the moment."

"But you and Treventon are engaged?"

"Meryon!" There was a rush and flutter, and Mrs.
Monder came running into the room. *"What's* that,
darling? Oh, how *wonderful*! Oh, I can scarcely *believe*
it! My dear, dear child, you don't know how happy I
am. Rex and you! Such a wonderful match. Why, *all*
our troubles are over."

Meryon sat down rather heavily. She felt utterly
and completely trapped, and the way her mother kept
on patting her and kissing her and exclaiming, only
made escape seem more impossible.

"We're not saying anything to anyone just yet,"
she repeated mechanically. "I didn't mean either of
you to know, only——"

"Oh, but why not, darling? How silly! Who *should*
know if not your own mother? And, after all, Gregory
is like one of the family, and good news should be
shared, shouldn't it, Gregory?"

Gregory assented, without much expression, to this
pretty generalisation.

"Besides, dear"—Mrs. Monder paused to look with
innocent surprise at her daughter—"what reason
could there *be* for not talking about it?"

For an hysterical moment Meryon wondered if she
would have to invent a fantastic clause to a will or
something equally improbable, but the next moment
her mind seemed to be acting more normally again, and
she said quite coolly:

"Well, we have scarcely got used to the idea ourselves yet. And—and, of course, we can't make definite plans until things are more settled at home."

"What things?" Mrs. Monder looked puzzled and not very pleased.

"I mean—not until Sally has got a job, and—and things are more stable for Gregory, and John is better."

"But"—Mrs. Monder's tone was faintly sulky—"you can't mean that you want to hang about, waiting until Gregory can look after his own family? I mean, Gregory himself wouldn't want that. Would you?" She turned to appeal to Gregory, quite oblivious of the nervous, angry colour in his cheeks.

But Meryon saw it, and she thought unhappily: "Oh, Gregory! I'm only increasing your anxieties, I believe, instead of lessening them."

"Meryon knows perfectly well that neither I nor the children would wish to stand in her light over this— marriage of hers," Gregory got out stiffly.

"There you are, dear!" began Mrs. Monder. But Meryon, feeling she would literally grow hysterical if she could not escape from this scene, grasped the nettle with a firm hand.

"The decision about saying nothing was taken to suit *us*, and I do beg you to respect it, Mother dear. I don't want the children told, and I don't want any of our few remaining friends told just yet. Please do understand that. Surely you can contain your—your gratification for a little while."

"We-ell," Mrs. Monder conceded, "of course, darling, it's just as you like. But I must say I think it's odd, don't you, Gregory?"

"I suppose Meryon may do as she pleases about her own marriage," Gregory said disagreeably and turned away.

Meryon got up and went with her mother to the

door. She felt a little sick, but vaguely thankful that this scene was over.

"Meryon," Gregory said quietly, without turning from the window where he was standing.

" Yes?" She came back a step or two into the room.

He held out his hand, palm upwards, still without looking at her, and she saw the crushed roll of notes.

"Oh—thanks." She took them and stood there fingering them nervously for a moment. Then, without a word, she went out of the room, closing the door behind her.

That terrible evening seemed interminable to Meryon.

Fortunately, Sally was not specially observant, and, in any case, she was used to being completely in the dark as to Mrs. Monder's moods. But once or twice Meryon thought it impossible that her mother's excited jubilation could pass unnoticed.

It was just as well, thought Meryon, that John was in his own room, for he would have known that something had happened. And she didn't think it would have taken him long to guess at something near the truth.

As for Gregory, he was in one of his silent moods when he sat in front of a pile of work he had brought home, apparently so much absorbed in it that he could only reply in monosyllables if anyone spoke to him.

When, at last, Mrs. Monder got up and said, "Well, I think I shall go to bed," Meryon thought it the sweetest and most sensible remark that had been made that evening. And it was only with difficulty that she concealed her frantic eagerness and managed to say calmly:

"Yes. It's really getting quite late. I shall come too."

Outside in the hall her mother gave her an affectionate hug.

"I *am* so happy, Meryon dear. You really must allow me to say that."

Meryon laughed a little, and felt both troubled and guilty.

"Thank you, Mother. I know you are. I'm sorry I had to be so stern about our not saying anything."

"Oh, that's *quite* all right, darling." There was not a scrap of rancour in Mrs. Monder's tone. "And, after all, it does add to the romance, doesn't it?"

"I suppose so." Meryon hoped that her smile was convincing, but she was thankful to escape from further comment on the pretext of going in to see that John was all right.

He had slept a good while that afternoon, and was awake now, reading by the light of the shaded lamp over his bed.

As Meryon came in he put down his book and smiled at her.

"Hello. I hoped you'd come in."

"Why, John? Did you want something?" She sat down on the end of the bed and looked at him affectionately.

"Oh, no. But I like to see you last thing. I think I told you once—you're very restful to the eyes."

Meryon smiled.

"I remember. It was the first time you saw me."

"Was it? Oh yes, so it was. And Father was quite shocked."

"Yes—so was Mother."

They both laughed.

"But you weren't shocked a bit, Meryon." He put out his hand and patted her arm. "Still, you wouldn't be, of course. We understood each other from the first."

"Yes." Meryon put her hand over his, and squeezed his fingers for a moment.

"I don't mind about being in this dreadful hole," she thought suddenly, "if only I can get him better."

"What's the matter, Meryon?"

"Nothing." She looked startled for a moment, and quickly tried to cover it with a smile.

"Oh, yes, there is. Did Dr. Trellor make gloomy prophecies about me?"

"*No*, John."

He considered her with that thoughtful little smile.

"Then have you quarrelled with Gregory?"

"No—no, of course not." Strictly speaking, that was true, of course.

"Sure?"

"Quite sure."

"Then I can't think what it is."

"Just—nothing, John, as I've told you."

He shook his head, still with that little smile.

"You keep that for blind people like Gregory," he said good-temperedly. "It won't go down with me."

"Why do you say that? About Gregory, I mean. I don't think he is inclined to be blind about things."

"Not about 'things,' Meryon. About you," John countered quickly.

"I don't know what you mean." Meryon felt an odd little stirring of alarm.

John didn't say anything for a moment, and then when he did, he spoke very quietly:

"You can tell me it's not my business if you like, but—you're awfully in love with Gregory, aren't you?"

There was absolute silence. Meryon could hear the ticking of the little clock on the table, and then, a long way away, the sound of a tram passing.

She could not imagine what to say. It was not so much that she was nonplussed by John's enquiry as that she was astounded at the way her own heart answered the question. She *did* love Gregory. Illogical, unsuitable, hopeless it might be—but she loved him. She loved him in his worst moods as well as his best moods, and, if anything, she loved him more now that the days of his success seemed a thing of the past.

She felt John take her hand—gently, almost apologetically.

"You mustn't mind my guessing, Meryon dear. Invalids notice things much more than people who can go about their own concerns. It's only natural."

She returned the pressure of his hand.

"Of course Gregory doesn't care in the least, you know," she said slowly.

"I don't think I should be so sure of that if I were you." John smiled a little again.

"What do you mean?" Meryon spoke rather sharply.

"Only that always when he's most tired or worried he seems to turn to the thought of you with instinctive relief. Just as I always like to think of you when I'm feeling specially rotten."

"Oh, John dear!" the tears came into Meryon's eyes. "What a sweet thing to say. I—I don't think I deserve it."

"Oh, yes, you do." John pulled her down suddenly and kissed her. There were very rarely any actual demonstrations of affection between them, and Meryon was touched beyond expression. She returned the kiss very warmly.

"Don't worry about this, will you?" she said earnestly. "I mean—I'm perfectly happy as things are, you know."

"Yes. I know you find a great deal in slaving for us all. You're that sort of girl. Very well—I won't worry. Maybe things will work out all right in the end."

"We'll hope so." She managed to smile quite cheerfully as she got up to go, though she felt that the chance of things "working out all right" were low at the moment.

Once upstairs in her room, she sat down in a chair by the window and tried to review the situation calmly.

It was difficult, because what John had just said kept on coming between her and the real issue.

She realised now that, at one time during the evening, the desperate idea had been at the back of her mind that she might let things take their course. She would let Rex see that if he repeated his proposal, the answer this time would not be "No." And then the situation which Mother had anticipated so joyfully would become an accomplished fact.

She had argued rather wearily that, after all, she did like Rex very much indeed, that his money would solve almost all the problems that surrounded her, that there need be no more anxiety about John, no more minor upheavals with her mother. The prospect had seemed almost attractive, as she sat there in the dining-room, trying to work things out.

But now she shrank from the idea. Something deep down inside her had been changed by those words of John. He had crystallised her own feelings, and he had thrown light on another side of Gregory which she could not—*could* not ignore.

One thing was certain in her mind now. She was not going to take the line of least resistance and let this fantastic engagement become an established fact. But, in that case, she must face an unreal and artificial situation, in which there was danger at every step.

With a sigh, Meryon began slowly to undress.

"It's a dreadfully stupid and unsafe position," she admitted to herself. "But what else am I to do? I *will* keep that money for John—it may mean his one chance of recovery." She was in a mood to face facts now. "Yet if I tell Gregory the real truth, I shall be made to send the money back, or else he'll provoke some perfectly impossible scene with Rex. He really is the most difficult person to have about."

But the smile she gave as she reached that point in her thoughts, showed no resentment of that "difficulty." And the last thing that passed before her mind's eye as she fell asleep was the picture of the vase of red roses which Gregory had bought "because it was pay-day and I do notice how much you do in this place."

The first thing to do next day was to seek out Dr. Trellor and tell him that the money for John's treatment would be forthcoming.

"But, if possible," Meryon explained, "I'd rather John had the impression that the treatment was free. He's—he's a bit inclined to take things to heart, you know, and I think it would worry him very much if he thought so much money was being spent on him."

"I understand." The doctor allowed himself a passing moment of curiosity as to how this pretty, earnest girl *had* obtained the money. But it was no business of his, of course. Possibly some remote and difficult relation had been persuaded to help. "There is really no reason why the financial side of the arrangement should go further than yourself," he assured her, and had to admit to himself that his curiosity deepened at the expression of extreme relief on her face.

"When can the arrangements be made?" Meryon asked eagerly.

"I'll get into touch with the Home at once, and if we are lucky with a vacancy, the sooner he is moved the better."

"Yes. Thank you so much. I'll go home and explain to him now. And—I know it sounds a little strange"—Meryon flushed—"but I am not telling *anyone* at home about the cost of this. You see, I—I don't want anybody else worried about it."

"I quite see," the doctor said soothingly. But when he had bowed her out of his surgery, he murmured, "I'm hanged if I do. I rather wish I did, to tell the truth."

And then, because he was a very busy man, he dismissed the matter from his mind, and, opening the door into his waiting-room, said, "Next, please," briskly.

Meanwhile, on the way home, Meryon stopped at a telephone box and rang up Rex.

"Yes?" His cool, rather lazy voice came to her over the wire.

"Oh, Rex, this is Meryon."

"My dear!" The tone changed slightly but quite perceptibly. It was warmer, much more personal. "What can I do for you?"

"Nothing, really." She smiled in spite of herself, because it was quite typical of Rex to put things that way. "I only rang to say that it will suit me better to meet you in Town on Thursday, rather than have you fetch me from home."

"As you like. Where shall I meet you?"

"At Piccadilly Circus? Swan and Edgar's corner about six-thirty?"

"Yes. I will be there."

She didn't wait to say any more, but as she stepped out of the telephone box, she had the sensation of having put some slight protection round herself. At least he wouldn't meet Mother in her present dangerous mood of happy effervescence.

Later that day, she began to ask herself with grim amusement, whether, after all, she were not a natural liar. It seemed comparatively easy, after the scenes of yesterday, to handle the fiction of John's going to the nursing home as a free patient.

Mrs. Monder accepted it unflinchingly.

"There now! Isn't it wonderful how things work out?" she cried delightedly. "Only yesterday you were saying how worried you were about him, and where was the money to come from and so on? And now he is to go there without any expense at all. And in addition——"

"Yes, Mother, it's wonderful," Meryon broke in firmly, just in time.

"Of course, dear." Mrs. Monder gave her a glance of such obvious and happy significance that John would certainly have suspected something if he had not been so much absorbed in Meryon's announcement.

"Meryon, is this true?" He looked flushed and touchingly eager. "Am I really to go to the Kurt Brahlen Home?"

"Yes. It's absolutely true. I—I told you it would be managed," Meryon assured him.

"You're a witch," John said, with a glance of affectionate admiration. "I can't think how you do these things. But I'm—very—thankful about this."

Even Gregory accepted her account of the arrangement with quite unsuspicious relief, and Meryon began to feel more confident and hopeful.

It was extraordinary how quickly things were arranged, after that. Dr. Trellor came round that evening to tell them that it would be possible for John to go to the Home almost at once.

"In fact, if you can make your own arrangements so soon, I will have an ambulance sent on Thursday morning, and we can have him settled there before the end of this week," he told Meryon.

It was obviously the best thing to do—although the suddenness of it all brought home to her how much she was going to miss him. But she agreed at once, promising that everything should be ready, and that she herself would go down to the Home and see John installed.

Later, Sally said to her rather wistfully:

"I shall miss John horribly, won't you?"

Meryon nodded. "Yes. I'm afraid we all shall."

"Only, you know," Sally added thoughtfully, "I've a hunch that this is going to be even more important than it seems. I mean——" She broke off, and then went on impulsively: "Meryon, wouldn't it be wonderful if this were the turning-point in John's illness? If somehow he could start getting really better. It would be worth almost anything, wouldn't it?"

Meryon looked at her curiously, a faintly superstitious feeling coming over her.

"Yes," she said slowly, "it would be worth *absolutely* anything."

Thursday came, bright and clear and "hopeful," as Sally said. She and John bade each other a laconic—but none the less affectionate—"Good-bye." And there was a great deal of affection too, Meryon guessed, behind Gregory's, "Good-bye, old man. Best of luck. I'll run down to see you on Sunday, and bring Sally with me."

Meryon was glad that Gregory would be safely out of the way before the ambulance came. Dr. Trellor was to be there then, and, although her faith in his discretion was complete, she thought that if Gregory started thanking him for all the trouble he had taken to arrange John's admission as a free patient, it might be something of a strain on the doctor's powers of deception.

Until now she had not made any attempt to alter her appointment with Rex because the journey to the Home was to be made in the morning. But almost directly after Gregory and Sally had left the house, a message came from Dr. Trellor to say that a re-arrangement had had to be made, and it would not be possible to send the ambulance until the afternoon.

"It doesn't matter," Meryon said, with as good a

grace as she could. But, actually, her heart misgave her a little that she had to alter her arrangements with Rex yet again.

She slipped out, however, on the pretext of doing some shopping, and telephoned to him. Rex himself was not at home, but his manservant promised to let him know as soon as he came in that Miss Dawling would not be able to keep her appointment, but would telephone again later.

"It's so complicated," Meryon thought, as she returned home. "But at least it's lucky that we can't afford a telephone of our own. If we had one, he would always be ringing when I was out. And then Mother would take the calls and just give everything away!"

As it was, however, it was safe to leave Mother in charge while she accompanied John to the nursing home that afternoon. And, to Meryon's extreme relief, the journey was accomplished without a hitch.

It was obvious from the first that the whole place made a happy impression on John, and the kindness and efficiency of the staff were beyond question.

Meryon watched with satisfaction the pleased way John's glance took in the details of the pleasant room, and the view of wooded hills which could be seen from the big, low window.

"I love it," John said slowly. "It isn't really like my room at Oldkeep, but somehow it suggests the atmosphere. I shan't be a bit lonely or miserable, Meryon, and you mustn't worry at all."

"I won't," Meryon promised, and then added with a smile: "At least, only a little bit about *us*, because it is we who will have to miss you."

"Nonsense! You'll have twice as much time to look after Gregory now," John told her with a quick smile. "Think how you'll love doing that."

Meryon laughed and coloured slightly.

"We'll come down and see you as often as we can," she said, avoiding an actual answer to his remark.

"Yes, please do. But Meryon, I do realise that fares mount up to a lot, you know, and that you can't always be chasing into Buckinghamshire to see me. Don't feel that you *have* to come. I shall quite understand. And, in any case, there's the question of using up everyone's time too."

"All right." Meryon patted his hand. "It's quite true, of course. But we'll manage the best we can."

And as she walked down to the station later, she thought: "He is a dear, thoughtful boy. He deserves to have people make an effort for him."

When she reached the station it was to find that she had just missed a train, and it was over half an hour until the next one. Even when that came, it proved to be a slow train, stopping at every station, and it was after seven before Meryon got into London.

"John was quite right about the journey taking time," she reflected ruefully as she stood waiting for the bus to take her the last stage of her journey, and she could not help giving a regretful thought to the rakish little two-seater which she used to drive in the old days.

Eight o'clock was striking as she turned into Beech-croft Crescent. Really, they would be wondering——

And then she stopped dead in dismay. For parked in front of Number Twenty-Two was Rex's unmistakable Packard.

With a heart that fluttered uncomfortably in her throat, Meryon walked down the road to the house. As she let herself in, she could hear her heart thumping —or perhaps it was only the sound of Mother's footsteps as she came hurrying out to greet her.

"Darling, whatever happened? Here's poor Rex

wondering whether you'd been killed or something.
He expected you to meet him this evening."

"But I telephoned." Meryon spoke almost in a
whisper, but sharply because of her alarm. "I left a
message to say I couldn't come."

"Well, he didn't get it. But, anyway, it doesn't
matter now. We've had *such* a charming talk, dear."

"Mother, you didn't—say anything—about——"
She couldn't get any further, and, at the expression
of guilty happiness on her mother's face, she felt herself
go cold all over.

"Well, darling, it was so *silly* to say nothing at all.
I was terribly careful, of course—just told him how
delighted I was that you'd changed your mind and
decided to marry him after all. I couldn't say less,
Meryon dear, because it's true. Now could I?"

Meryon didn't answer. She just stared wordlessly at
her mother.

Then, gently putting her out of the way, she went
towards the dining-room door.

CHAPTER IX

REX WAS STANDING over by the window when she
came in, and, with an instinctive movement that must
have caused some surprise to Mrs. Monder, Meryon
shut the door on her, and leant against it nervously.

He didn't move for a moment, and Meryon had time
to think how dark and overwhelming he looked
against the light. Then he crossed the room quickly
and his hands were on her—lightly but very firmly.

"Darling, don't look so scared! You mustn't mind
that your mother told me your feelings had changed.
She had no idea I was in the dark about them. She
thought I knew, too."

"But it wasn't that. She didn't know. I mean—
I didn't tell her—anything." Meryon groped hopelessly for words to hold back the tide of joyful tenderness let loose on her. But it was useless. He was scarcely
listening to what he took for mere confusion and
embarrassment.

"Never mind, dearest. It doesn't matter how she
knew. The point is that she innocently let me know
too. God bless her for her blundering!"

Meryon was powerless to echo that—or, indeed, to
answer anything at all. A sort of heavy, despairing
resignation was closing in on her. She felt him take
off her hat and smooth her hair—very tenderly, but
with an indefinably proprietary air that frightened
her.

She was his now. He was rejoicing in the fact—

not ungenerously, but with perfect confidence. And what could she say to stop him? "It's all a deception. I pretended we were engaged because I knew I had no right to take the money unless we were. And now, in addition to giving me the money, will you please pretend something that will hurt you terribly, because I want my people to think I've behaved decently even if I haven't?"

It was impossible! No man on earth would submit to that. No man on earth should be expected to submit to it.

Then—what else? She couldn't even make a full confession and beg him to take back the money. She was already committed to the spending of that money. John's chance of life and health depended on it.

And—as so often in the past few days—at the thought of John, her resolve hardened. There was one course—and one course only.

She heard Rex say, "Aren't you going to look up and let me kiss you now?" And, with a feeling of final surrender to overwhelming odds, she held up her face to his.

Meryon had never indulged in easy love-making, and no man had ever kissed her like this before. She knew that if things had been as they should have been, she would have experienced her first thrill of eager, happy awakening. But as she felt Rex's firm, possessive kiss on her mouth, she experienced nothing but a deepening of her despair, and a certainty that her life lay in ruins.

He released her at last, and she said quickly, nervously:

"It's a shame to keep Mother outside now. I—I'd better go and speak to her."

"As you like." His indulgent expression said plainly that she might do what she pleased about most things, and, with a gasp of something between relief and anxiety, Meryon escaped out of the room.

Mrs. Monder had retreated from the hall to the kitchen by now, but she was doing nothing useful there —only standing looking out of the window into the garden, with that expression of guilty happiness which somehow touched Meryon, even while it irritated her.

Poor Mother! How could one expect her to be anything but overjoyed? Happiness for her consisted in spending money—usually unwisely—and knowing there was plenty more to spend when that was gone. Now, after financial anxiety beyond her blackest nightmare, she was to see her daughter married to an exceedingly wealthy man. No wonder she smiled like a pleased child who half-distrusted its good fortune.

Meryon went over and kissed her. It was impossible not to.

"Oh, Meryon dear!" Mrs. Monder returned the kiss. "Isn't everything *wonderful*? And you're not cross with me, are you?"

"No, I'm not cross with you," Meryon said gently. And then, a little mechanically: "And everything is wonderful, of course."

"It's just as I always hoped, darling—all that time ago—do you remember? In Scotland."

"Yes. I remember."

That was before she had even known Gregory existed—or John and Sally either, come to that. Before the crowd of dear but heavy responsibilities had pressed around her. It seemed to Meryon now that the Scottish visit was the very last time she had known complete peace of mind.

Then Mother had told her about their vanished money, and after that—well, one thing had piled on another until here she was, engaged to a man she didn't love—tied to him by her obligations to the people she did love. And Gregory——

But it was no good thinking about Gregory. He wouldn't think of her. At least, not for long. He would just remember her as the girl who had helped well in a crisis—and then married a "gilt-edged security."

"Meryon dear, you are *funny*!" her mother interrupted plaintively at that point. "Not a bit like a girl who's just become engaged. You don't seem specially happy, and you scarcely have a word to say."

"I'm sorry." Meryon forced a smile. "It's really just that I'm tired and—and everything seems so sudden."

"Oh, hardly *sudden*, darling!" Mrs. Monder protested. "It was all settled in private days ago, wasn't it?"

Meryon agreed rather desperately that it had been, and muttered something again about being tired and not having had any dinner.

"Poor child! Of course, you're *hungry*," cried Mrs. Monder, in the tones of a charity worker to a starving waif. "Oh, dear, and I'm afraid I forgot what you told me and cooked *all* the steak, dear—in fact, just a little *over*cooked it—that is, it was rather queer and hard, and now if we warm it up again——"

A significant pause described the probable result more eloquently than words.

"It doesn't matter," Meryon said. "I'll have bread and cheese."

"Indeed you will not, my child. You'll come with me, and in twenty minutes I'll have you sitting in front of the best meal in town," Rex's voice informed her from the doorway, and, turning, Meryon saw that he had followed her out into the kitchen, having tired evidently of waiting for her return.

"Oh!" she began. But her mother snatched the decision out of her hands.

"How splendid, Rex dear! Exactly what the child needs. Not too much of a celebration. Just a quiet but gay little meal to make her realise that there is someone to look after her at last."

Rex put a careless but compelling arm round Meryon.

"Is that right, sweetheart? May I do everything I can to make you feel someone is looking after you?"

She tried to think of a refusal that would be in the remotest degree gracious. But it was impossible, and as his lips lightly touched her cheek, she gave a hasty assent, more to stop any further coaxing caresses than anything else, she supposed.

After that, they scarcely gave her a chance to say more than that she had seen John comfortably settled, before Rex shepherded her out of the house with an air of happy possession, while Mother waved approval and congratulation from the front door with a faintly damp handkerchief.

Once they were in the car, Meryon tried to pull herself together. After all, she had set her feet on a pretty difficult path. It was no good flagging in the very beginning. And, turning to Rex with a convincingly bright smile, she said:

"Sorry, Rex dear, if I seemed a bit dumb and stupid. I had a rather tiring journey back from the nursing home, and I'm only just reverting to normal."

He gave her a glance of affectionate amusement.

"Don't be silly," he retorted gently. "You know you don't have to apologise to me. And as for reverting to normal—I hope you won't do that if it means the same thing as coming down to earth. For my part, I feel I shall never be quite normal again, but slightly and deliciously mad for the rest of my days."

She didn't answer that with anything but a friendly little pat on his arm, and that came fairly naturally, because, of course, he *was* a dear—even if one had to marry him.

"So you're quite satisfied about John?" he said after a moment, as though to give her a chance of speaking of other things.

"Oh, yes." Her face brightened genuinely. "I'm so thankful to you for arranging that."

"That's all right, my dear. I was only too happy to do it for you."

"It was for John, too," she corrected before she could stop herself, but Rex laughed carelessly and said:

"John owes any luck in the matter to being *your* favourite."

"But you like him, don't you?" It seemed so important, somehow, even now, that John should have something to do with this bargain. "I mean, you're glad that your money should make him better."

Rex shrugged.

"All right, then. To please John, I might put my hand in my pocket, but to please you"—he hesitated—"I would commit murder," he finished with a smile.

"Oh, Rex, I hope I shall never need that," Meryon said, with a slight laugh that was meant to keep things on a half-flippant basis.

"I hope not," he agreed carelessly. And then they drew up outside the restaurant, and a few minutes later he was making good his promise to give her "the best meal in Town."

Meryon tried not to feel that it was a perfectly hateful evening. In the ordinary way, she would have enjoyed dining like this with Rex, but now, with all it implied, she could only long for the moment of release. And the handing over of the final fifty pounds only made her feel a degree more miserable.

Fortunately, in his new-found rôle of guardian of her health, Rex had no intention of keeping her up late when she was obviously tired, and it was scarcely eleven o'clock when the car stopped once more outside the gate of Number Twenty-Two. Even so, the house was in darkness, and the street so quiet that they seemed alone in the world.

She steeled herself for the moment when he should take her in his arms, but, instead, he just took her hands and looked at her.

"Good night, darling. I hope you are as happy as I am."

"Oh, yes," Meryon assured him quickly. "I'm terribly happy, Rex. It's all so—so sudden, but I'm terribly happy."

He kissed her then, and she returned the kiss convincingly. Perhaps she was improving with practice, she thought a little forlornly. And then she went into the house.

Impossible not to remember that other time—only a week or two ago—when she had come in to find Gregory asleep. She had been secretly treasuring that scene, she realised now, but of course she must not think of it any more, now that everything had changed.

There was no sign of Gregory this time—only a note from her mother on the dining-room table. With that strange disregard for pronouns which afflicts some people every time they put pencil to paper, Mrs Monder had written:

"Can lock up, darling, as are all just going up to bed. Told dear little Sally the news as seemed silly to make a mystery now. Love. Mother."

The unusually affectionate description could only mean that dear little Sally had reacted satisfactorily, Meryon supposed, and with a slight smile she locked the front door and went upstairs to bed.

As she quietly crossed the upstairs landing, a hissing whisper from Sally's room said, "Meryon, is that you?"

"Yes."

Meryon went into the room and, switching on the light, Sally leant up on her elbow, blinking a little.

"You ought to be asleep," Meryon said.

"Yes, I know. But I was reading until about ten minutes ago," Sally confessed.

"You shouldn't really do that, particularly when you have to get up early, you know."

"No, I know. But it was a terrific thriller, and I had to find out who did it. I'd suspected every man in turn, and in the end it was a woman."

"How extraordinary," commented Meryon dutifully.

"Yes, wasn't it? But I didn't want to talk about that. Isn't it exciting about you and Rex? I'm not a bit surprised."

"Aren't you?"

"No. In fact, it means I've won two shillings," Sally admitted shamelessly.

"Sally! How?"

"I bet John two bob that you'd marry Rex in the end. His money was on Gregory, but I never quite knew why. You don't really like Gregory much, do you?"

"Of course I like Gregory," Meryon said a little too quickly. "But, anyway, it wasn't at all a nice thing to do, Sally."

"No. I know. It was awful, really," Sally agreed. "But you ought to be feeling so over-the-moon that you could forgive anything. Are you frightfully happy, Meryon?"

"Frightfully," Meryon said mechanically, and found the word peculiarly apt.

"When are you going to be married? And can I be a bridesmaid?" Sally wanted to know.

Meryon experienced another of those very disagreeable shocks at hearing anything so definite in connection with it all.

"We haven't really settled anything," she explained quickly. "And, in any case, I couldn't think of making arrangements until we see how John is when he comes home."

"Oh, no, of course not. How is John? Your mother said he seemed very comfortably settled. Did he really like the place?"

"Yes. I think and hope it's going to do him a lot of good."

Sally hugged her knees and looked thoughtfully at Meryon.

"Of course, if John really got well, and I had a job and Gregory went on getting rises as quickly as this last one, you could marry your Rex almost right away, couldn't you?"

"I don't know—perhaps—we could see. But, anyway, what is this about Gregory getting a rise? I didn't know."

"No—nor did we until this evening. He got it last pay-day."

"*Did* he? But he never told us."

"He said it didn't seem important beside the fact of your getting engaged. Apparently he knew about you and Rex some days ago?"

Meryon didn't answer the enquiring look. She just said:

"Not *important*?" and then was silent because her throat contracted most strangely.

She didn't need to be told how wildly, gloriously important it must have seemed to him, as he came home with the news. His first triumph in his new job —a triumph that would affect all the family and make them proud and happy, instead of worried and sympathetic. It must have appeared far more important than any unexpected piece of luck in the old days.

And then, when he came home, it was too late. Meryon had acquired a rich fiancé, beside whose fortune any little increases in the family budget would seem pitiful and slightly ridiculous. She bit her lip very hard, with something of the pain of disappointment that Gregory himself must have felt. Then Sally's cheerful voice recalled her to the present:

"Anyway, it's all very lovely, whichever way you decide to fix it up. I'm awfully pleased, Meryon dear—and at the week-end we'll go and tell John all about it, and I'll claim my two bob."

"Perhaps that's not due until the actual wedding," Meryon forced herself to say with a smile. "And the future is never quite certain, you know."

"Don't be cynical," Sally retorted comfortably as she lay down again. "An engagement is halfway to a wedding, so *one* shilling is mine, anyway."

"Perhaps you're right," Meryon said, and managed to laugh as she finally bade Sally "Good night" and went out of the room.

.   .   .   .   .

The next morning Meryon had every intention of saying some word to Gregory about the rise, but somehow the opportunity never came. She told herself that it was difficult in the hurry of early-morning breakfast but actually, she knew, the difficulty was in herself.

She felt desperately nervous and self-conscious in his presence, aware that, like Sally, he must probably have heard a good deal from Mrs. Monder about the latest development. And if he could not find it possible to say anything but the merest civilities to her, she, in her turn, felt just as frozen and unable to speak.

When he and Sally had gone, Meryon set about clearing up the room, and in doing so, she had to move the vase of roses he had brought her. Until now they had remained amazingly fresh and complete, but as she lifted them this morning, they seemed to fall to pieces in a shower of dark red petals.

With a slight exclamation, she set down the vase again and, kneeling on the carpet, began to gather up the petals. Her heart felt indescribably heavy, for there was something almost symbolical in this, she thought. The one bond between herself and Gregory had flowered so sweetly but so briefly, and now it was all gone— just a handful of dying petals.

She heard her mother coming downstairs at that moment, and on an impulse she could not herself explain, she caught up an envelope from the writing desk and crushed half a dozen of the rose petals into it. There was no time to hide it anywhere in the room, and, with something very much like a sob, she thrust the sad little memento down the front of her dress, and was kneeling on the floor again, gathering up petals, when her mother came into the room.

"Dear, dear, what a mess," was Mrs. Monder's mild comment. And Meryon thought: "Yes. It's the sort of mess I've made of my life." But she only said:

"I suppose they've lasted as long as one could expect. Even the loveliest flowers can't last for ever." To which Mrs. Monder assented with an absent murmur, before becoming absorbed in the less important columns of the morning paper.

If Meryon had hoped that open discussion of her engagement would give it a more real touch, she had ample opportunity of testing this theory during the next few days. Mrs. Monder and Sally both found it a topic of inexhaustible interest, and Meryon was hard put to it to equal their enthusiasm herself.

"What sort of ring are you going to have?" Sally wanted to know the very first evening.

"I don't know. I haven't thought about it yet."

"Oh, but, Meryon, you *must*. What about a very gorgeous pearl? You could have——"

"Pearls for tears," quoted Mrs. Monder a trifle dramatically. "I shouldn't have a pearl, darling."

"I don't know." Sally twirled a curl thoughtfully round her finger. "I read a story once about a girl whose engagement ring was a single black pearl. It said——"

"*Black!*" Mrs. Monder gave a slight shriek. "Sally, what a *dreadful* idea for an engagement ring. How can you?"

"It was very valuable," Sally retorted inexorably, whereat Mrs. Monder shuddered slightly, to indicate that the monetary value of a thing left her entirely unimpressed.

"Diamonds are nice," ventured Meryon, hoping that her voice held the correct note of romantic interest.

"Except that *everyone* has diamonds," countered Sally. "Do you like emeralds? What about a square-cut emerald?"

"Green," objected Mrs. Monder cryptically.

"Well, what about it?" Sally was growing impatient.

"Green is so unlucky, darling."

"Oh, nonsense. Besides, Meryon quite often wears green."

"Yes, I know. And see how unlucky we've been," replied Mrs. Monder with an air of gentle triumph.

Sally frowned, and shifted her ground a little.

"Well, what do *you* suggest?"

"I scarcely know." Mrs. Monder looked thoughtful. "Of course, some antiques are very beautiful. And they so often have a romantic history." She sighed a trifle sentimentally.

"Including a murder or some other form of sudden

death," commented Gregory from behind the pages of the *Daily Telegraph*.

"Gregory!" Mrs. Monder was almost personally offended by this contribution to the discussion. "What a horrid thing to say."

"I'm sorry." But he sounded singularly unrepentant.

"Well, what would you think a nice engagement ring for Meryon to have?" Mrs. Monder wanted to know, in a laudable effort to draw him into the conversation.

"I haven't the slightest idea," Gregory assured her, still without lowering his paper. "And I can't see that it concerns any one of us except Meryon."

Whereupon the discussion died a natural, though slightly embarrassing death.

During the next few days, Gregory's attitude of complete detachment from the whole subject obstinately continued, and Meryon could scarcely conceal her dismay when it appeared that only she and Gregory would be going down to visit John on the Sunday. Sally had developed a cold which would certainly make her an unwelcome visitor in any nursing home, and Mrs. Monder insisted that she would much rather stay at home with Sally than "spend half the day travelling."

"It looks as though you and I shall have to go and represent the family, Meryon," Gregory remarked coolly. "That is, of course, if your fiancé can spare you."

"Oh, yes, I shall certainly come," Meryon assured him hastily. "I promised John that I would."

Though, when Sunday afternoon came, she very much wished that she could have taken back that promise.

However, like many other disagreeable tasks, this had to be faced, and, when it came to the point, the journey down at least was not so embarrassing as she had feared. For one thing, their train was fairly full, and for another, as they walked up from the station, they fell in with an elderly couple who were going to the nursing home too. So Meryon was saved a *tête-à-tête* with Gregory at any stage of the journey.

They found John in bed, but extremely gay and talkative, and when Meryon compared his present state with the languor of a week ago, she could not doubt that already there was a marked improvement.

That in itself set a very cheerful tone to the conversation, and for a while, in listening to John's lively description of life in the nursing home, Meryon almost forgot her own worries. Then John smiled at her and said:

"But what's the news of the family—apart from poor old Sally's cold? Anything interesting happened?"

"Yes——" began Gregory a trifle drily. But Meryon broke in quickly:

"Yes, rather! Gregory got a handsome rise last pay-day."

"How did *you* know?" Gregory asked not very graciously.

"Sally told me. I've been wanting for days to—to tell you how pleased and thrilled I was, only there never seemed to be an opportunity."

"Why shouldn't she know, anyway?" John enquired innocently.

"Oh, I hadn't told her myself—that's all." Gregory seemed supremely indifferent all at once.

"Not told Meryon! But she's more interested than anyone in any family triumphs."

"It didn't seem such an extraordinary triumph," Gregory said rather stiffly. The tone was perfectly cool and composed, but, right at the back of it, Meryon heard—or thought she heard—an oddly forlorn note.

"Don't be an ass," John retorted affectionately. "It's of almost national importance at the moment. I'm surprised you and Meryon aren't wearing flags in your hats."

Gregory grinned then, and said much more naturally:

"It is rather exciting, I suppose."

And Meryon wanted very much to hug John, because it was such an enormous relief to hear him saying the things she had longed to say herself and could not.

After that, tea was a very gay affair, and Meryon found, to her relief, that she and Gregory were talking quite naturally to each other now, instead of talking *at* each other through a third person, which had been their miserable and self-conscious substitute for conversation during the last few days.

Even when it came to saying "Good-bye," and she had to face the journey home again alone with Gregory, she felt none of the dismay she had experienced earlier in the day.

"Take good care of her, Gregory," John said with a smile. And, although Gregory immediately raised his eyebrows rather quizzically, he replied quite gravely:

"I will. I promise." And he refrained from making any remark about her engagement or the fact that it was someone else's business to look after her now.

As they came out of the nursing home, Gregory said:

"Let's take this path across the fields. It follows the direction to the station, more or less, and this isn't the kind of evening to be walking on roads if one can find a path instead."

Meryon agreed and, passing through a gate, they followed the uneven path which wound its way along by the hedge until it lost itself in a little wood beyond.

At first they were silent—Meryon, at least, soothed by the comparative quiet which was broken only by the friendly sounds of the countryside.

Seeing John so happy and so obviously better already had quieted a great deal of the wretchedness in her heart, and now, as she strolled through the evening sunshine with Gregory, she felt even a certain happiness of the moment herself.

It was he who broke the silence first, speaking a little abruptly:

"You didn't say anything to John about your engagement. But you could scarcely have forgotten it. I suppose the silence was intentional."

"Yes."

"Why, Meryon? Sometimes I think your attitude towards this engagement of yours is rather strange."

"Do you? But I assure you I—I feel quite normal about it."

He didn't comment on that. He said instead:

"May I say something that you probably won't consider my business?"

"I—suppose so." But her heart misgave her.

"It's just this. Though you may be trying not to believe it yourself, you are *not* the kind of girl to be happy on money alone."

"Oh, Gregory!" Meryon's voice was exceedingly troubled, for she hardly knew whether to argue with him or to leave him in possession of a theory which would at least supply an explanation for her actions.

"What is it?" He spoke rather gently, and she thought how much he had changed from the days when he used to set his own opinions stonily against any argument.

"Only that I wonder why you are still so sure that I set a high value on money—even to the extent of doing violence to my better feelings, which I suppose is what you mean this time."

He looked troubled in his turn then, and when he answered, his voice was very earnest:

"Meryon, don't think I still class you as a gold-digger. I did once, but I'll own that knowing you has proved me completely wrong."

She half put out her hand at that and, catching her fingers, he held them tightly as they walked slowly along together.

"It's only—well, I've realised lately that things could never have been very easy for you," he went on thoughtfully. "I suppose it was always a case of there not being quite enough money, so that a big income naturally seemed the most important thing on earth. Then when your mother married again, everything must have been wonderful—except that it lasted such a little while. And after that, poverty must have appeared more appalling than ever."

Meryon laughed slightly, but her eyes were very gentle as she glanced at his earnest face.

"It's nice—and so odd—to hear you making excuses for me, Gregory dear, but you needn't really, you know. Things are not quite as you think. To begin with, I hadn't the faintest idea we *were* short of money until about a fortnight before Mother married your uncle. We'd really been blithely living on capital according to some crazy theory of Mother's. But I didn't know about that. I don't believe I ever thought much about money, one way or the other, in those days."

"You mean—the first time you ever knew real shortage of money was during these last months?" He sounded thunderstruck at the sudden collapse of his theories.

"Well—yes."

They walked on in profound silence until they came to a stile. He climbed over first, and gave her his hand to help her, still without saying anything, and at that point Meryon felt impelled to ask a question in her turn. Sitting on the top bar of the stile, she looked down into his serious grey eyes.

"Gregory, what is it? Has something I said troubled you very much?"

"It's not that." He leant against one of the posts, looking up at her. "But I must ask you something—and I can't help it if it sounds crude. Am I to understand from all this that you're *not* marrying Treventon for his money?"

She saw then how she was caught. It was too late to go back. She was going to have to take her stand quite definitely—either as a gold-digger or as being genuinely in love with Rex. But, even so, she tried a moment's desperate prevarication.

"Gregory, you really have no right to ask me such a question. I——"

"No, I have no right. But if you care one atom for my peace of mind, I beg you to answer."

"But——" She paused, and then went on desperately: "Well then, it is *not* because of his money. Of course it isn't."

She heard him give a slight gasp, as though he had been holding his breath. Then, without a word, he put his hands lightly round her waist and lifted her down from the stile.

"Come on, or we shall be late for our train."

"Gregory"—her voice sounded almost timid now—"what had my marrying for money to do with your peace of mind?"

"Nothing," he said curtly, "since the money doesn't enter into things after all. It was only that I'd been kicking myself every day for the last week to think I hadn't asked you to marry *me*, in the days when I had enough money to make you say 'Yes.'"

CHAPTER X

THERE ARE SOME REMARKS that simply shriek for an answer and yet, try as one will, one cannot find the words. And Meryon, as she walked, thunderstruck, beside Gregory, searched her mind in vain for something to fill the awful gap of silence.

"But I had no idea." "I suppose that is a joke." "Gregory, I'm awfully sorry." They all seemed equally fatuous, and as minute followed minute, she realised there was nothing that *could* be said.

It was not that one thing held her silent. *Everything* did. Her duty to the man she had agreed to marry, her sense of responsibility towards John, even her hope that Gregory would some day find happiness himself. They all demanded that she should rouse no further doubts or questions. And when she finally found her voice, it was not to say anything in answer to him. It was merely to remark in a strangely toneless way:

"I think if we cut through here we come out just beside the station."

"Yes, you're right. And we certainly need a short cut."

He too implied by every inflection of his voice that nothing really important had been said. And after that it seemed that the only matter of moment was to be sure they caught their train.

Later, sitting in a corner seat, and gazing out at the darkening fields and hedges, Meryon allowed her thoughts to return to what he had said.

Had he meant that he loved her? Had he meant it was something he would now get over? Had he meant that he just didn't like her going away and he wished—more than half seriously—that he had done something to keep her?

It was impossible to say. She would never know the answer to any of these questions, because never again must they come near discussing the subject. The very thing which meant most in life to her must remain a closed book.

When they got home Rex was there, sitting in an armchair and talking to Mother with that air of indulgent amusement that so enchanted her.

"Hello, dearest." He got up at once and kissed Meryon. "How d'you do, Monder?"

"How d'you do?"

"I've been *so* anxious for you to come in, darling." Mrs. Monder was evidently excited. "Such a charming suggestion of Rex's! You and I are to go and spend a week or two at his country house. He says you need a holiday. It's true, of course. In Hampshire, darling, near the New Forest. Isn't that splendid?"

"It's awfully sweet of you, Rex." Meryon contrived to sound more pleased and surprised than she felt. "But I don't know really how I can get away just now. You see——"

Rex took her gently by her arms and smiled down at her—quite good-temperedly, but with complete determination.

"Now look here, darling. If you start pushing your family down my throat again I shall be really angry with you. You've sacrificed yourself quite enough for them already." Meryon felt, rather than saw, Gregory stiffen with furious resentment. "They aren't so completely helpless as you seem to think. John is all right at this nursing home without your running in and out perpetually to see him, and Sally is going to stay with some friends. They're the people of one of the girls at the business college, and they seem anxious to have her."

"Yes, you see, Meryon dear, it's *perfectly simple!*" Mrs. Monder was evidently delighted with the whole arrangement.

"But Gregory——" began Meryon defensively.

"Don't be absurd. I can manage all right," Gregory assured her curtly.

"Oh, yes, I'm sure Monder can look after himself very well," Rex agreed. "He could have most of his meals out and——".

"Thanks. I really can map it out without your assistance," Gregory informed him coolly. And then, as there was an uncomfortable little silence: "When do you intend to make a start ?"

"Wednesday, if Meryon thinks she can be ready by then."

"I think so—that is, if Sally's cold is better."

"Sally's cold is already better," Rex assured her a little drily, and then Meryon wondered if she had really sounded very ungracious and ungrateful about the whole thing.

She slipped her arm into his with an eager, friendly air.

"It was nice of you to arrange it, Rex dear. I shall love a country holiday, really, and I know Mother will."

"I hope so." He smiled and patted the hand on his arm. "Anyway, I thought it was time you saw your new home. Then if there's anything you want to have altered, we can have it done in good time."

"Oh, thank you. But—but I don't expect I shall want anything altered," Meryon said. And, all at once, she felt miserable and profoundly depressed.

Her new home! Of course he was right. But, oh, how she hated the words!

It wasn't a difficult matter to make what Mrs. Monder called "all satisfactory arrangements." She herself took very little part in these, but found innocent pleasure in instructing everyone else from the depths of her own ignorance. Even the good-tempered Sally said at last:

"It would be lots simpler if you just took a nice book and went and sat in your own room quietly until everything was ready."

"And left Meryon to do everything! Sally, my dear, I'm not so selfish!" Mrs. Monder exclaimed indignantly.

So they let her stay and make what happy muddle she liked.

On Tuesday evening Sally left to take up her new quarters with her friend. Meryon, who had already met the girl once or twice, liked her very much, and she had no doubt whatever that Sally would be safe and happy. John, too, of course, was in the very best hands possible, so that there was really not the slightest need to worry.

As for Gregory, no doubt he *could* look after himself, as he said, and, having arranged that a daily woman should come in to make his breakfast and tidy up, Meryon found that there was nothing else she was allowed to do for him.

"Do go and enjoy yourself, Meryon," he told her. "I want you to, and no one ever deserved it more."

She smiled at that, patted his arm with sisterly affection—which was, of course, the warmest expression of feeling she could allow herself. And the next morning Rex came in the big car and collected her mother and herself for the holiday, which was vaguely defined as "two or three weeks—or perhaps even longer."

It was a beautiful day, with the sun shining out of a clear, blue sky, and as the Packard hummed along and a soft, warm breeze blew through the open window, Meryon leant back in her seat and thought it was very good not to be washing up and making beds on a day like this.

Little exclamations of pleasure and interest from Mrs. Monder, in the back seat, punctuated the pleasant silence from time to time, but Meryon was affectionately amused, rather than irritated, by such things as:

"Look, Meryon dear! Primroses. No, no—there, on the left. You missed them? Oh, what a pity. Well, perhaps they couldn't be primroses at this time of year. But! anyway, yellow flowers. Very charming." Or: "Look! Isn't that like the Cunninghams' old house?—except that theirs was red brick, of course, instead of grey, and the porch was on the other side."

It was getting near lunch-time when Rex finally said:

"If you look through the next gap in the trees on the right, you'll get your first glimpse of the house."

It was little more than a glimpse, as a matter of fact, but Meryon could see how beautiful the surrounding land was, and a few minutes later they turned into a wide, well-kept drive, where the sunlight through the trees made a subdued, golden-green light.

For half a mile they drove under an archway of trees, and then the pathway opened out in front of them, to display a house of that slightly formal beauty in which the Regency period excelled.

"Oh!" Meryon clasped her hands in an access of such real pleasure that the colour was shocked into her face. "Oh, Rex, what a perfectly heavenly house!"

He didn't say anything until he had stopped the car, but his smile said very plainly how pleased he was, too. Then, coming round, he opened the door for her and literally lifted her out.

"I'm glad you like it, darling," he said. "It's every stone of it yours, you know." And he kissed her in that quiet but passionate way that disturbed her so profoundly.

"Sim-ply charming!" Mother was saying as she got out of the car. "My dear child, what a lucky girl you are!"

Meryon supposed she was, and murmured something appropriate. And then they went into the house.

Mother was perfectly right—the whole place was simply charming. Large, admirably proportioned rooms, where wide windows looked on to beautiful formal gardens or equally beautiful parkland. Furniture that had been chosen, piece by piece, for its elegance and its comfort. Silver and china that a collector might have envied, and everywhere a suggestion of quiet luxury which only unlimited money can provide.

It would have been hard to imagine anything less like the comfortable but everyday usefulness of the rather sparse furniture at home, and even Meryon's heart warmed and expanded at the sheer beauty and tastefulness of her surroundings.

Her mother and she had rooms side by side, with a communicating door between, and during the few minutes that they were up there, before the lunch-bell sounded, Mrs. Monder kept on running in and out in a happy fever of congratulation and excitement.

"Darling! Did you ever see *anything* quite so delightful? And to think it's all of it yours? I can't tell you how happy I am on your behalf. It's just *exactly* what I would have chosen for you."

"Is it?" Meryon smiled at her indulgently. "Well, I can't imagine a more beautiful place myself."

"Nor I. And I'm sure you'll be wonderfully happy here, child."

"I should be very ungrateful if I were not," Meryon said slowly, and she meant that from the bottom of her heart. For everything of beauty in this new home that was to be hers reminded her of the fact that she could not only take things. She *must* give something in return. And the least that she could do for this man who lavished generosity on her was to make him believe that she was as happy as he wanted her to be.

It was not so difficult, either, in the first day or two, for there was so much to see, so many things to admire and enjoy. Sometimes Mrs. Monder came with them if there was anything very special to be seen, but at other times she exercised what she fondly imagined to be tact, and insisted rather ostentatiously on letting them go alone.

"No, no! You don't always want an old lady with you," she would say brightly, and then wait with transparent pleasure for them to protest at the absurd description of herself. They never failed to supply her with this simple means of gratification, and then, after the pleasant little comedy had been played once again, they would go off to explore the woods nearby, or walk up to the farm which supplied most of the needs of the house, or perhaps take the car and drive for miles through the sunshine and shade of the New Forest.

It was when they were on one of their woodland walks that he gave Meryon the engagement ring he had chosen for her—a single diamond of such purity and beauty that Meryon thought, with a passing smile, even Sally must be satisfied.

"How wonderful, Rex! I've never seen such a beautiful ring," she said earnestly.

"You like it? I'm glad. I chose the stone before we left London, but they took a little while to make this special setting. That's why you haven't had your ring until now."

"I didn't mind waiting. And the setting is as beautiful as the stone. Rex, you're so much too good to me," she exclaimed impulsively.

But he laughed at that, and passed his arm round her waist.

"Darling, you make me uncomfortable when you say such things," he told her, with, however, no outward sign of embarrassment. " 'Good' is hardly the word to describe me, I'm afraid, and sometimes I wonder if you know what a very imperfect proposition you are taking on."

Meryon pressed his arm.

"You've never been anything but good to me," she said. "I shall continue to think you that, whatever you say."

He gave her a glance of amused affection, in which there was more than a touch of ruefulness as well.

"I wonder what, in your opinion, constitutes a 'good' man," he remarked thoughtfully.

"Well," she began, and then was silent. "I suppose," she went on at last, "I meant particularly that you are always so kind and generous to me, that you think of everything you can to give me pleasure, and then you supply it in the nicest and most tactful way possible."

"There's nothing very virtuous in a rich man spending money in the way that gives him most pleasure," Rex said quizzically.

"Oh, Rex!" she smiled protestingly. "Are you *trying* to belittle your own good points and make yourself out to be an unworthy sort of person?"

"No." He smiled reflectively in his turn. "But when I find you polishing my non-existent halo, I feel I

ought to do something about it, for sheer decency's
sake. I suppose if I were another type of man, I
should feel rather tempted to confess a few specific
sins."

Meryon didn't say anything for a moment, thinking
with more than a hint of amusement of Sally's senti-
mental: "I suppose if he asked you to marry him, he'd
tell you everything and ask your forgiveness."

Aloud, Meryon said:

"Do you think one ever does any good by that?"

"No," he said frankly, "I don't. That's why I'm not
allowing myself the indulgence."

"And, anyway, I don't know that it's my business,"
Meryon added thoughtfully.

"Maybe not. But few people attain such magnificent
detachment," he said with a smile. "How do you
arrive at it? By arguing that it's my future and not
my past that is your concern?"

"I suppose so."

"You're an extraordinarily unjealous woman,
Meryon," he said curiously.

"Am I?"

"I think so. I cannot imagine that most women
wouldn't have questioned me for that reason alone."

"Oh—I see. You mean, of course, that there have
been other women?"

She said that quietly, but she knew how startled he
was from the profound silence that followed the
question.

"I suppose it would be silly to expect you not to
have heard some of the stories about me," he said at
last rather curtly.

"Yes. But I'm not prepared to accept gossip of that
sort at its face value. I'd rather have your word. *Were*
they true—these stories?" she asked, with a coolness
that surprised herself.

"Many of them not, I expect. Some of them—yes."

There was silence again.

"Do you mind very much?" he said finally in a rather low voice.

"No," Meryon replied slowly. "No, I can't honestly say that I do."

"Meryon!" His arm tightened round her. "Are you super-human? How can you say such a thing?"

"It's rather as you suggested, I suppose—that I can't feel I have any right to your past, only to your future."

But as she spoke, she knew that was not the reason at all. The fact was that she didn't love him—that was the beginning and end of it. She knew he would treat her well in the future, that he would behave decently by her, and she didn't want any more than that. She *couldn't* agonise over any other woman in his past, because she simply didn't care. If it had been Gregory now—— But here she stopped her thoughts, for of course they could not run on those lines. And, anyway, Rex was kissing her and saying in a quick, low voice that was full of emotion:

"My dear, you must be the most generous woman alive."

She wasn't, she knew, because generosity had nothing to do with it. But she couldn't explain that to him— she could only accept his kisses in silence, and return them as warmly as she might.

He didn't speak of the matter again after that, either then or during the next few days. But once or twice Meryon found him looking at her with a tender air, and there was more than a suggestion of puzzlement in the glance, which she found hard to explain.

She and her mother had been down there almost a fortnight already, and Meryon was astonished to find how quickly and pleasantly the time had flown. How

lovely it was to slip away from the burden of household worries!—to live in a world where beds were
things to be slept in instead of made, meals were things
to be eaten instead of cooked, and china was something
to be admired instead of washed.

"It won't take long to train me into a life of luxury
once more," Meryon thought. And she tried to make
herself think that that made the shadow of her
approaching marriage less alarming.

From Sally there came a cheerful note, during the
second week, conveying little information beyond the
fact that she was well and happy, while from John
there was a much longer letter, with a more detailed
account of what he was doing.

Evidently his health was improving extraordinarily
well—even the writing showed that—but there were a
few sentences which gave Meryon a little thrill of
disquiet.

*"Sally came down on Sunday and we had a good time,
chewing over all the news. Gregory didn't turn up, after all,
but he sent me a note. It seems he's got a cold this time—
caught Sally's, I suppose, just before she went away. I
haven't heard if he's better yet. Have you?*

"Now, about your engagement——"

Meryon put down the letter and frowned. No—she
hadn't heard whether Gregory was better. She hadn't
even heard that he was ill—and that was worrying.
Or was it just that Gregory had nothing special to say
to her and so saved himself the time and trouble of
writing?

She supposed that was really much the most likely
explanation. And, telling herself sharply that she was
in danger of developing into a perpetual fidget and
bore, she tried to dismiss Gregory and his cold from
her mind, and go on reading John's letter.

She was amused, but faintly disturbed, to notice with

what grown-up diplomacy he contrived to comment on her engagement without once disclosing his own opinion.

She knew now why she had shirked telling John the news herself. He was far too observant and far too quick-witted for her to want to discuss the matter with him until he had got used to the whole idea. Besides—Meryon bit her lip as she remembered the fact—John was the only one out of all the family who knew the real state of her feelings. It was not going to be easy to throw dust in his eyes, or to pretend that her feelings had undergone an extraordinarily rapid change.

Still, she would have to see about that when she got home. No point in climbing her fences before she came to them.

It was only a couple of mornings later that Meryon came down to breakfast to find an unexpected letter beside her plate.

Replying a little absently to Rex's "Good morning" kiss, she glanced in a puzzled way at the envelope. It was not a handwriting she recognised at all, yet only someone who knew her very well could know where she was staying.

Opening the envelope, she took out the single sheet of paper and looked at the bottom of the page.

"*Yours respectfully, Mrs. Glenby.*"

Mrs. Glenby! That was the daily woman who had been called in to look after Gregory.

With the strangest sense of foreboding, Meryon went back to the beginning and began to read the letter.

"*Dear Miss Dawling, I hope you will excuse me writing but I think you should know Mr. Monder is very bad, the doctor says pneumonia and what with my family to look after I can't keep on coming in. Doctor says he could get a nurse but if you would rather come back there it is. Hoping you are well and had a good holiday. Yours respectfully, Mrs. Glenby.*"

It was Rex saying, "What on earth is the matter, my dear?" that told her how white and frightened she must be looking.

"It's Gregory—he's ill—pneumonia. I must go at once." She spoke jerkily, curling the edge of the letter nervously in her hand as she spoke.

"Go at once? But you can't. Don't be absurd, dear. We can make some other arrangement." Rex's voice was extremely determined. "Who is it who has written?"

"Mrs. Glenby. The woman who goes in to clean. She says he's very ill. If you'll drive me to the junction I can get the eleven-thirty. I *must* go."

"Wait a minute." Rex had never spoken to her with quite that tone of authority. "You're not going rushing up to London in this heat to do sick-nursing, simply because your mother happened to marry Gregory's uncle. We can easily arrange something else. He has no claim, and——"

"I am going."

"My dear, be reasonable. May I see that letter?"

She handed it over without a word, and he read it rapidly.

"But you see what she says: the doctor will get in a nurse. It's perfectly simple, child. Why on earth should you get into this state? We can telephone to Dr. Trellor right away, and ask him to arrange to get in a nurse—two nurses, if you like. But I'm not going to have your one decent holiday and rest interrupted like this. It will undo all the——"

"I am going to London," Meryon said flatly. "You can say what you like, but I'm going back to London. I'm not going to leave Gregory alone and ill, and just being nursed by strangers."

"Meryon, it's ridiculous!" Rex was obviously controlling his temper with difficulty. "At every turn there's some fresh demand that these people make on you. If John isn't ill with spinal trouble, Gregory must needs get pneumonia, or Sally is too young to be allowed to do some perfectly ordinary thing on her own. It isn't even as though they're your own family."

"They *are* my family," Meryon said. "I've made them my family. I've worked for them, and they love me and trust me. They'd no more expect me to desert them now than they'd expect the sun to set at midday. I can't help what you think or what you want—I'm going to Gregory now. And if you won't drive me to the junction, I'll walk to the nearest station and pick up a slow train. But *I'm going.*"

"Well, of course, if you feel as strongly as that"— Rex's voice held very little expression—"there's no more to be said. I'll drive you to the junction, naturally, but I'm afraid I simply can't come with you to London, my dear. I have to see my bailiff on some very important business."

"You don't need to come with me," Meryon said quickly. "I don't see what you could do, Rex, if you came. I'll be awfully glad if you'll just drive me to the station—and I'm so sorry it means a disappointing end to the holiday for you."

"It isn't that. I hate the thought of your slaving again, that's all."

"I won't slave, I promise you. If—if he's very ill, I'll get a nurse as well, but I must be there."

"All right. What about your mother? She, at least, had better stay on here, don't you think?"

"Oh, Rex—if she could—it's awfully kind of you. It certainly would simplify things for me."

"Very well. That is settled. And then if you find you can get away again in a day or two, I can come and fetch you to rejoin her here."

"Oh, thank you."

"Now please make some sort of breakfast, child, if you're going on a journey. You'll still have time to pack a few things before I bring the car round at eleven."

"Packing! Who's talking of packing?" demanded Mrs. Monder, as she came into the room. "So *very* sorry I'm late, my dears, but it was one of those mornings when everything seemed to go wrong—you know how it is. But what's this about packing?"

"I have to go back to London this morning, Mother. Gregory is ill with pneumonia, and there's no one to look after him, you know."

"Gregory—pneumonia—go back to London!" gasped poor Mrs. Monder. It was indeed one of those mornings when everything seemed to go wrong.

"Yes. But Rex very kindly suggests that you stay on here for a little while, in case it's not so serious as it sounds, because then I could come back and rejoin you. It's really much the best way, Mother, since Rex is so kind."

"Well—I don't know—it's all so sudden."

Meryon wanted to say that pneumonia usually was, but, of course, one never said impatient things like that to Mother. And after a while Mrs. Monder consented to accept the arrangement made for her, and not to say anything more than:

"Pneumonia—dear, dear! That can be very serious, of course."

Meryon bit her lip, but managed to keep back the little groan of fear that rose in her heart.

Pneumonia *was* serious—that was the worst of it. People even died of pneumonia—quite often. But it was absurd to entertain ideas like that! She must be perfectly calm and collected, and soon she would be in London and finding that things were nothing like so serious as she had feared.

Rex was very quiet on the way to the station, but he seemed to have recovered entirely from his momentary flash of temper. There were only a few minutes to wait before the train came in, and he walked up and down the platform with her, pausing for a moment to buy her magazines which she knew she would not read and fruit which she knew she could not eat.

Then the train came in, and he handed her into a first class carriage, since he himself had insisted on getting her ticket.

"Thank you, Rex. You've been an angel to me," she said, as she kissed him "Good-bye." "And if I was cross, you must please forgive me. It was simply that I was nervy."

"You weren't cross, my dear. And if anyone is an angel, it's you. Have a good journey, and I hope you find Gregory better already."

He stepped back as the train began to move, and waved to her. She waved in return, and then, as the train rounded a bend, she sank back into her seat, and Rex passed completely from her mind.

Gregory! She was going back to Gregory at last! But he was ill—perhaps dangerously ill—and anything might happen. *Anything.* He was so tired and over-worked; the last six months had been such an unspeakable strain. He wasn't in a condition to stand up to a serious illness.

But she *must* not think like this. She mustn't form thoughts whose very shadows terrified her.

The world without Gregory. She couldn't imagine such a thing. Her life without Gregory was something she had forced herself to face for some while now, but that was different. He would always have been there—somewhere in the world—even if he must mean nothing personally to her. But that he should not be there at all! Meryon felt her face go cold and wet at the thought.

Waterloo was reached at last, and the Underground took Meryon to within five minutes' walk of the house.

Everything looked so very much as usual in the afternoon sunshine. There was the baker on his "round," and the little girl who always swung on the gate of the corner house smiled and said "Hello", as though she had never been away.

Meryon ran up the steps of Number Twenty-Two and opened the door with her key. As she did so, Mrs. Glenby came out of the kitchen with a relieved expression on her face.

"Well, Miss Dawling, you have been quick and no mistake. I'm glad to see you, I can tell you."

"How is he?" Meryon put down her case and began to pull off her gloves.

"Not too good." Mrs. Glenby shook her head. "He's been talking ever so queer. Little bit off his head, you know, but that doesn't always mean danger. My eldest two were like that with measles, but, bless you, they was eating their heads off a week later."

"I'll go up at once, and then I'll come and talk things over later, if you can wait just a little while," Meryon said.

It seemed that Mrs. Glenby could wait, and very quietly, two steps at a time, Meryon ran up the stairs.

The door of his room was ajar and she went straight in. As she crossed the room she could hear his hoarse, heavy breathing, and it frightened her terribly, though her face remained perfectly calm.

He was lying on his side, half turned away from her, his fair hair very tumbled and his face flushed and restless. His eyes were almost closed, and when she spoke his name he took no notice at first.

"Gregory," she said softly again. "Gregory dear, it's Meryon."

This time he turned his head and stared at her with

bright, fevered eyes. Then he groped rather feebly for her hand and put it against his burning cheek.

"Oh, darling," he muttered, "is it really you at last? I thought you'd never come. It's been weeks and months."

CHAPTER XI

IT WAS PERHAPS the sweetest and yet the bitterest moment of Meryon's life—this realisation that Gregory not only had loved her, but did love her still.

Bending down, she slipped her arm round him, raising him slightly so that she could turn the hot, crumpled pillow. When she would have laid him back again, he clung to her like a sick child.

"No—don't put me down. If I let you put me down, you'll go away. And then you won't come back—you never do come back." His voice trailed away, and for a heavenly second or two Meryon held him close, feeling that he was the most precious thing in the world, and it didn't matter if she showed it just now, because no one would ever know—not even he himself.

Then he stirred against her and spoke again, still in that hoarse, feeble voice, but more coherently this time:

"Why, Meryon, is that you? I thought—you were miles—away."

"Yes, I was. But I've come back now to look after you."

"Have you?" He looked puzzled, but he smiled faintly. "How very nice. I'm not really ill—just a heavy cold. I'll be back at the office soon."

"Well, we'll see about that," she said soothingly. "Now I must go and speak to Mrs. Glenby. I'll have to put you down for a little while. Do you mind?"

"No—of course not." He looked surprised, and she

smiled slightly, thinking what odd deceptions the conscious mind could play.

She very gently laid him back, put the clothes round him and went out of the room.

It was strange how light-hearted she felt, in spite of her anxiety. He was hers for a little, little while! Hers to look after and care for and pet. No one could object, no one could interfere. Even such sympathetic witnesses as Sally and John would not be there. She could do as she had always wanted to do—wait on him hand and foot, and know that he was her own dear care and responsibility. No one could even think it was wrong. It was, in fact, the only right and proper thing.

Downstairs she found Mrs. Glenby waiting with an air of overwhelming patience. Meryon apologised for the length of her absence.

"That's all right, miss," Mrs. Glenby said, in the tone one reserves exclusively for occasions when it is not all right. "But if you don't mind, I'll have to go now."

"Yes, of course. Only, tell me first—has the doctor been to-day?"

"Yes, miss. But he's coming again about six."

Meryon's heart missed a beat.

"He thought it necessary to come twice a day?"

"I suppose so, miss." Mrs. Glenby was not going to commit herself on the subject of the doctor's motives. "Some of 'em just keep on coming to make the bill big, of course, but he didn't *seem* that sort. Quite the gentleman, in fact."

"Of course." Meryon paid hasty but absent tribute to the gentlemanliness of Dr. Trellor. "But he must think Mr. Monder very ill."

"It looks like it," Mrs. Glenby admitted.

"Did he come twice yesterday?"

"Yes, miss. But only once the other days. I kept the number of visits so as you could check the bill." She still seemed much more concerned with the honesty of Dr. Trellor than the seriousness of the patient's illness, and Meryon decided not to press her questions further.

It seemed that Mrs. Glenby could still come in regularly every morning. "And I can always do any little bits of shopping for you, miss, if you can't get out in the afternoons," she offered good-naturedly

Meryon accepted this gratefully, and decided that unless Dr. Trellor emphatically recommended having a trained nurse, she herself could manage very well, both the sick nursing and looking after the house.

Dr. Trellor, when he came an hour later, seemed satisfied with the suggested arrangement.

"There shouldn't be an abnormal amount of nursing," he said. "And, unless the patient takes a turn for the worse, I don't think there is likely to be anything which you couldn't manage, Miss Dawling."

"Then he isn't *very* seriously ill?" Meryon wished she could sound cool and efficient instead of deadly anxious.

"Pneumonia is always serious," the doctor pointed out.

"Yes, I know, but——"

"With good care and attention—and I am sure he will have both—I see no reason why he shouldn't make a complete recovery."

Meryon's breath escaped in a sharp gasp of relief.

"But he must get rid of this ridiculous idea that he is going back to his office in a day or two," the doctor added sternly.

"Oh, yes, of course. I'll see he takes a more sensible view of that," Meryon assured the doctor with entirely groundless confidence.

"Is it rather a serious matter for him—being absent on sick leave?"

"I don't know." (It was strange how one anxiety could wipe out another. She had never once thought of this aspect of the case. All that mattered now was that Gregory should be well again.) "Anyway, we can worry about that when he's better," she added with a smile.

"No doubt that is the best way of looking at it," Dr. Trellor agreed, smiling in his turn as he took his leave.

As soon as he had gone, Meryon ran upstairs again. It was indescribably pleasant and exciting to have the place to herself like this, except for a quiet, weak Gregory, who seemed content to lie there and watch her or to obey her few sick-room orders with most unusual meekness.

"What does Trellor say?" he asked, after watching her in silence while she quietly put one or two things to rights.

"That you're getting on quite nicely, but that you must do exactly what you're told," Meryon said, standing at the end of the bed and smiling at him.

He grinned feebly back at her.

"You must be in your element. You love telling people what to do."

"Gregory! That sounds as though I'm a horribly bossy young woman."

"So you are," he told her with an affectionate glance.

For a moment it shook her to have him regard her with such frank liking. Then she realised that, weak as he was, he could not keep up the barrier that usually stood between his feelings and the outside world. When he looked at her now it was as he wanted to look at her, not as he felt he should look at her. That, too, was going to add the sweetest danger to this short time together.

"Well, if you know I'm a tyrant already, I can add

a few more orders without giving a shock to your
system," Meryon said. "And as a beginning—no more
talking. You mustn't waste your strength, especially
if it means criticising me."

He accepted her ruling with that docility that seemed
so strange in him, and made no more attempt to talk.
Only when she went to sit down he said:

"No, don't sit there. I can't see you. Come a little
further this way."

She obeyed without protest, and he lay there watching her with contented eyes, while she pretended to
read, though really she was just allowing her thoughts
to roam where they liked.

"It's a long while since you've turned a page," he
said at last.

She immediately turned one guiltily, whereat he
gave a feeble little laugh, and she laughed too, though
her colour rose.

"All right. It's natural for your thoughts to be in
Hampshire," he said in that rather slow hoarse voice.

"Hampshire?" She looked vague.

"Isn't that where Treventon lives?"

"Oh—oh, yes. Of course." Meryon blushed more
deeply still at the ridiculous slip, but Gregory obviously
attributed her colour to other thoughts. He was silent
again for a moment or two. Then he said:

"Didn't Treventon raise creation when you wanted
to come back to nurse me?"

"No. He—well, no, of course not."

"Delighted, in fact?"

"Hardly that," Meryon admitted. "But when I had
explained the circumstances, he quite realised I must
come."

"Charming disposition the fellow has—or else he's
a perfect fool," Gregory murmured ungratefully.

"I did say 'no talking,'" Meryon reminded him

with a touch of severity. And after that there was silence until it was time to give him his very light supper.

"It's stupid being so weak," he protested with a frown, when she had to put her arm round him to support him, and almost literally to feed him.

"No. It's quite natural. You've had a high fever for several days." She spoke very coolly, but, looking down at his head very near her shoulder, she had an almost irresistible longing to kiss the tumbled fair hair.

"Have I?" He sounded faintly interested. "How did you know I was ill, by the way? Neither of the children knew."

"No. Mrs. Glenby wrote and told me."

"Mrs. Glenby?"

"The woman who comes in to clean."

"Good Lord!" And then: "Well, bless Mrs. Glenby for her interference."

Meryon laughed softly and tightened her arm slightly.

"I don't want any more, Meryon." He leant his head back against her with a sort of weary content that touched her deeply.

She didn't say anything—just sat there holding him —and presently she saw his dark lashes droop. Once —twice they flicked upwards again, like those of an obstinate child who was trying to stay awake. Then they came down once more very firmly, and there was no further movement.

For a long while she sat there holding him for the sheer pleasure of the contact. Gregory in her arms! It would have been incredible twenty-four hours ago. She felt a moment's guilt for her overwhelming happiness, but it was hard to believe there was anything really wrong in caring for a sick Gregory. And after a while the tremors of conscience passed, and only the happiness remained.

There followed for Meryon three or four enchanted days. The peak of Gregory's illness had really been on the day she returned, so that now there was little to do but nurse him carefully and watch his slow improvement.

Most of the time he was too languid to talk much, but he liked to have her there in the room, and by common consent she spent a great part of the day there—sometimes reading to him, sometimes sewing or writing letters—but always within his range of vision, because he grew strangely restless if he could not see her.

Once he asked idly: "To what do we owe the very welcome absence of your mother?"

Meryon hesitated.

"I'm sorry you don't like Mother," she said a little sharply, without answering his question.

"Oh, but I do. She's the most gloriously inconsistent and illogical person I ever came across. I always think she must have been a special invention of the Almighty when he was in a very humorous mood."

"Gregory!"

"But I like her nowadays. One simply can't help it. She'd be so ludicrously astonished if one didn't, for one thing."

Meryon laughed vexedly.

"It's quite true. She does expect everyone to like her. But then that's partly because she likes everyone herself."

"A very laudable state of mind," observed Gregory gravely. "But you haven't told me where she is."

"Oh, she stayed on down in Hampshire. Rex suggested she should in case—well, in case I should be rejoining her in a little while."

"And shall you?" Gregory looked rather fixedly at a fold in the window curtain.

"No." Meryon was quite emphatic about that. "You'll need careful nursing for quite a long time. I shouldn't dream of leaving you."

"That's very nice of you." Gregory didn't shift his gaze, and, if anything, his expression became more wooden. "But our devoted Rex won't like that, will he?"

Meryon was silent. She supposed he wouldn't.

"Well, it would be silly to get in a trained nurse at this point," she said at last. "I think Rex will agree that I had much better finish the job myself. And, anyway, Sally will be back soon, and Mother will be returning then."

"That certainly will satisfy the proprieties a little better," Gregory agreed gravely. "Do you realise, Meryon, that you and I have been rather flouting convention during the last few days?"

Meryon smiled.

"It did strike me once," she admitted. "But with you ill and—and Mrs. Glenby coming in—I mean, anyway, it's ridiculous," she finished rather confusedly.

"Pneumonia and Mrs. Glenby seem rather odd chaperons," Gregory said reflectively. "But perhaps, as you say, it's all right. Anyway, if your mother and your fiancé are satisfied, who are we to raise queries?"

Meryon laughed, but the phrase "your fiancé" was a cold wind that blew aside much of the magic of the last few days and emphasised the fact that it was all cruelly short in any case.

Perhaps he followed the same line of thought, because after a moment that air of mock gravity left him and he said rather deliberately:

"When does Rex propose to put a plain ring beside that very handsome diamond you are wearing?"

"Oh, I don't know—we haven't settled—there's

so much to arrange." She spoke hastily and not very coherently.

"There's not so very much to arrange really, Meryon." Gregory's voice was unexpectedly gentle. "Things have been smoothing themselves out in some ways—and Heaven knows! you deserve that they should."

"What do you mean?"

He didn't answer that at once, and she waited with a sort of loving impatience for him to speak.

"Do you remember," he said at last, "when you first took on the job of making a home for us all, you soothed your mother's objections by telling her it wouldn't be for always?"

"Yes, but——"

"If I remember rightly, you said that one day I should be 'earning a wonderful salary again and able to pay a real housekeeper.' We none of us believed that at the time—not even you, for all your dear insistence on the fact."

Meryon was perfectly still, remembering that scene with poignant clearness, terribly moved by the expression he had used, and all the more so because he spoke so quietly.

"I didn't believe it either, Meryon dear. It was simply *your* determination that kept us all going at that time. I knew it even then, and sometimes I wanted to tell you so and to thank you for giving us all the courage to go on. But I couldn't. There was that queer barrier of antagonism between us. I know—it was I who had erected it, and by some strange whim of Fate if was *you* who had to take it down. I couldn't, however much I tried."

She put out her hand and took his, holding it in a close grip that said more than any words.

"And during all the time that you were giving so

much help to me, I wasn't really helping you at all because I didn't know how to reach you."

"Gregory, that isn't true! You did help me."

"How?"

"Oh, by—by being your dear, hard-working, worthwhile self, of course. *I* couldn't have gone on unless I had known *you* were there to rely on."

"Well," he smiled at her, "that's a nice way of putting it, and I'd like to think that in some small measure you're right. But I must confess that what really gives me pleasure now is the realisation that things seem like working out almost as you prophesied. Your judgment is vindicated in every sense, Meryon." And he smilingly patted the fingers that were curled so tightly round his.

"Is it?" She looked enquiringly at him. "How do you mean?"

"Curiously enough, it came out of my illness. I had had a disturbed idea that if I were absent from the office for a long while, they might discover they could do without me altogether. But it seems that something like the reverse was the case."

"Gregory!"

"I had an extremely cordial letter from Mr. Crimley —that's the senior partner, you know—this morning. He actually says something about how valuable they realise my services were, now that I'm no longer there. (Very gratifying from such a cautious old bird as Crimley.) And that when Vandar retires in November they intend to promote me to his position. It means nearly double the salary right away, and—what's much more—a chance to use the particular kind of brains I do possess."

"Oh, my dear!" Meryon's eyes were shining with pride and joy. "Doesn't that *show* how clever you really are?"

Gregory laughed softly.

"Dear Meryon! Hers is a wonderful family, isn't it?" he said teasingly.

"I think you *are* a wonderful family. And I ought to know, if anyone does. Imagine their talking about promotion so soon after your last rise! And you haven't been long in the firm. They must think the world of you if you've made an impression so quickly."

"Well, they did know my work before they took me on," Gregory pointed out with a smile. "But, anyway, it's very heartening. And the great thing is that you can get married now just as soon as you like, and not have a single qualm of anxiety about your blessed family."

"Oh—yes. Of course."

Meryon felt as though she had suddenly been dropped from a great height.

Her marriage with Rex. *That* was supposed to be her reason for rejoicing. Not the wonderful success that had crowned Gregory's work. She could be pleased and congratulatory about that, of course, just as she might about some success of Sally or John. But the real point was that it made her marriage almost an accomplished fact.

Happy Meryon! She could shorten her engagement as much as she liked now. And the shorter it was, the happier she was expected to be.

Somehow she made a more or less graceful escape to her own room, and there she cried the first tears she had allowed herself since Rex had put his ring upon her finger.

But what was the good? She was right up against the facts at last. Nothing stood between her and her marriage to Rex. She must face it.

Two days later her mother came home.

"*Such* a pity you couldn't stay the last few days,

darling. We had some really lovely weather at the end," Mrs. Monder said, ignoring the fact that they had had beautiful weather all the time. "And Gregory doesn't look *very* bad to me." She had come into Gregory's room to greet him, and now stood looking at him with an air of kindly reproach.

Gregory smiled at her.

"I've been at death's door," he asserted firmly.

"No! Really? Has he, Meryon?"

Meryon exchanged an amused look with Gregory.

"He's been pretty bad," she said, and very lightly touched his hair. "But he's better now."

"Yes. I'm sure. All men are like that—if you'll forgive my saying so, Gregory dear. Just big babies. Think they are going to die as soon as the doctor appears. Now, women are *quite* different."

"I'm sure they are," Gregory agreed meekly, whereupon Mrs. Monder immediately countered generously with:

"Still, pneumonia *is* a nasty thing, and I'm very glad to see you better, my dear. Meryon is a very good nurse, of course."

"She's wonderful," Gregory said gently, and Mrs. Monder looked extremely pleased.

Later she said to Meryon:

"You know, darling, Gregory has *mellowed*. He's nothing like so difficult as he used to be."

Meryon very much wanted to say indignantly that he never had been "difficult," but truth and a disinclination for a long argument held her silent.

Rex had not returned to Town with Mrs. Monder, which rather surprised Meryon, but a very affectionate letter explained at some length the various matters on the estate which kept him there for a short while longer.

She wrote, assuring him that she quite understood,

and then felt a hypocrite because, for very decency, she had to say that she missed him.

However, the return of Sally and the resumption of the normal running of the household took most of her thoughts, particularly as Sally brought with her the first hint of wonderfully good news of John.

"We didn't write and tell you about all the ups and downs, Meryon, because John said there should be something definite before we started bothering you," Sally explained.

"You don't bother me," Meryon said, smiling into Sally's bright, eager face.

"No, I know. But—well, anyway, we wanted something definite. And, even now, I'm not really supposed to say much——"

"Sally dear, do come to the point," Mrs. Monder interrupted with gentle firmness. "Nothing is more annoying than to have someone wander round and round the subject."

Sally looked astounded at such a charge from such a quarter—as well she might. Then she shrugged her shoulders good-temperedly and said:

"Well, the point is that he's making the sort of progress none of us ever dreamed of. It isn't only that he's walking about a little again. He does more every day and it's becoming the natural thing with him, instead of the exception. Even the doctors and nurses at the Home are astonished, and though they won't commit themselves much to John himself, his own special nurse let out that they look on him as one of the possibilities of a complete cure."

"Sally dear! What wonderful news! Why ever wasn't I told before?" Meryon almost hugged Sally.

"Well, it was only the last time I went down that there was any *real* confirmation of our hopes. And John insisted that you had quite enough worries without having your hopes raised and then all squashed."

"Very thoughtful of him," observed Mrs. Monder approvingly, while Meryon smiled, not quite steadily, and said:

"John has more thought for others than anyone else I know."

Sally nodded, with an assumption of sisterly indifference that deceived no one—not even herself.

"D'you remember I said in the beginning that I had a hunch this treatment would have wonderful results?"

"Yes, I remember," Meryon said.

"Well, dear, there was nothing remarkable about that. We *all* knew it was the best treatment possible," Mrs. Monder pointed out.

"And you said then that it would be worth almost anything to have him well," Sally added, amiably ignoring the interruption.

"I said 'worth absolutely anything,'" Meryon amended with an odd, reflective little smile. "And I meant it."

"And then it cost nothing after all!" Mrs. Monder summed up brightly. "Just think of that! It's really wonderful."

Meryon looked very thoughtfully at her mother.

"Yes," she said. "It's really wonderful."

The next day, when Dr. Trellor came to see Gregory, he, too, had a talk with Meryon about John. The medical authorities at the Home had written to him, and he had also had a long telephone talk with the principal doctor in charge.

Dr. Trellor was a good deal more technical than Sally, and not quite so sensational, but the general conclusion was much the same. John was not only improving rapidly. Even a complete recovery might reasonably be expected in time.

"It isn't suggested that he should remain at the

Home longer than was originally arranged," Dr. Trellor explained. "He can come home here at the end of next week, and provided you can make arrangements for him to attend the North London clinic once a week, another five or six months of quiet, restful life should see him pretty well able to consider himself cured."

"It's more than I'd ever dared to hope," Meryon said.

"Yes." The doctor smiled at her. "Both your patients have done remarkably well. You can feel very well satisfied, and leave them without anxiety. I understand from Mrs. Monder that they can't expect to enjoy your good nursing much longer."

"Oh"—Meryon looked faintly put out—"I don't know that I'm going to desert them just yet."

"Well, shall I put it that someone else is going to have a more pressing claim to be looked after?" the doctor said, and went off chuckling at what he considered his neat way of putting things.

For one reason or another, Meryon found it impossible to go down to see John during the rest of the time he was at the nursing home. Not only was she very busy at home, but Sally explained elaborately that he was not having visitors for long at a time just now, and he himself wrote to say it was scarcely worth while her coming so far for so short a time when very soon he would be home.

In the ordinary way, Meryon would scarcely have agreed to being put off like this, but, with Gregory convalescent, she had her hands full, and although he never put his thoughts into words, she knew he felt better and happier when she was in the house.

She was a little surprised, really, when she found that the rest of John's stay at the nursing home had slipped away, and before she had had time to visit him again, they were discussing arrangements for bringing him home.

In the end, it was Dr. Trellor who fetched him in his car. Meryon had fully intended to go too, but Sally insisted so firmly on the fact that John himself wanted a "proper home-coming party" that it was decided that everyone should be waiting at home to greet him.

Dr. Trellor had promised to arrive about tea-time, and Sally and Meryon were very busy all the afternoon making what Mrs. Monder called "festive preparations."

It was a cool day in very early autumn, and Meryon had lighted a fire, because, as Sally said, "Even if you don't need it for warmth, a fire is the best thing in the world for a family to sit round." And soon after lunch Gregory, still rather weak but looking much more himself, came down to sit beside it.

"It's funny how patiently we've waited all these weeks and now it seems stupid to have to wait an hour," Sally declared.

But even Sally's patience was not too severely tried on this occasion, for as half-past four struck there was the sound of a car drawing up outside, and, running to the door, Meryon saw Dr. Trellor get out, followed by John.

With a little gasp of delight and wonder, she realised then why both the children had managed to keep her from going to see him during the last weeks. They wanted the full force of his recovery to come at once. The boy who was coming up the steps and into the house was a completely transformed person—a John Meryon had never even hoped to see. He walked almost briskly, his eyes looked bright and eager, and a clear, fine tan replaced the delicate pallor of two months ago.

Without a word, she flung her arms round him, and not until he said teasingly, "Now, Meryon, don't start crying or I shall, too," did she realise that there were tears in her eyes.

After that there was a perfect storm of greeting and congratulation, during which everyone talked and nobody listened, but everyone was very happy. Dr. Trellor stayed long enough to see his patient a little more quietly settled, and then took his leave, after having been congratulated by Mrs. Monder on what she apparently believed to be entirely his work.

Tea was a very happy though spasmodic sort of meal, in which everything was discussed, except, Meryon noticed, her own engagement. Perhaps John meant to speak of that when they had a minute or two alone together, but, anyway, no reference at all was made to it now, though once she saw his glance go very reflectively to her engagement ring.

After tea, when everything had been cleared away, they sat round the fire, and Sally said, with a contented sigh:

"Isn't it lovely to have a real family discussion again?"

"Yes. Though I'm afraid we've said nearly everything there is to say," Mrs. Monder objected.

"We might begin all over again and say it once more," suggested Gregory lazily, leaning back in his chair and looking at his young cousins with much the same affectionate satisfaction as Meryon.

"Nonsense! There must be lots more things to discuss," declared Sally.

"Yes," John agreed, smiling round from one to another. "And there's one subject particularly that *I* want to talk about. Who paid for my treatment in the nursing home, and how on earth was it done?"

Three pairs of astonished eyes were fixed on him.

"Why, no one paid," Mrs. Monder replied at last. "It was free. Don't you remember? I'm sure you heard about it at the time, my dear."

"No," John said slowly, "it was not free. I found

out by chance on the very last day, when I was talking to my nurse. There are only two free patients at that nursing home. I knew them both. Someone paid for me, so *one* of you must be a guardian angel in disguise. Which is it?"

There was a second's silence again and then, as though by instinct, they all looked at Meryon. She was not looking at anyone. Her lashes were down and her colour unusually high.

"Very well," she said at last. "I did arrange it."

For once in their lives Sally and Mrs. Monder spoke together in exactly the same words:

"But, my dear, where on earth did you get the money?"

CHAPTER XII

MERYON CLEARED HER THROAT NERVOUSLY, firmly conquered the absurd feeling of guilt that had come over her, and said:

"We didn't mean to tell you, but—it was Rex who provided the money."

"Rex!" exclaimed Sally, John and Mrs. Monder in varying keys of astonishment.

Gregory didn't say anything at all. He just sat there with his eyes on Meryon, his hands gripped tightly over the arms of his chair.

"There! We might have known!" Mrs. Monder said quite incorrectly.

"Why might we have known?" Sally demanded. "I don't see any reason why we should have guessed."

"Well—I mean—dear Rex always comes to the rescue in some way or another. What it is to have money *and* a generous heart!" And Mrs. Monder beamed round on everyone, entirely unaware of any tension.

"It must have been a good deal of money, Meryon," Gregory said quietly at last.

"Yes. It was a good deal of money."

"Something like a hundred pounds." His voice shook slightly.

"Something like that."

John moved slightly in his chair.

"It was very good of him indeed," he said in a disturbed tone.

"*Good* of him? I think he's a peach," Sally retorted.

"Fancy our having a man like that in the family.
Honestly, we are lucky. And to think he wanted to
keep it all quiet, too."

"I agree with you, Sally, that we're astonishingly
lucky in the relations we acquire," Gregory said slowly.
"But, personally, I should instance Meryon rather than
Rex."

"Oh, of course, Meryon's a darling, too. She knows
we think the world of *her*." Sally smiled brilliantly at
Meryon, who managed to produce a faint smile in
return. "But, after all, this is such a surprise about
Rex. He scarcely *is* the family yet, and he's done this
marvellous thing. Weren't you bursting to tell us
really, Meryon?"

"It was better not to say anything at the time,"
Meryon replied, to which Mrs. Monder said:

"I don't quite see why."

Meryon didn't offer to explain further, but Gregory
spoke again in that same strangely quiet voice.

"Perhaps the fact that they were not even engaged
then had something to do with it."

"In fact—Oh, Meryon, how romantic!" exclaimed
Sally suddenly. "Was it over that that you and
Rex——"

"No, dear. Don't be silly," lied Meryon desperately
before Sally could complete the sentence. Then, somehow, she managed to drag the conversation away from
the subject, and no one was gayer or more amusing
than Meryon after that, for no one had a more pressing
reason for avoiding awkward, reflective silences.

It was not possible, of course, that no further
reference would be made to what Rex had done, but
gradually Meryon began to hope that at least the train
of thought which seemed to her so obvious, might not
necessarily appeal to the others as the inevitable
one.

John's wonderful recovery and Gregory's good fortune at the office proved such profitable sources of discussion that her fears began to subside presently, and when she saw how casually and unselfconsciously Gregory seemed able to address her, she thought: "Of course, things look so different when you view them several weeks later. Even if Gregory thinks there is some connection, he isn't very likely to get the events in their right order. Besides, he doesn't even *know* how Mother innocently forced the issue."

The evening slipped away almost without their knowing how it had gone, and, remembering Dr. Trellor's warning that they must not judge entirely by John's remarkably strengthened appearance, Meryon insisted on a fairly early bedtime for her two convalescents.

"Come in and say 'Good night' to me before you go to bed yourself, Meryon," John said. "Then I shall really know I'm home."

She laughed at that and promised to come, very glad to have John there once more, with his spontaneous bursts of affection which showed how young he really was.

Meryon had one or two things to put to rights before she went to bed, so that she was later than she intended when she did finally go into his room, and she half-expected to find him asleep. However, his "Come in" in answer to her knock sounded anything but sleepy.

He hadn't even been reading, she saw, when she came in—just lying there luxuriating in the fact that he was home again, she supposed.

Standing by the bed, she smiled down at him.

"It's nice to see you in this room again, John."

"Yes." He dismissed that almost absently in favour of what he intended to say. "Why on earth are you marrying Rex?"

The question was so completely bare and unvarnished that Meryon gasped slightly.

"Well—why do you think?" she parried.

"I don't know. I've been asking myself that ever since Sally told me the news, and I haven't found the answer yet." Putting out his hand, he pulled her down gently on to the side of the bed. "Look here, I know Rex is a nice fellow, and personally I like him, but—he didn't present you with some sort of ultimatum over this money for me, did he?"

"No, John, certainly not." That at least she could say with perfect truth.

"Do you give me your word on that?"

"Absolutely." There was no mistaking the sincerity in Meryon's voice. "Rex isn't that kind of man at all."

John gave a slight sigh of relief.

"No, I must say he never struck me as a melodramatic villain. I'm glad. But in that case—*why*, Meryon dear?"

"I might say it's hardly your business," she pointed out gently.

"Yes, you might, of course. But that's the sort of stupid remark one keeps for people who don't matter or don't understand. I hope you won't mortify me by dishing it out to me."

Meryon smiled slightly. It was difficult to resist John when he spoke like that.

"Well, then, my dear, it is simply that I *want* to marry Rex, so don't waste any more time looking for obscure reasons."

John frowned.

"You know why I can't just swallow that whole, don't you?"

"Yes. You have some idea I'm still in love with Gregory." Meryon could scarcely have believed it possible to bring that out so calmly, but she had been steeling herself to say it during the whole of the conversation. She saw John was taken aback by the frankness of it.

"Well"—he hesitated—"if you're *not*, I'm a little surprised that you didn't raise the point right away."

Meryon produced a slightly embarrassed laugh—without much effort, to tell the truth.

"There is such a thing as feeling a bit of a fool when one can't explain one's own change of heart," she said.

"Oh, I see. I—I'm sorry, Meryon. I'm afraid I pushed into something that was hardly my business."

"Never mind. It doesn't matter."

She meant that. It *didn't* matter. Nothing mattered if John would only accept her protestations at their face value. If he guessed for one moment that a chain of rather tangled links connected the need of money for him with an unwanted marriage for her, then half of her sacrifice was wasted.

Meryon held her breath with anxiety. Then after a moment he smiled at her doubtfully.

"Then it's really all right? You're awfully happy and all that?"

"Very happy," Meryon said in a perfectly convincing tone.

John took hold of her left hand.

"It's a nice ring," he observed critically.

She smiled. "I'm glad you like it."

"Are you going to be married quite soon?"

"I—dare say. We hadn't really fixed anything, but Rex will be back in a day or two and then we shall talk things over."

"I see. Poor old Gregory," John said carelessly.

It was so absolutely unexpected that she could not control the quick spasm of pain which made her hand

ighten on John's. But perhaps he didn't notice that.
At any rate, he gave no sign whatever, and finding
that she was apparently reluctant to take that up, he
didn't press the point any further.

"I hope I shall see Rex soon," he remarked, "and
be able to thank him myself. It was really most awfully
good of him. I'd like him to know how grateful I
feel."

"Oh, you're certain to see him some time during the
next few days," Meryon said. "I had a letter this
morning to say that he expected to be in Town before
the end of the week. I rather think he will be going
back to the country later for a little while, but he's
certain to come here as well as taking me out with
him."

John nodded.

"Then I won't write. I'd much rather say it. When
you start writing down thanks for anything like that, it
always sounds frightfully pompous and stilted."

Meryon agreed with a smile, and then they said
"Good night" and she went to her room.

Had this awkward fence been safely surmounted?
She supposed it probably had, and, telling herself that
for this at least she might be thankful, she rather
wearily got to bed.

The very next day, there was a telegram from Rex,
saying that he was returning to London that afternoon,
and unless she left a telephone message at his flat to
the contrary, he would drop in for tea.

"Isn't it lovely? Everything is happening at once,"
exclaimed Sally.

"Lovely," said Mrs. Monder, and:

"Lovely," agreed Gregory. But their tones were not
identical.

When Rex arrived, rather late that afternoon,
Meryon met him in the hall alone and, taking her in

his arms, he kissed her several times, as though it were many months since he had seen her.

She returned his kisses—gratitude for John's recovery making them genuinely affectionate—and then he said quite frankly:

"I've not been able to get rid of the feeling that I was unkind and unreasonable the day you went away. It's good to see you again, darling, and to know that everything is all right."

"Oh, Rex, you were never unkind or unreasonable to me in your life. The fact is that you spoil me."

"Do I?" He smiled at her and touched her cheek with light, caressing fingers. "What ought I to do with you? Beat you occasionally?"

Meryon had a silly impulse to say that it would make her feel slightly less conscience-stricken about some things if he did. But of course she repressed the thought as soon as it came, and made some non-committal reply as they went into the dining-room together.

"Rex dear! Isn't this splendid!" cried Mrs. Monder as though welcoming him back from the interior of China. "And what a lovely secret we've just discovered about you!"

"Really?" Rex looked amused and mystified. "Sure it's not a guilty secret?"

Mrs. Monder paid that absurdity the tribute of a smile.

"No, my dear, of course not. It's just that John has something to say to you."

Everyone looked faintly uncomfortable at this somewhat crude stage-managing of the occasion, and Rex still looked genuinely puzzled.

"Hello, old man." He held out his hand to John. "I'm glad to see you looking so much better. What's the dark secret that you and I are sharing?"

John took his hand very warmly.

"Meryon told us yesterday about your putting up the money for me at the nursing home. I'd no idea before. It was most frightfully good of you. I can't tell you how grateful I am."

For the first second Rex's eyes had widened in an almost startled expression. Then he patted John's shoulder carelessly.

"That's all right. I couldn't have Meryon breaking her heart over her favourite like that, you know. And I'm delighted the results were so good."

"Yes—just imagine, Rex dear! They think he will be completely cured in time," Mrs. Monder broke in. "You must feel very proud and pleased with what you've done."

"Yes," Rex agreed just a trifle drily. "I am very pleased indeed." Then, to John, in something more like his usual casual tone: "Why don't you come down to my place for a week or ten days? I shall be going back in a day or two, and I could run you down. I'd like to have you."

"Oh, Rex"—Meryon came and slipped her arm into his—"that would be simply marvellous. It would do him so much good."

From the sudden pressure of her arm against his side she knew she had been right in supposing that his real idea had been to give pleasure to her.

"I'd like it awfully——" John began.

"Then it's settled," Rex said. "I suppose there is no chance of your coming too, my dear?" He didn't actually look at Meryon, but the pressure of his arm again told her whom he meant.

"I'm afraid I couldn't just now," she pleaded a little nervously. But there was really no need for the nervousness, for he said at once:

"Very well. I'll see John has a good time, even if he must be rather quiet."

Meryon felt a lump come into her throat. She wished passionately at that moment that she *could* love Rex. He was so good to her—it was horribly ungenerous not to give him the very best in return. Perhaps as time went on things would change. She might even grow to be glad that events had worked out as they had, for, of course, people *did* change with the years, and liking *did* sometimes grow into love.

But it was hard to believe there would ever be a time when one glance from Gregory's cool, grey eyes would not be worth all the generosity of Rex.

The two men, though slightly distant to each other, contrived to be perfectly courteous, though certainly Rex made no hospitable suggestion that Gregory should come and convalesce at his country house.

Perhaps he thought Gregory already had more than his share of good fortune in having so much attention from Meryon. Certainly his eyes followed her with rather close attention when she went near Gregory or spoke to him.

"Ah, Rex, it's no good expecting to persuade Meryon to run away on any more holidays," Mrs. Monder declared with a smile. "You'll have to take her away altogether when you do it next time."

"So I imagine," Rex said pleasantly. "How you must all hate me for proposing to take her away."

Meryon laughed a little uncomfortably, and Gregory said, "Oh, we do." But so coolly that it was perfectly obvious even to Mrs. Monder that dear Gregory was not meaning to be rude this time.

"Are you going to be married quite soon?" Sally asked candidly.

Rex smiled.

"You must ask Meryon that. The decisions are all in her hands, you know."

Meryon forced herself to meet his eyes and smile, though she was burningly aware of the fact that Gregory was watching her.

"Quite soon, I think," she heard herself say calmly. "Some time before Christmas certainly." For it had gradually come over her during the last half-hour that she *must* marry Rex soon. It was terribly unfair to all of them if she shirked the issue any longer.

Rex stayed quite late that evening—very much at home with Sally and John, charming and slightly teasing to Mrs. Monder, sufficiently cordial to Gregory, and affectionately attentive to Meryon.

She looked at the others once or twice and saw in Sally's and her mother's eyes their certainty that anyone *must* be happy in Rex's company. John, she knew, was genuinely attached to him too. And Gregory? Ah, well, of course, it was wiser not to guess at Gregory's thoughts—just as it was better not to examine her own too closely.

During the next day or two Meryon found little difficulty in avoiding a conversation with Gregory alone. For one thing, he scarcely seemed any more anxious for it than she. And for another, now that Rex was in Town for a week, it was very natural that she should spend most of her time with him.

John and Gregory no longer required any actual nursing, and with the invaluable Mrs. Glenby still "coming in," as she put it, there was no hardship to Mrs. Monder and Sally in leaving them to manage the household sometimes.

Rex could be just as charming and entertaining company in the town as in the country, and he arranged that Meryon had a pleasant round of theatres and concerts and dinners with him, to make up for the weeks of hard nursing which she had had.

Quite often it acted as a pleasant drug which enabled

her to forget how near she was to losing the life which
meant even a sight of Gregory, for she knew now she
must take great care to see practically nothing of him
once she was married.

"It's no good taking a difficult decision and then
playing with fire," Meryon told herself firmly. And to
Rex she said: "Would it be possible for us to do quite
a long tour abroad as our honeymoon?"

"Why, of course, my dear." He seemed very pleased
at the suggestion. "A tour round the world if you
like."

Meryon smiled. He was really going to make it as
easy as it could possibly be.

"I should love that," she told him.

"Then perhaps your mother would like to spend a
good deal of the time down at the place in Hampshire?
I think she would enjoy playing hostess there to some
of her old friends."

"I'm sure she would," Meryon said, touched that he
should have so much thought for her mother too.

"And you really mean that we shall be married
before Christmas?"

"Yes—of course. Say the end of October or—or
November." (November was a strange month for a
wedding, of course, but perhaps that scarcely mattered.)

When Mother heard she didn't seem to think it
mattered at all. She merely said:

"Velvet, dear, of course. A velvet wedding can be
so pretty. Not dead white—something a shade warmer.
You don't want to risk looking cold and yellow if it's
foggy. Very, very faint peach colour, I think." She
began to look dreamy, and all Meryon had to do then
was to say, "Yes, Mother," at intervals.

At the end of the week Rex and John left for the
country. They went down by car, obviously such good

friends that the holiday could scarcely be anything but a success. And Meryon set to work in earnest then to make the preparations for her rather simple trousseau.

Rex, she knew, wanted to heap every extravagance upon her, even now, but she preferred that until she actually went to him as his wife, she should preserve some sort of independence. And he was willing to respect her wishes.

Perhaps it was the sight of these definite preparations that brought Gregory's nerves to a fine edge again. Certainly they must have been cruel enough in the circumstances, and Meryon became aware that, instead of avoiding a talk alone with her, he was definitely seeking an opportunity for one now.

It was impossible to put him off indefinitely, of course, for, with Sally out of the house most of the day, there was only her mother to play a necessary—or unnecessary—third. And one afternoon, two or three days after John and Rex had gone, Gregory followed her into the lounge, where she had gone to put some flowers in water.

She realised with a nervous thrill of apprehension that he had closed the door behind him, and was coming across the room to her, but she refused to turn round. The flowers in the bowl were already satisfactorily arranged, but in an access of nervousness, she began to rearrange them with very great attention.

"Meryon." He was behind her now. "I've tried to make up my mind not to force a scene on you, but there's something I simply must say."

"Well, you have a very good opportunity now," she told him, almost praying that she would be able to keep up this cool but friendly air of finding nothing wrong.

He didn't give her much chance, however. Taking

her gently by her arm, he turned her to face him.

"That money you had in your bag that day——"
He spoke rather jerkily. "It was for John, of course?"

"Yes. It was for John."

"Did you agree to marry Treventon because you
needed his money for someone you loved?" His expression was deadly earnest and his eyes never left her face.

"Gregory, don't be absurd! You and John do run to
melodrama. You both seem to think that because I
thankfully accepted Rex's offer, I must have agreed
to some villainous bargain. You haven't much opinion
of Rex's decency or my good sense, have you?"

"It isn't that. But there's something desperately
disquieting about the facts that keep on coming out.
You say John had the same suspicion as I. Why?
Because it's the perfectly obvious suspicion. We know
quite well that you would sacrifice yourself for the
people you love and——"

"I am not sacrificing myself," Meryon said almost
coldly. "I am marrying the kindest and most generous
of men because I want to marry him. Surely that
should be enough to convince even you."

"If Rex Treventon had been a five-pound-a-week
man who couldn't raise a finger to help John, would
you still be marrying him?" Gregory asked point-blank.

"You have no *right*——"

"I have every right!" Gregory caught hold of her
suddenly in a passion of despair and anger. "You know
I have, and you know why. We've never had anything
put into words between us, but we'll have it now. Since
before we came into this house——"

"Gregory!" She stopped him, almost more by the
quiet intensity of her voice than by the fact that she
actually put her hand against his lips. "Won't you
realise that there are some things which are so much
better never said."

"Do you mean that you don't *want* to hear what I would say?"

"I mean that it isn't any good." Meryon suddenly sounded very weary and dispirited. "Nothing that either you or I can say now could make any difference."

"But, my dear"—he spoke much more quietly now —"don't you see that I'm horribly—hopelessly in the dark? I only know that you're making some decision which must spoil my whole life. If it is for your own good and happiness—well and good. I hope I have the decency to lose as quietly and philosophically as most men. But nothing you have ever said or done has convinced me that you *are* acting in the interests of your own happiness. Can't you—won't you be more frank with me?"

Rather nervously, Meryon passed her hand up and down his arm while he was speaking, but at the last sentence she stopped and looked up at him.

"Very well," she said slowly. "I will tell you. And perhaps you're right. Perhaps you ought to know the whole thing, because it does concern us both."

"Thank you for that admission," he said very gently, and, lifting the hand that rested on his arm, he kissed it gravely.

She didn't speak for a moment, and when she did her voice was very low, but every word distinct.

"When I first heard how much money was needed to send John to the nursing home, he was desperately ill. It wasn't just a case of trying to make him better. It was a question of seeing that he didn't grow terrifyingly worse. The money was horribly—crushingly necessary, and we hadn't got it."

"But we *had*, child!"

"No. Only if we drove ourselves to the brink of financial disaster. I *would* not have that."

"But how much better, surely, than that you should make some abominable bargain with Treventon?"

"I made no bargain with Rex. He isn't that sort of man. I know he has his faults, but he never forced anyone in his life. He simply found that I was desperate for money and he gave me what I needed. Gave it absolutely freely and generously, without any thought of return. Do please remember that because it is what ties my hands now."

Meryon was very pale, and the shadows round her eyes made them look even larger than they were. Gregory said nothing now, only watching her with that terrible air of anxiety deepening every moment.

"When I came home, there was that scene with you." Gregory gave a slight exclamation. "I was so afraid you would make me give the money back that I took refuge in that silly lie about being engaged."

"But why didn't you tell me the truth, Meryon? Surely that would have been much simpler?"

She looked squarely at him.

"At that time would you *really* have let me take Rex's money for any reason whatever, if we had not been engaged?"

"I——" Gregory hesitated. Then he said doggedly, "No. I suppose I shouldn't. I should have insisted on our spending our own money."

"Which would have left us with practically nothing, and then perhaps you would have lost your job. I wasn't prepared to have the others take the risk, Gregory. There were the children and Mother to think of. I was satisfied in my own conscience that it was right to accept the money, but I knew I could never persuade you. It was stupid to invent that story, but I hadn't much time to think of an alternative."

"Do you mean that you calmly landed yourself with an engagement to Treventon rather than——"

"No. I didn't mean it to become a fact. I meant to use the story long enough to get John safely settled." She smiled very faintly. "It was a bit unscrupulous, I suppose, but I had very little choice. Then Mother came into the picture, and of course the danger was doubled. As a matter of fact, it was she who innocently congratulated Rex on what she believed to be my change of feelings. He was overjoyed—simply thought I had been afraid to tell him myself. And before I knew where I was, I found myself overwhelmed by his happiness and affection." She paused.

"Yes. Go on."

"What could I do, Gregory? He was good and kind. I like him—I like him awfully. He will be a good husband to me—no one could be a better one. And I am horribly in his debt. He would make any woman happy."

"Not you." Gregory's voice was low and strained.

"Yes—me."

"That's not true. You know it. You're not that sort of woman. Only one man could make you happy—and that is the man you love."

"Gregory"—Meryon very lightly put her hands on his shoulders—"many women end by being happy with the second-best. I don't know even why I'm saying so much to you, but——"

"Yes, you do."

"But I must explain and you must understand. Circumstances have put me where I am. I can and I will make the best of it—and there is very much in the best of it."

"There's never anything—sense or decency or anything else—in marrying one man while you love another," Gregory said almost violently.

"Yes, my dear, there *is* both decency and sense in this. And, above all, there is decency. Rex has been good to me beyond any demand of friendship or generosity. If he had tried to make terms, that would have been different, but he never did. He has been goodness itself, and if I backed out now, only he would be unhappy. *He* would have to pay a bill which he never incurred. I can't do it and I won't do it. It isn't right or just."

"But, Meryon"—he gently took her hands from his shoulders and held them in his—"can you possibly suppose you can make him happy, feeling as you do?"

"Yes," she said very deliberately, "if you don't make it too hard for me. I can give him very nearly the best —I doubt if he ever expected more. I won't pretend that you and I could not have found something much better"—their hands tightened in unspoken communion —"but, strange though it may seem, that is beside the point."

"Meryon!"

She was silent, though she winced slightly at the pain in that exclamation.

"Don't you think," he said at last, quite gently, "that your sense of duty is out of all proportion?"

Meryon shook her head slowly.

"No, Gregory. I know it's old-fashioned and emotional to talk of duty nowadays. But it's only another way of saying 'decent responsibility towards other people.' It's a daily thing now for people and even whole nations, to shirk their decent responsibility because it's crushingly hard to face. Well, I can't do it. I know that it was *my* deception that brought on this situation. *I* must pay any price—not Rex—and my one hope is that he will never even know that any price was needed."

"I shall pay, too, you know," Gregory said in a very low voice.

Meryon hesitated before she answered, because this was the hardest thing of all to say.

"You were a little to blame, too," she told him gently at last, "because it was your obstinate determination to force your views that pushed me into a corner. It is a price out of all proportion, whoever has to pay it, but why should Rex be the one to pay, when he is the only one of the three who is entirely blameless?"

Gregory was silent, staring at the hands that he was holding. Then suddenly he bent his head and put his cheek against them.

"Darling, you're so much better than I shall ever be. God forgive, me if I should make things harder for you than they are already."

And, turning, he went out of the room, leaving her alone.

CHAPTER XIII

WHEN GREGORY HAD GONE, Meryon stood there for a long while, absently rearranging the bowl of flowers yet again. Then, as though it suddenly came over her what a foolish thing she was doing, she sighed impatiently and, going over to the fire, sat down in a low chair and gazed into the flames.

She had done it at last—broken the last link. Now she would have no more trouble, even with Gregory himself. It somehow soothed her to know that he actually understood her point of view. He didn't like Rex —that was too much to expect—and he thought she set too much store by duty. But he did see that the whole situation was something very different from having been engaged to a man and then having found that one had honestly made a mistake.

A definite course had been taken, a horrible muddle had resulted, and someone had to stand by the cost. It must not be Rex—that was all.

Just for a moment, she wondered idly what would have happened if she had done what her mother had wanted a year ago and married Rex then. That would have involved scarcely knowing Gregory, of course, or, at least, only knowing him casually as a remote relation of her mother by marriage.

It would have saved a good deal of pain and unhappiness, she supposed, and, anyway, now the end was the same—she was to marry Rex. It was almost a pity she——

"No!" thought Meryon at that point. "That isn't true! I wouldn't have been without the experience of this last year—not to save myself every bit of unhappiness now. It's wonderful to have known Gregory and John and Sally, and to have worked for them. And it's been worth almost anything to have found a real sense of values, and to know that loving people means doing the best for them and hoping they will learn to love you in return."

Nothing could ever take this year away from her, and if half that Gregory said was true, she had left something worthwhile with every one of them too. With John his new-found health. With Gregory his restored confidence. And with Sally a contented, happy view of life.

Oh, yes, it had been a very good year. Never mind if it had meant some unhappiness at the end.

The door opened and her mother came into the room.

"Hello, darling. Is anything the matter with Gregory?"

"I—don't think so. Why?" She managed not to sound at all concerned.

"Oh—nothing, except that he seems just a little short-tempered these days. I was asking him just now whether Rex had said anything to him about acting as best man, and, really dear, he was quite *rude.*"

Meryon looked at her mother in silent dismay, but Mrs. Monder noticed nothing, for she was ambling off on another tack.

"Of course, it may be that he's rather hurt because Rex *hasn't* said anything. Perhaps I ought to drop a tactful hint to Rex about it."

"Oh, no, Mother," Meryon said, with something like horror at the recollection of her mother's ideas on tact. "I don't really think I'd say anything about it if I were you. After all, it is a question for Rex to settle."

"Well, I don't like the idea of Gregory being left out of things," Mrs. Monder objected generously. "He's rather easily *hurt* dear, Sometimes I think you don't quite realise that."

"Don't I?" Meryon said rather dully. "I'll—see what Rex has to say about things, then." Which fortunately pacified her mother completely for the moment.

The remaining week without John and Rex passed uneventfully enough. Gregory was back at the office now, and Meryon found that she saw very little of him. He was quiet and friendly when they did meet, but, in a curious way, almost formal, and she guessed that the strain was as great for him as for her.

Perhaps it was that which brought her to the sudden decision that when Rex came back with John, she would ask him if they couldn't be married by special licence—quickly and quietly, and without any fuss.

Mother would not like it at all, of course, but for once that really couldn't be allowed to count.

However, on the afternoon of John's arrival, Meryon was surprised to see that Rex was not there and that the chauffeur was driving.

"Why, what happened? Surely Rex didn't stay on in the country?" she said when she had greeted John.

"No. We dropped him at the flat first. He'll be seeing you later. There was something he wanted to arrange." For a moment she thought there was the slightest sign of evasion about John's manner, and that was something so extraordinary in him that she felt puzzled. But, after watching him for a little while as he answered all the family enquiries, she decided she had been mistaken. He was as frank and open as ever—and he looked wonderfully well.

Presently, when she went into the kitchen to put
on the kettle for tea, he followed her out there.

"Meryon."

"Yes?" She turned from the stove with a smile.

"I've got a message for you."

"Have you? From Rex, you mean?"

"Yes."

There was a short silence, and she forced herself to
say with assumed lightness:

"Well? Very much love, and he is longing to see
me?"

"Not exactly." John frowned. "He wants you to go
and see him at his flat this evening, Meryon."

"Does he?" Meryon looked surprised. It was the first
time Rex had ever suggested anything that was even
remotely unconventional. "But why doesn't he come
here to see me?"

"I suppose he wants to talk to you without any fear
of the rest of us barging in."

"He usually takes me out to dinner in that case."

There was another silence—and suddenly Meryon
glanced sharply at John.

"You haven't been—saying anything you shouldn't
—have you?" she said a trifle jerkily, and with the first
sign of anger she had ever shown towards him.

"I don't know what you would consider as 'anything
I shouldn't say.'"

"You're prevaricating!" Meryon flushed and then
paled. "Have you been presuming to—to make con-
fidences to Rex?"

"No."

"What, then?"

"Meryon—occasionally someone asks one a question
to which one *must* give a comparatively truthful answer.
Will you please go and see Rex this evening and let
him say what he wants to say himself. It isn't fair

to him or you to have me act as a sort of go-
between."

She didn't answer for a moment—struggling with
the desire to ask frightened, half-angry questions.
Then, with an effort, she realised that what he said
was true.

"Very well." Her voice was very carefully con-
trolled. "Go back into the dining-room. I'll come in a
minute."

He glanced at her, almost as though he would make
some form of protest or apology. Then he made a little
gesture of acceptance and went out of the room.

Tea was a difficult matter for Meryon. So was the
hour that followed, before she could make some sort
of excuse to slip away out of the house.

What did John mean exactly? What had he said to
Rex—or Rex to him? She felt she couldn't bear it if,
in addition to everything else, she was faced with
having to remove doubts and questionings from Rex's
mind.

Surely, surely she had faced enough without this?

On the way to Rex's flat she thought again of John's
odd expression, "Occasionally someone asks one a
question to which one *must* give a comparatively
truthful answer." Well, who had asked such a question?
And, above all, what had that question been?

But, of course, it was ridiculous to torment herself
like this. Sometimes she felt that her thoughts ran
in one groove, and one groove only. Why *should* she
suppose John would take it upon himself to throw
doubts on her feelings to Rex. He had accepted her
protestations completely that last time they had
discussed things. She was just looking for trouble.
It was some matter that could be put right in five
minutes.

Her bus stopped at the end of the road leading to

the great block of luxury flats where Rex lived. She had only been there once before for a few minutes, but she remembered the way, and as she went up in the lift to his flat on the top floor, she tried to tell herself that the beating of her heart was not so heavy as it had been.

She knocked a little timidly at the great dull silver knocker, and almost immediately the black, polished door was opened by a very discreet-looking man-servant.

Rex was in, it seemed, and she was taken at once into the square, soft-carpeted lounge which she re-membered.

"Oh, Meryon, my dear! How good of you to come so soon." He got up from the armchair where he had been sitting, and came to take her coat himself. She took off her hat, too, and ran her hand rather childishly through her hair, disturbed and puzzled that, in spite of his friendly air, he made no attempt to kiss her.

"Come and sit down."

She came over to sit by the open fire-place, where a small but cheerful fire was burning.

"Did you have a good journey this afternoon?" One must ask a few conventional questions first, she supposed.

"Yes, thank you." Pause—and then: "I suppose, since you are here, that John gave you my message."

"Yes. He said you—wanted to speak to me about something and were anxious that no one should interrupt us."

"I think that describes it quite accurately." He smiled slightly.

With an effort, she raised her eyes and looked up at him as he stood on the rug in front of her.

"What is it? What did you want to ask me?"

"I wanted," he said slowly, "to ask you the question

which no chivalrous fiancé is ever supposed to ask.
Would you be horribly shocked if I told you that I
didn't want to marry you after all?"

The silence was so profound that he heard her
swallow nervously.

"Why, Rex," she began at last, and then stopped.
"I—I wouldn't want you to marry me if—you didn't
love me enough to be happy with me," she finished
helplessly.

"And I wouldn't want *you* to marry *me*, dear, if you
didn't love me enough to be happy with me," he told
her gently.

"No—of course not. But I am—I mean—that is
—if you want me——" She stammered into silence,
horribly unsure of which way to turn.

And at that he gave a slight, affectionate laugh
and, sitting down on the arm of her chair, put his arm
round her.

"You've been in love with your Gregory almost
since you knew him, haven't you?"

"Rex!"

He put his cheek lightly against the top of her head.

"I'd be much more gratified and flattered if you'd
pay me the compliment of telling me the truth, child."

There was another difficult silence.

"Has John been—saying stupid things?" she
whispered at last.

"No. John merely confirmed what was almost a
certainty in my own mind already."

"I'm sorry, Rex, if I ever gave you the impression
that I——"

"You have nothing to be sorry about, my dear,"
he told her. "You really played up magnificently, but
—I'm thankful to say—the rôle was just a little bit
beyond you."

"Oh." It made her feel very helpless to have him

speak so quietly and confidently, but she must make one more effort. "Then you're not prepared to believe that I—was very fond of Gregory once, but that my —that my feelings changed?"

"No. I'm afraid I'm not prepared to believe that, though it's a nice little story." She knew from his voice that he was smiling again.

"Rex, I could be very happy with you."

"No, dear, you couldn't. And, to tell the truth, I couldn't be happy with you in the circumstances."

Her head drooped a little lower.

"I'm so miserable and ashamed," she said in a very small voice.

"But why, darling?"

"I ought to have been able to do it better."

"I'm very glad you couldn't."

She looked up quickly.

"Do you *really* mean that?"

"Of course. You don't suppose I wanted you eating your poor little heart out for another man, do you?"

"It wouldn't have been like that—always."

"No? Well, it will be something so very much better than that for you now."

Instinctively she pressed a little against him, with a spontaneous affection that had never been there before.

"But what about you? Are you going to be— terribly miserable?" she asked, almost shyly.

He smiled and slightly shook his head, his eyes still on hers.

"I won't pretend that any man could let you go without a wrench, Meryon. But there's nothing quite so cooling to love's fever as the realisation that one simply doesn't count."

"Oh, Rex!" She gripped his fingers remorsefully.

"No, darling. Don't mind my saying that. It would

have hurt ten times more if you had loved me once and then changed your mind. I probably *should* have spent my life then fretting after the thought that perhaps I could get you back. As it is"—he shrugged, and gave a rather wry little smile—"since you never have been mine really, I must put you among those lovely, unattainable things for which one doesn't even struggle. I hope I am a philosopher enough not to let something inevitable blight my life."

"You're saying all this just to comfort me, aren't you?"

"Well, I should like to think it does comfort you." He touched her cheek lightly with his fingers. "But, in any case, Meryon, there's stern common sense in it, too. And common sense is so much better than sentiment at such a moment."

She put up her hand and took his fingers in hers.

"Rex, you're so good. There's something almost heroic about you."

"Because I can face life without you?" he said teasingly. "Yes, I think perhaps that is the test of a hero."

"Oh, no! Not that. But—everything. The way you put everything right, regardless of yourself, and——"

He interrupted her with a laugh of genuine amusement.

"No, no, Meryon dear. I'm sorry to have to refuse this crown of glory, but I'm not quite the selfless creature you seem to think."

"Yes, you are. Look at the way you gave me the money for John, without any thought of return."

He made a slight face.

"How do you know I had no thought of return?"

"*Had* you?"

"I was not quite so ingenuous as to refrain from hoping it would have some effect," he said drily.

"Well, I think that's only reasonable."

"Maybe."

There was silence for a moment. Then she said:
"When did you first begin to—to have any doubts
about my feelings?"

"Almost at once."

"Did you!"

"But I thought I might change that. Then something happened which made me see that you were not
the least bit in love with me—it was only friendship
and a sort of gratitude."

"When? What made you think that?"

He looked rather thoughtful.

"That time you asked me if there—had been—
anyone else. No woman who was genuinely in love
would have displayed such masterly tolerance over the
reply."

"Oh!" Meryon said in a small voice, because she
saw that, even now, there was something in that which
afforded him slight, grim amusement.

"However—not being quite the first-class character
you imagine—I made no offer to release you. I thought
that time and my money might play into my hands.
And then your confounded Gregory had the good
fortune to develop pneumonia. It was when you
insisted so fiercely on going to nurse him that I began
to realise what I should have realised long ago. Your
liking for me could never be anything else, because
Gregory had everything else already."

"Oh, Rex, these haven't been easy weeks for you
either!"

"Well"—he shrugged and smiled—"they've been
rather a harrowing muddle for us all. But I'm afraid
I didn't give the right solution as soon as I might.
You'll scarcely believe it from anyone of my noble
character"—his eyes twinkled and Meryon gave a

relieved little laugh—"but I was not prepared to resign in favour of Gregory even then. It was not until I started talking things over with John——"

"John!"

"Yes. That's an extraordinarily nice boy, by the way," Rex added reflectively. "I hope you're going to lend him to me as a companion on that world tour which you will *not* be taking with me."

"Rex! Would you like that?"

"Very much indeed. And I think he would, too."

"Of course he would. What a wonderful opportunity for him! But, tell me, what did John say?"

"Not much at first, until I asked him point-blank if you were in love with Gregory, and assured him—in my essentially noble fashion—that what I really wanted was your happiness."

"And then?" Meryon squeezed his fingers again in that movement of half-nervous sympathy.

"Then he told me that, although he couldn't explain your actions, he was convinced you *were* in love with Gregory."

"But I *told* him I wasn't!"

"How extremely wrong of you," Rex said gravely. "An absolute and unvarnished lie which deserved to be disbelieved."

Meryon smiled faintly.

"I wonder why he was so sure." She spoke half to herself.

"Well, I think you were unwise enough to let him keep hold of your hand while you were discussing the point. When he expressed sympathy for Gregory, you gave yourself away so badly that no protestations could cover it up again. I'm afraid, my poor little Meryon, that deception is not an accomplishment of yours." And he laughed again with affectionate but real amusement.

"Oh," Meryon said soberly, "that certainly was very stupid of me."

"But very fortunate."

"Do you *honestly* mean that?"

She looked up at him and he nodded.

"I don't think any of us would have made very much of the other arrangement," he said. And she hoped with passionate eagerness that his air of grave sincerity was genuine.

There was silence for a moment or two. Then he said:

"Now will you promise me not to work up any absurd sense of guilt over this? And then we can consider the whole episode closed and all explanations made."

"I feel simply awful about all that money," Meryon said unhappily.

"Why, my dear?"

"Oh, it—it seems as though I had it on false pretences."

"But you did nothing of the sort. Don't you remember? I told you that I never lend money to my friends, but sometimes I give it. Well, I gave this to you—as my friend. Nothing else. If you like, you can consider that I gave it to John—as my friend."

"Oh, in *that* case——" She looked up eagerly, but a sudden flash of intuition told her that she must not take away that one thing which had given him so much pleasure. "No," Meryon said slowly. "No. I would much rather think that you and I are such real friends that even a gift of money between us only increased the friendship instead of ruining it."

"Thank you, my dear." He bent his head and kissed her gently, and, without any hesitation, she kissed him warmly in return.

"And now"—he stood up and lifted her gently to

her feet—"I think it's time you went home and told Gregory that everything is all right."

Meryon laughed a little at his way of putting it, but, at his words, the first real glow of indescribable relief began to warm her.

It was true. She *could* go home and tell Gregory that—comparatively speaking—everything was all right.

Rex held her coat for her, and as she slipped into it and then reached for her gloves, a final thought came to disturb her content.

"Oh!" One hand went over the other rather nervously.

"What is it?"

"My ring. I——" She began to take it off.

"No—please." For a moment his hand was on hers, but he withdrew it almost immediately. "Do keep your ring, Meryon. I would like you to."

"Oh, but when a girl breaks her engagement she always——"

"And when a man breaks an engagement he usually asks the girl to keep the ring," he reminded her with a smile. "Will you please keep your ring—in acknowledgment of the fact that *I* broke this engagement."

"Oh, Rex! Well, of course, I couldn't refuse to keep it if that's really how you feel."

"I do," he assured her. And then he took her down in the lift and summoned a taxi for her. He didn't attempt to kiss her as he handed her in—and she hardly expected him to. That one kiss of complete friendship which they had exchanged in the flat made any others unnecessary.

He paid the driver and then turned back to her again.

"Good-bye, my dear. Don't forget that I want to take John abroad with me, sometime before the New

Year. Tell him I shall be writing to him about it."

"I will, Rex. And—thank you. Thank you a thousand times for everything."

He smiled, and made her his usual charming bow as the taxi started. Glancing back through the window, she saw him standing there, looking after her. Then the taxi turned a corner, and Rex and his luxury flat and that chapter of her life seemed to sink away from her consciousness. She was alone in the taxi—driving home to Gregory.

Carefully she drew off her ring now and slipped it into her handbag, for, of course, Rex would hardly expect her to go on wearing it—at any rate at present.

Her hand felt curiously light and free without the ring, and she curled and uncurled her fingers in an access of pleasure.

She was free!

She couldn't quite imagine just how she and Gregory would work things out together—just how Mother would accept what must be a great disappointment for her—just how they were going to balance responsibilities and future joys so that one was not entirely lost sight of in the happiness of the other. But for the moment none of these things mattered. They could work them out later. The only thing that mattered now was that she was free—and going home to Gregory.

As the taxi drew up outside Number Twenty-Two, Meryon glanced at her watch and saw to her astonishment that it was scarcely half-past eight even now. Less than two hours had sufficed for the journey to Rex's flat and back, and the conversation which had changed her life.

She went into the house, and as she did so, Sally came out of the dining-room and went towards the kitchen.

"Hello. You're just about in time for supper."

"Hello. Yes—I suppose I am. I won't be a minute."
And she went upstairs.

How funny it was! Everything was perfectly normal
and yet really everything had changed.

"Is that you, dear?" her mother called out from her
room. "You're just in nice time for supper."

"Yes, Mother. I'll take off my things. I won't be a
minute."

How was one going to start turning calm into drama?
She really couldn't imagine. If anyone else told her she
was in good time for supper she thought she would
begin to laugh hysterically.

But no one else did. Downstairs in the hall once more
she met John, and his expression was by no means
casual and unknowing. His eyes went to her left hand,
and then he said quite baldly:

"Gregory's in the lounge if you want him."

Something in that tickled Meryon's sense of humour
irresistibly. She *did* want him, of course, very decidedly.
But the schoolboy directness of John's tactics had
something very funny about it.

"All right, dear. I don't know that I'm in quite such
an indecent hurry," she said with a smile.

John's anxious expression gave way then, too, and,
with a relieved laugh, he flung his arms round her and
kissed her.

"Is it quite all right, Meryon?"

"I think so. At least—it's going to be."

"Then do go and tell poor old Gregory something
about it—decency or no decency," John said. And,
still smiling a little, she went towards the lounge.

He was sitting at a small table writing when she came
in, and evidently he had already been interrupted once
or twice that evening, for he deliberately took no
notice of the opening and shutting of the door.

She came forward into the room, waiting for him to

ook up. But he went on writing instead, apparently
thinking it was either Sally or John. At last he said
absently:

"Yes? What do you want?"

"You, Gregory," Meryon said, and watched with a
sort of half-frightened joy as the pen fell from his
hand and rolled on the floor.

"What—do you mean?"

Gregory pushed back his chair and got to his feet a
little unsteadily.

She didn't know what to say to him then, and, half
nervously, she held out her hands to him. He took
them with a puzzled, eager gesture, and she saw how
pale he was. She felt his fingers, tight and nervous, on
hers—and then suddenly they gripped hers in a way
that almost made her cry out.

"Meryon! Your ring—it's gone."

"Yes. I know—that's it—I wanted to tell you——"

"Darling!" He gathered her into his arms before she
could finish, and began to kiss her rather wildly, first
on her cheeks and then on her mouth. "You changed
your mind! You did break your engagement. Oh, I
could——"

"No, I didn't," she gasped. "That wasn't the right
way out. It was Rex who decided to break it."

"The damned skunk!" Gregory said indignantly.

"Oh, *no*! You mustn't say that. It's not true. He did
it because he found out that I—loved you."

"You told him?"

"No, no. He just—guessed. And then something
John said—anyway, he found out how things were,
and he wouldn't hold me to our engagement after that.
He wouldn't *let* me marry him—even insisted that it
was he who broke the engagement! That was the most
generous bit of all."

"Yes," Gregory said slowly, "that certainly was

amazingly generous. I've a horrid feeling I shouldn't
have been anything like so generous in the cir
cumstances."

"Oh, yes, you *would*."

He smiled slightly and shook his head, watching her
all the while, as though he could never look at her
enough.

"No. I'm sorry, darling. With you only just in the
circle of my arm, I know that I wouldn't give you up
to anyone now on any pretext whatever."

"That's natural at the moment."

He laughed.

"Is it? Well, perhaps you're right. Not very noble
but very natural. Are you sure you prefer naturalness
to nobility?"

"Certain."

"I feel I ought to give you a list of my faults, dearest
and point out that I'm far from being the paragon that
your first fiancé was."

"You don't need to," Meryon assured him. "I've
been one of the family quite long enough to know all
about your faults."

"Little beast," he said and kissed her fondly. Then
he added reflectively, "I wonder how the family will
take *this*, by the way."

"John will be delighted."

"Yes. I know that."

"And Sally? I think Sally will be very pleased
too."

"Probably."

They looked at each other and laughed.

"Yes, of course, Mother is the doubtful quantity,"
Meryon said. "It's difficult to know what she'll say."

"Shall we go and see?"

"Perhaps we'd better."

They hesitated a moment longer, their hands clasped,

their eyes smilingly seeking each other's. Then Sally's voice called out prosaically from the hall:

"Supper's ready, you two. Better come while it's hot." And together they went out of the lounge and into the dining-room.

CHAPTER XIV

MRS. MONDER WAS STANDING by the fire, warming her hands, and Sally was putting chairs round the table when they came in. Neither of them noticed Gregory and Meryon specially. But John did. He took one look at them and smiled.

"Two bob, Sally," he said, and held out his hand to his sister.

"What do you mean?" Sally turned from the table in surprise.

"You owe me two shillings on our bet. Meryon's going to marry Gregory, after all."

"Meryon's going to—— My dear, don't be so *silly*," Mrs. Monder said reprovingly. "That isn't at all in good taste."

"Perhaps not, but it's true," John assured her.

"Yes, Mother. It's quite true." Meryon's voice sounded much smaller than she had meant it to be. "I'm going to marry Gregory."

"But you *can't*, dear! You're going to marry Rex." Mrs. Monder spoke as though there really were a case of bigamy in question.

"No. I—we've broken off our engagement. It's Gregory I really want."

"But it *can't* be. Not that you're not very nice, Gregory dear, but——"

"That's all right. Don't mind my wounded feelings," Gregory assured her with a grin. "I quite understand that, in competition with Rex, I can't expect to be placed."

"No, no. It's not that. But—oh, Meryon, what *is*
it all about?"

Meryon left Gregory's side and came over to put a
reassuring arm round her mother.

"Please don't be upset, Mother dear. It was just a
series of mistakes over Rex. He's the best friend
possible, but I never really loved him. It was always
Gregory—only we took a long time to work things out.
You do want me to marry the one man who can make
me happy, don't you?" she pleaded.

"Well, of *course*, darling. Only——"

"And you know you're thoroughly fond of Gregory."

"Oh, yes, yes—certainly. I don't want to hurt your
feelings, Gregory. I *am* very fond of you."

Gregory nodded sympathetically.

" 'Not that I love Cæsar less but that I love Rome
more,' " he suggested helpfully.

"Well, I don't know about that," Mrs. Monder
said. "I don't see that Rome has anything to do with
it."

Gregory smiled at her with a kindness and understanding he would not have shown in the old days.

"I do understand what is wrong, really. You're
afraid I can't give Meryon half the things that Rex
could. And she's such a darling that she deserves everything good in the world."

"Yes. That's it." Mrs. Monder nodded, very much
relieved to have Gregory himself put her doubts into
words.

"Well, it's quite true, of course, that I couldn't give
her the things Rex could. But I'm beginning to do
pretty well again now, you know, and I'm going to do
very much better. She shan't want for many things,
I promise." And Gregory smiled very tenderly at
Meryon.

"I couldn't want for anything now," Meryon said

quietly. And at that Mrs. Monder began to fumble sentimentally for her handkerchief.

"Well, of course, darling," she began, "if that's how you feel——"

"It's worth two bob," finished Sally.

Meryon smiled and kissed her mother.

"And, after all, it *was* you who first suggested I should marry Gregory, you know," she said teasingly.

"*Was* it? Nonsense, dear. Such a thought never entered my head."

"Oh, yes, it did," Gregory reminded her gently. "It entered your head the first time Meryon came into my uncle's house. You said so perfectly clearly—in the drawing-room, before Meryon had even sat down in the house."

"Oh, *that!*" Mrs. Monder bridled a little. "That was only a joke. And, anyway, Gregory, you couldn't know anything about that," she finished triumphantly. "*You weren't even there.*"

There was a moment's silence, while Gregory looked both amused and reflective.

"Wasn't I?" he said. "How very odd. And I've always believed that I remembered every detail. Strange what mistakes I seem to have made in the past. I must really try not to make any more in the future." And, drawing Meryon to his side, he kissed her very tenderly.

Something for Nothing?

WELL, not exactly for nothing, but just for the price of a postage stamp, you can get much more pleasure from your reading.

You can make sure that you are never at a loss for a book to choose. You need never miss a book by a favourite author, and each month you'll have information on all the new and forthcoming titles.

There is no magic about it. Just send us a stamped addressed envelope, and ask for our Happy Reading Collection. The Happy Reading Collection is published every month and gives details of every book we are publishing as well as interesting news of the authors. You really ought to have it. Thousands of readers do already and know that it is too good to miss.

Therefore, wherever you live, here in England or thousands of miles away, just send off for our Happy Reading Collection and make sure of hours of pleasant reading.

MILLS & BOON READER SERVICE
P.O. BOX 236
CROYDON, CR9 3RU